WAHIDA CLARK PRESENTS

# THE ULTIMATE SACRIFICE IV

BY
ANTHONY FIELDS

This is a work of fiction. Names, characters, places, and incidents either are the product of the author's imagination or are used fictitiously, and any resemblance to actual persons, living or dead, business establishments, events, or locales are entirely coincidental.

Wahida Clark Presents Publishing
60 Evergreen Place
Suite 904
East Orange, New Jersey 07018
973-678-9982
www.wclarkpublishing.com



Library of Congress Cataloging-In-Publication Data:
The Ultimate Sacrifice Part 4 by Anthony Fields
ISBN 13-digit 978-1936649-67-9 (paper)
ISBN 10-digit 1936649675
ISBN (e-book) 978-1-936649-14-3
LCCN 2015902379

1. Urban- 2. Washington DC 3. Drug Trafficking- 4. African American-Fiction- 5. DEA-

Cover design and layout by Nuance Art
Book design by NuanceArt@aCreativeNuance.com
Sr. Editor Linda Wilson
Proofreader Rosalind Hamilton

Printed in USA

# PROLOGUE

## AMEEN

"What's up, ock? Surprised to see me, huh?" Ameen said, looking over Khadafi's shoulder and checking on the woman sitting in the truck. *Is she the woman that Shawnay told me about?* Ameen wondered. Once the woman made no attempt to exit the truck, he focused on the man standing in front of him. Khadafi's eyes searched his for answers he knew weren't there. His eyes were no longer readable. Being a free man teaches one to mask all emotion. Khadafi's gaze then fell onto the gun in Ameen's hand and at the body sprawled out at his feet.

Slowly, Khadafi's eyes found Ameen's again. "Is this the part where my life ends by your hands? Are you finally gonna finish the job that you left undone in that rec cage and in the hallway of the jail?" he asked.

"Naw, ock, if I wanted you dead, it wouldn't have really mattered to me who killed you, as long as the end result was that you were dead," Ameen explained, shaking his head. "I could've let Lil Cee do you in, but that's not why I came here tonight. There's a reason I did what I just did."

Khadafi glanced down again at the body at his feet and asked, "Are we gonna stand here all day, or are you gonna tell me why you did it?"

"I saved your life to prove that our beef is over. I think I proved that through my actions, so there would be no misunderstanding my intentions. I gave Shawnay my word that I wouldn't beef with you anymore, and I'ma try doing everything in my power to keep that word. That is, unless you give me a reason to go back on my word."

"Why would I do that?" Khadafi slightly held out his arms to drive his point home.

"There's been a lot of blood shed between us, ock. You know as well as I do what the last four years have been like between us. But if you say you wanna squash all beefs between us—well, that's good enough for me. I'ma take you at your word now and pray that you never decide to break your word later."

Khadafi nodded in the affirmative. "I know my word ain't exactly iron with you the way it was at one time. But cuz, I know I crossed lines that weren't supposed to be crossed. You ain't ever gotta worry about me tryna bring you a move. By Allah, I give you my word that what happened between us on all fronts is over."

"Like I said, I'ma take your word and roll with that."

"But, I gotta ask you one thing though, cuz."

"What's that, ock?"

"How did you know Lil Cee would be here tonight trying to kill me?"

"Simple, ock. Lil Cee wanted us both dead. I figured that out when he got on the stand and lied. I realized he wanted me to beat the beef so that hopefully one day he'd have the chance to kill me. He blamed us both for what you did to his family. I always knew that if I ever ran into him as a free man that I would have to kill him. I just didn't know when that would be. I hadn't heard anything about him over the years, or since I'd been home, but I knew he was out there somewhere. By chance, or either it was the will of Allah, I was downtown one day seeing some people, and I thought to myself that your trial was going on."

Khadafi's eyes narrowed in surprise.

"Yeah, I kept up with you. Anyway, I decided to see what was going on in the trial. I only made it as far as the gallery, when I spotted him. He was dressed in a suit and his look was different, but I recognized him instantly. I smiled and said 'All praises due to Allah' as I envisioned myself knocking his head off. Lil Cee was sitting in at your trial, and I felt it was my destiny to crush him." Ameen stole another quick glance at the body.

"Later that day, I waited for him outside. All I thought about was the look on his face when he walked into my trial in Texas and the fact that he killed my brothers. Although I didn't mess with them niggas at all, that still didn't give Cee the right to take their lives. After all, they were my blood. So, for that reason as well, I planned to do him real dirty. I wasn't paying attention to the two women walking ahead of him. I just thought Cee was going to his car. When I bent the corner and saw him crush the two broads—that threw me off."

"So, Lil Cee killed that cop bitch and Strong's girl, huh?"

"Yeah . . . You thought it was me?"

"Naw . . . I really didn't know who did it, but I never thought it was you."

"That broad day double murder made me 'noid, so I broke and decided to catch Cee another day, if Allah willed it. At the time, I didn't know who the two women were, but I found out later when the news came on, and instantly I knew why he did it. He wanted you to beat your beef so he could kill you. When he didn't get caught for killing them two broads, I knew what came next. All he needed to hear was that you were being released from jail. Once that happened, I knew what the play was. All I had to do was come here and wait."

"I'm glad that you did, cuz. And I will never forget what you did in Beaumont when you took the beef to free me *and* what you just did. I owe you," Khadafi said with humility.

"You don't owe me nothing, ock. Just thank Allah for the good. And welcome

home," Ameen said without smiling.

"The same to you, cuz. And let me ask you for one thing before we part." Khadafi looked down momentarily before meeting Ameen's gaze dead on.

"What's that?"

"No matter what happens to me, please take care of my son."

Ameen thought briefly about the events that led to Khadafi having a son by Shawnay and got upset. He quickly shook off those thoughts and replied, "Like he is my own, ock. Like he is my own." The two men parted ways, with all scores settled.

As Ameen drove through the city en route to Virginia, he thought about many things. Lil Cee was the first person he'd killed since killing Cochise Shakur in the stairwell at the jail, and for some reason he felt different. Ameen couldn't put a finger on why, but all he knew was that he felt different. Maybe it was the fact that all the people he'd killed in his life were enemies, but he'd never killed a friend. Maybe it was the stark realization that Keith Barnett's murder had indirectly claimed another life. That one murder that happened in the shower room at Beaumont had changed the lives of everybody involved. If it had never happened, many people would still be alive. Maybe something inside him grew tired of killing, tired of seeing and smelling blood.

A smile crossed Ameen's face as he wondered if Khadafi had shit himself when he saw him step out of the darkness after blowing Lil Cee's brains out.

Since it was well after midnight, the streets were clear and it didn't take long to get home. To Ameen, his beef with Khadafi and the Keith Barnett murder chapter in his life were closed. It ended with the death of Lil Cee and the conversation he had with Khadafi. It was time to move on with his life and open his store. That was what was important to him now.

He pulled into the driveway and exited the car as quietly as possible, entering the house through the basement. After he ejected the clip out of the gun and detached the silencer, he put everything away with the rest of the artillery and ammo that he purchased on the streets when he first got home. It was always better to be safe than sorry. Ameen's war chest was a metal locker that resembled a small safe. Silently he prayed to Allah that after this night he would never have to open that locker again, because if and when he did, someone was gonna die. And he didn't want that. After moving the locker out of sight and making sure it was secure, he undressed down to his boxer briefs and walked upstairs. Climbing into bed beside Shawnay, he got directly up on her butt and kissed her neck. Minutes later, she stirred.

"Antonio . . . stop it . . ." she moaned. "Your body is cold. Where have you been anyway?"

The lie slipped from his mouth effortlessly. "I couldn't sleep, so I ended up riding around for a while, and then I decided to go through Congress Park just to see the old stomping grounds and reminisce." He wished he had the type of ride or die relationship with Shawnay that some couples shared, but they didn't. He couldn't force her to accept the fact that the man she loved was a cold-blooded killer. So lying was his only option. "I needed to get that out my system, and therefore, I never have to go back to the projects again. My past was there, but my future is here with you, and that's where I belong. Which reminds me, I got some unfinished business I need to handle."

"And what's that, Antonio?" Shawnay asked as she rubbed her butt all over his hard on.

"Let me do you one better and show you." Ameen reached around Shawnay's waist and found her pussy. His fingers entered her panties and found her clit. They moved with familiarity and made Shawnay hiss and squirm. "Ooooh . . . shit . . . Antonio! You gon' make me cum all over your fingers . . ."

"Do it then, and then I got something else for you to cum on."

"Oooh . . . my . . . gawd . . . Antonio. I love you so much."

"I love you, too, baby. Till death do us part."

# CHAPTER ONE

## KHADAFI

What had just happened at the jail wouldn't leave Khadafi's mind, but at the moment his eyes were glued to the back of Marnie's heart-shaped ass as she climbed the stairs to her apartment. The pink skirt hugged her every curve, and his dick was ready to explode. Once they were safely inside the apartment, he grabbed her, felt her ass, and kissed her ear.

"Stop it, Khadafi," Marnie whined as she turned to face him. "I wanna know what that was all about back in the jail parking lot. And I ain't giving up no goodies until you tell me."

"C'mon, cuz, with that bullshit. How you gon' do a horny man like that after he been in jail over a year? Besides, you just saw what happened back there."

"You don't understand how terrified I was when I thought that, that dude was gonna kill you, and I was helpless to stop him. Who was he, and why was he there trying to kill you? Who was that other dude that appeared out of nowhere and saved you? What the hell just happened back there?"

"What did I just tell your ass in the truck?" Indignantly, Khadafi let her go and started to remove his jacket and shirt. "Didn't I ask you to just leave it alone? Damn! Let it go!"

"I can't let it go. I just witnessed a murder, and I almost witnessed you get murdered. How can I just act like all that never happened? And you . . . how can you just act like there wasn't a gun at your head thirty minutes ago? Like it's all good and something like that happens to you every day. And what were you and the other dude talking about for all that time?"

"Cuz, you nosy as shit."

"So what? Do you want some pussy or not?"

"Of course I do."

"Well, I suggest you start talking, brother. And why does it seem like trouble and death stick to you like flies on shit?"

"That's the way my life is . . . I can't explain why I always end up with blood on my hands. Death is always lurking around every corner for me. Always has been . . . I don't know why. But what I do know is that this is what you signed up for. This life is what you wanted. It's what you chose. And you can't have it both ways. From day one, you knew what you were getting with me. I am who I've always said I was. I live by the gun and I'm an outlaw. Remember the night you told me you were pregnant, and I told you that I was going back to Kemie?"

Marnie nodded. "Please don't remind me."

"I tried to give you a way out that night. I was trying to tell you in so many words that I wasn't gonna live long and you should find someone else to love. But did you listen? No. Not you. Not your wannabe Sista Souljah ass. You wasn't tryna hear that shit. You latched on to my ankle and held on for dear life. So why are you suddenly becoming undone over what you just witnessed in the parking lot? You wanted to be the wife of an outlaw. So, now that you are, don't nut up on me now with a million questions about what you saw. Just deal with it."

This was the moment where a normal female would've run or cried, begged and pleaded for him to change his life and all that, but Marnie was not a normal chick. She smiled and said, "Oh, so I'm an outlaw's wife now, huh? Does that make me wifey, or am I gonna really be your wife? There's a difference, ya know?"

All he could do was shake his head. Marnie wasn't working with a full deck. "You crazy as shit, cuz. No bullshit."

"Crazy about you, baby. Crazy about you. But let's not get sidetracked here, and you getting all dramatic and shit does not change the fact that I still wanna know what the hell happened back there."

"You know what happened. Fuck that shit, cuz. I'm tryna worry about the here and now and me getting some of that wet-wet."

"The quicker you talk, the quicker you can get some of this wet-wet. Now talk."

Khadafi exhaled in defeat. Then he told Marnie everything starting at the beginning.

"That was Ameen? Shawnay's Ameen?"

"That was him. I thought he was gonna kill me. I thought he killed Lil Cee because he wanted to kill me himself, to finish me. That's what I thought, but that's not what he wanted."

"What did he want? What did he say to you?" Marnie asked. "And how did he know that the dude was gonna be there like that? Or did he know?"

"That's the exact same thing that I wondered. So I asked him, and he said he came there to kill Lil Cee and prove to me that he and I could live in this world together and not kill one another. I'm not gonna sit here and get all into how he knew this and how he knew that. Let's just say that he did and he got his point across to me. I'm here and you're here and we need to be doing other things besides talking. I've been in jail for fourteen months, and I need some sexual healing. I promise you that tomorrow I will tell you anything you wanna know, but right now I'm tryna fuck." He unzipped his jeans and pulled his dick out. "I need you to speak into this mic, so I can hear your complaints and questions better."

Marnie walked over and got on her knees. She kissed his dick, then looked up at him with lust in her eyes. "Tomorrow we gon' talk about a lot of shit, nigga. Did you hear that? Can you hear me now?" She sucked Khadafi deep. "Can you hear me now?"

*****

After Marnie washed, conditioned, and braided Khadafi's hair, he told her he needed to make an important run. Without question, she handed over the keys to the Escalade, kissed him on the lips, and told him to take her cell phone in case of an emergency. Although she never said a word, Khadafi knew deep down inside that Marnie knew where he was headed. On Sheriff Road in Northeast, he stopped at a flower shop and copped a bouquet of pink roses, Kemie's favorite flowers. Minutes later, he reached his destination.

Climbing out of the truck at Harmony Cemetery, Khadafi picked up Marnie's cell phone and dialed a familiar number. Kemie's mother, Brenda, answered on the first ring.

"Hello? Ms. Brenda?"

"Khadafi?"

"It's me. I got out yesterday, and I want to visit Kemie's grave site."

"I'm glad you made it home, Khadafi, and I'm sure had Kemie lived to see this day, she would have been excited for you and for herself." Brenda Bryant's voice broke, and he knew that she was crying. She gathered her composure and eventually gave him the info he needed.

Fifteen minutes later, he knelt in front of a marble tombstone with a gold nameplate and a small photo of Kemie encased in glass. Placing the roses at the base of the stone, tears welled up in his eyes. The wind picked up suddenly, causing him to button up his Yves St. Laurent pea coat.

Was the strong gust of wind really Kemie's spirit letting him know that she was there? Khadafi read the name Rakemie Bryant over and over again and let his tears fall. *I still can't believe that my baby is really dead. Gone from me forever. The ultimate partner, the love of my life, my soulmate.* He thought about the day Kemie killed Phil Bowman to prove her love. He would miss her forever. Her body lay in a casket six feet below where he now kneeled. Khadafi stared at the photo of Kemie on the tombstone. *So full of life.* He couldn't seem to grasp the fact that she'd been dead for eleven months. Something inside him still hoped and prayed that this was a long nightmare that he still hadn't awakened from. At some point he'd wake up, and his life would be as it was the day before Kemie got shot.

His chest constricted, and he felt trapped in a bad, dark comedy movie, and it wasn't funny anymore. He wiped at the tears on his face to stop them from falling, but it wasn't meant to be. His tears had a plan of their own. They obeyed his heart, and at the moment his heart commanded them to cry. Every part of Khadafi's body was hurting. He cried and could barely breathe, and as terrified as he was, suddenly, he knew why he couldn't breathe. His heart was gone. His life's blood was flowing through his veins but going nowhere. In his most vivid nightmares he never imagined Kemie leaving the world before him, especially not by a hand other than his own. Khadafi was a cold-blooded savage, the beast, the animal marked for death. His enemies were too numerous to count. So how could Kemie have possibly been killed before him? An uncontrollable rage began to build inside Khadafi, one that he knew all too well. The rage screamed and begged to be released upon someone, anyone. If only to stop the dull ache in his heart just for a short while. That anger showed him TJ's face, and he had to remind it that TJ was already dead. Killed by Bay One because he killed Esha. Khadafi's mind searched to remember any of TJ's relatives that he could kill to feed the beast, but he drew a blank. Everybody close to TJ was already dead. He tried to think of anybody else that had crossed him in the past, or while he was locked up, but again, no faces or names came to mind. The vibration from the cell phone in his pocket broke the reverie. He pulled it out. "Hey," he said into the phone and listened as Marnie talked and made him smile. She was a comedian just like

Kemie. Khadafi knew he loved Marnie a lot and he appreciated her, but no one would ever replace Kemie in his heart. And deep down inside he believed Marnie knew that too. "I'm on my way back there now. You want me to stop and pick up anything? No . . . A'ight, I should be there in twenty minutes. Love you, too."

Khadafi stood, wiped all traces of tears from his face, and said his goodbyes to Kemie and prayed that she could hear him. He walked down the hill feeling as if a boulder had been lifted off his shoulders, all the while knowing he had to pick up the pieces and get on with the rest of his life, no matter how hard that, that would be. The rest of his life was calling, and although his heart was broken, he still had to answer it.

# Chapter Two

## Ameen

One year later . . .
February 14, 2013

"Daddy! We can't find Kashon and everybody is waiting for you!" Asia announced in a panic as she rushed inside. She found her dad on the ground with his head bowed, hands cupped in front of him, praying to Allah and thanking him for all the blessings he'd bestowed upon him.

"What you mean you can't find Kashon?" he asked, finally rising to his feet.

"I took him to the bathroom, and then we went to help Mommy get dressed. As soon as we finished, and I turned to take Kay Kay with me to come get you, he was gone. And they're ready to start the wedding too."

"I'll check outside and you check inside." Ameen quickly slipped on his Ferragamo shoes, hoping Khadafi hadn't reneged on their oath. "Did you tell your mama?"

"No, because I didn't want anything to mess up her day. I told her I sent him in here with you."

Ameen opened the closet door and snatched his Ferragamo suit jacket off the hanger and slid his arms into it. Suddenly he slowed his pace, grinned, and told Asia, "Never mind." His body relaxed as he straightened his cuff link.

"What you mean 'never mind'? Daddy, come on! We gotta find Kay Kay." Asia's gaze asked if he was serious. Didn't he realize her three-year-old brother could have wandered off anywhere?

Ignoring his persistent daughter, he dropped to one knee in front of Kashon, who stood inside the closet giggling, looking just like his father, Khadafi. "You ready to do this, little man?" Ameen asked.

"Yup." Kashon nodded, looking over his black tailor made suit jacket, a replica of Ameen's. "I look good!" His reddish brown curls were untamed and a sprinkling of freckles dotted his nose and cheeks.

Asia glared at Kashon. "I'm gone make you look bad, if you run off like that again," she threatened. "Daddy, I'm about ready to kick his little butt. Scaring me like that."

"He won't do it again. Right, Kay Kay?" Ameen asked.

"Right. I won't hide nooooo more," Kashon said, stepping out of the closet.

"And you got the rings, right?" Ameen asked.

Affectionately called "Kay Kay" by everybody in the family, Kashon nodded again, reached into both jacket pockets, and produced two small jewelry boxes.

"You're doing good, little man. I'm proud of you. C'mere." He pulled Kashon into a tight embrace. His love for the kid was genuine. Ameen kissed him.

"Daddy," Asia implored, "would you and bratty boy please come on now? Everybody's waiting for you."

Ameen stood. Then he turned and grabbed her, hugging her. "Awww, are you jealous? Gimme some sugar."

Asia wiggled and freed herself from his arms. "Stop it, Daddy! You gonna mess up my hair. And I am not jealous." She grabbed her little brother's hand. "Come on, Kay Kay, let's go take our positions like we practiced."

Like a proud father, he watched them rush out of the room before eventually following. On the other side of the door was his destiny fulfilled. This was a day Ameen had dreamt about for years, and now it was finally upon him. Still, he couldn't believe that all the tears, all the pain, the trials and tribulations had culminated into this one moment.

Slowly, he walked into the ballroom at the Elk's Lodge, where friends and family, both his and Shawnay's had gathered to witness their special day. When they first planned their wedding, Ameen promised to respect Shawnay's individuality and her desire to remain Christian. So they mutually agreed to be married in a neutral site. No religious themes or overtures allowed. Just a decorated ballroom, family, friends, and the Justice of the Peace. He walked down the aisle until he reached the raised platform where Judge Lewis Paterson stood, ready to connect Shawnay and him in matrimony.

Ameen had been home fourteen months, and it felt like an eternity already. All the things that happened over the last twelve years were never far from his mind. As he stood on the platform and waited to become one with his soulmate, flashes of the events from the last six years replayed in his mind.

His nostalgic moment was broken when music started playing. Ameen looked down the aisle and saw Asia marching forward spilling rose petals in her path. She was the most beautiful flower girl he had ever seen. Kenya, Ameen's oldest daughter, marched behind her, serving as her mother's bridesmaid. She was all grown up and a replica of Shawnay. He smiled as her eyes found his. The rest of the bridal party soon followed. Lastly, came Shawnay, dressed in a white, custom made Vera Wang dress that made her appear as a princess. Her hair fell down her back in layers, flat ironed to perfection. Her caramel complexion shined and radiated, accenting the fuchsia polish on her nails. She looked breathtaking, escorted down the aisle by the best man and ring bearer, Kashon.

Now, with the wedding party on the raised platform, Shawnay took her position at Ameen's right hand side as they both turned to face the Justice of the Peace.

"The bride and groom have elected to recite their very own nuptials. Since it's always ladies first, Shawnay, you go ahead," Judge Peterson said.

Shawnay turned to Ameen and their eyes locked as they held hands. A feeling he couldn't describe washed over him and tears threatened to fall.

"Antonio Tariq 'Ameen' Felder, I take you to be my lawfully wedded husband. I love you now more than I ever have in my life. You are and always have been the air I breathe, my comfort in troubled times, my knight in shining armor."

"Mommy, but I'm supposed to be the knight," Kashon interrupted, half upset and confused.

"You are," Ameen and Shawnay said at the same time, gazing down at him with compassion. The wedding attendees laughed.

"It can be more than one knight?" Kashon quizzed, thinking it over.

"Yes. First Daddy, then you. Now, can I finish my vows, Kay Kay?" Shawnay asked.

"Yes, Mommy!" He nodded vigorously.

The crowd chuckled.

Shawnay turned back to Ameen, her smile replaced with an expression of grave honesty and sincerity. "When I was fourteen years old, I met a boy who has now become a man, a father, a provider, a husband. And I have loved you ever since the first time I laid eyes on you. Take this walk with me and never leave my side." She gripped his hands tighter. "Comfort me, cherish me, help me, desire me, and none other. Make me better; make me whole. You and I have seen the eye of the storm. We've been to ground zero and faced obstacles that would've broken other couples. Our fortitude and perseverance, our strength and love has proven we are not easily broken. Stand by my side and lead me where you want us to be. Head my house and make it your own."

Ameen nodded slightly, enough so that Shawnay knew he understood her every word.

"I love you. You are my soulmate, my best friend, and my rock. Now I ask you to be my husband. Will you be my husband?"

"I will," he replied.

Shawnay got the jewelry box from Kashon, opened it, and extracted a ring. After handing the box back, she turned and took Ameen's hand and slid a platinum wedding band onto his ring finger.

Then it was his turn.

Just over Shawnay's shoulder, Ameen thought he saw an unwanted familiar face standing by the exit. Swiftly, he glared at Kenya, but placed his focus back on the beautiful woman in front of him. "Shawnay Maria Dickerson, from this day forward, your name will be Shawnay Felder, if you'll have me as your husband and become my wife. I too recall the day when I first laid eyes on you. I remember telling my friends, 'There goes my future wife.' After that day, you changed my life. You gave me two of the most beautiful children in the world. But all of that wasn't enough to stop me from going down a destructive path." His last five words made him steal a second glance at the exit, but the phantom young thug was gone. "And through it all, I've ended up right back next to you, where I belong." Antonio recited lyrics from Gerald Levert's song, "Made to Love You." Shawnay's eyes watered because the lyrics fit them perfectly. He ended his vows with, "And I thank Allah for you, for us, for our family. We were made to be together. So, will you be my wife?"

With tears falling down her eyes, Shawnay replied, "Yes, baby. I will be your wife."

"Gimme the box, Kay Kay," Ameen said. Kashon handed him the box, and he opened it to find it empty. Judge Peterson, Shawnay, and Ameen laughed. "The other box, Kay Kay."

Kashon instantly realized his blooper. He smiled, went into his other pocket, and pulled out the right box. Ameen extracted a five carat, VVS diamond wedding ring and placed it on Shawnay's ring finger. They both turned and faced Judge Peterson.

"By the power vested in me, by the District of Columbia, I now pronounce you man and wife. You may kiss the bride," Judge Peterson said.

And that's exactly what he did. Ameen grabbed Shawnay and kissed her.

Forty minutes later, the reception got underway and was one Shawnay would never forget. After an afternoon of dancing and eating, Ameen surprised her by having the singer Sisqo serenade her with the song "Incomplete." Shawnay and most of the females present were in awe and shed tears. Later, she tossed the bouquet into the crowd of frantic women, and after serving cake and doing more dancing, Ameen and Shawnay said their good-byes to their family and thanked everybody for sharing in their special day.

"Nana is gonna take care of you until I get back," Shawnay told a crying Kashon as she and Ameen sat in the limousine that would whisk them to the airport to begin their honeymoon. "You be nice to her and your sisters. I'ma call you every day, okay? I love you," Shawnay said. Kashon hugged her neck tight and kissed her face before she handed him back to Asia.

Finally, Shawnay hugged Kenya and Asia before saying, "I want y'all to mind Grandma. Help her with Kay Kay, and make sure y'all text me every day in the morning and at night. Understand?"

"Understood, Mommy," Asia replied.

"I got you, Ma. Y'all have fun," Kenya added.

Ameen hugged both of his daughter's fiercely, as if it would be their final time. Lastly, he grabbed Kashon and whispered that he was in charge. That made him giggle. Ameen kissed Kashon and held him tight. Then he handed Kashon to Asia. He stepped out of the vehicle and pulled Kenya to the side.

"Can I trust you?" he asked. "Can we trust you?"

"Yes, Daddy," Kenya answered, but didn't sound certain.

"*Yes, Daddy,*" he mocked. "Was he here today? I thought I saw him at the door."

Kenya knew exactly whom he was referring to. "No! Why would I invite him to your wedding?"

"'Cause you think you're smarter than your mother and me."

"No I don't."

"Good, 'cause you're not. So, can we trust you?"

"Yes, Daddy. You and Mommy can trust me."

"So that means no talking smart to your great grandmother. You gotta help her with Asia and Kay Kay, and no telling lies, right?"

"Yes, Daddy."

"That also means that you will go straight home to Great Grandma's after school, right?"

"Yes, Daddy."

"And stay away from them projects around your old way *and* that dude. What's his name?"

"Tyjuan."

"Yeah, him," he said dryly, wondering if Kenya had actually invited the young thug to the wedding. "Stay away from him, Kenya," he warned.

"Okay, Daddy."

"Don't 'okay, Daddy' me. Do what I tell you."

"Okay, Daddy . . . Dag! I hear you. You don't have to tell me that all them times."

"C'mere," Ameen said before embracing Kenya in a bear hug and picking her up.

"Daddy, put me down!"

"You're my little lady, and I love you with all my heart. Don't make me lose my trust in you."

"I won't, Daddy. Now, put me down!" He did as she requested. "Bye Mommy, bye Daddy."

"Bye sweetheart."

The last thing Ameen had for Kenya was genuine trust, especially when it came to this new boy Tyjuan she'd been bringing around. He represented everything he once thought he loved, but now hated with extreme prejudice.

# Chapter Three

## Kenya

Kenya's cell phone blasted "Dangerously in Love" by Beyoncé and woke her up. She grabbed it off the pillow beside her and checked the caller ID. Tyjuan. She pushed the talk button. "Hello?"

"Kenya?"

"It's me. What's up?" she answered, sounding groggy.

"You sleep?"

"I was, but not anymore, thanks to you."

"You miss me?"

"What time is it, Tyjuan?"

"Let me check my phone, Yah-Yah. It's 11:15. Why?"

"I told you not to call me that, boy. I thought it was later than that. It feels like I've been asleep longer than just two hours. And I always miss you."

"I can't tell. Why are you sleeping so early anyway?"

"Because I got up early. I been up since five a.m. helping my mother get ready for the wedding."

"Damn, my bad! I forgot all about your parents getting married today."

"Well, I didn't and it was beautiful. My mother's dress, her red bottom shoes, the decorations, the food, all those people that came, it was unforgettable. And guess what?"

"What?"

"My dad thought he saw you at the wedding."

"What! That's crazy!"

"Same thing I thought."

"He must be paranoid."

"I know, right? Anyway, you're not gonna believe this, but my dad had Sisqo sing to my mother. He serenaded her at the reception. Oh. My. Gawd . . . I wanted to die. I couldn't believe it. He was so—"

"Sisqo? What Sisqo?"

"Duh? The singer with Dru Hill."

"That little gold-haired nigga? He's a fag."

"He is not. Stop hating, boy. Sisqo is not a fag. And for your information, his hair is not gold."

"What color was it then?"

"It was red, flaming red."

Tyjuan laughed uncontrollably before saying, "Like I said, he's a fag."

"Whatever, Tyjuan. It was beautiful, though. Today made me think about the day when we get married. Ours will be very similar to my parents, but I wanna get married in Las Vegas."

"Las Vegas? And who do you think is gonna pay for all that?"

"Tyjuan Dewayne Glover. That's who. And why haven't I heard from you all day?"

"Because I was caught up doing something all day."

"Did that something include you putting your dick somewhere it didn't belong?"

"Not at all. My dick ain't have shit to do with what I was doing."

"It better not have." Kenya yawned. "Damn, I'm tired as hell. After the wedding reception, I had to help my grandmother and nem' clean up the Elk's Lodge. Then I had to bathe and put my little brother to sleep."

"So your mother and father went on and jumped the broom, huh? That's a'ight, in a good way and a bad way."

"How could them getting married ever be a bad thing, Tyjuan?"

"Because it takes your mother off the market, and she phat as shit, that's how."

"Boy, don't play with me like that," she insisted, getting upset.

"Damn, Kenya, I'm just playing, boo. Your butt's way phatter than your mother's."

"No it's not."

"Yes it is, but you can't deny that your mother is a milf."

"Bye, Tyjuan! I'm about to go back to sleep."

"A'ight, a'ight, boo, I'ma stop playing. Speaking of your butt, I need to see it. I mean—you."

"See me when?"

"Right now."

"Tyjuan, are you crazy? I can't see you right now. My grandmother is probably still woke. You tryna get me killed?"

"Stop the bullshit, Kenya. Grandma old as shit, she ain't gon' kill you."

"Grandma? Who said anything about Grandma? She won't kill me, but she will tell my mother. Then she'll tell my father and he'll kill me. Antonio Felder ain't going for the bullcrap."

"Maaaannnn," Tyjuan groaned, "fuck your father!"

"You really gon' make me hang up on you now. Keep it up."

"Real talk, though, Kenya. Your father be hating like shit. He be hanging the phone up on a nigga when I call y'all house phone. He act like I ain't good enough for you or something. Like him and your mother ain't originally from the projects in Southeast."

"It ain't that. You gotta understand that my father went to jail for murder when I was four. He's been home over a year, but he's still trying to get used to the fact that I'm almost grown. In his mind, I'm still his little girl and he wants to protect me."

"Protect you from what? From who?"

"From mistakes and eighteen-year-old thugs like you. Dudes who prey on sixteen-year-old girls like me and steal our innocence, then leave us with children and no father to raise them. He always tell me to find a nerd type dude, not a street dude."

"I feel that, but slim gotta respect my gangsta—"

"Your gangsta?"

"Yeah, my gangsta. I know he did a bid on a body and caught a body in the joint. My big homies know your father. In the joint they call him Ameen."

"I know that."

"Well, I do my thing too and I bust my gun. Man, fuck all that. Come outside and see me."

"Come out where, Tyjuan? Where are you?"

"Outside your grandmother's house."

"You what! Where?" Kenya jumped out of bed with the phone still to her ear. She walked over to the window and pulled the curtain back. "Boy . . . What are you . . . Where are you?"

"I'm in the champagne Porsche truck with the rims. See it?"

Kenya spotted the Porsche Cheyenne. "And you've been parked out there for how long?"

"The whole time that I've been talking to you."

"Boy, whose truck is that? Did you steal it?" she asked with her eyes glued to the beautiful SUV with the chrome 26-inch rims.

"You gon' disrespect me like that, huh? Like I'm a car thief. You wrong for that. This my man, Squirt's joint. He got my Charger for the weekend. Are you coming out or what? I said I need to see you," Tyjuan said as he exited the Cheyenne dressed in jeans, Nike Foam Posites, and a Louis V sweater with a Louis V scarf around his neck.

Butterflies instantly gripped her stomach as she watched him from the window. He always had that effect on her. Kenya felt like a groupie whenever she saw him. Tyjuan's swagger was on one million. He was fine as shit and resembled Waka Flocka. His clothes were always designer, and they draped his 5-feet 10-inch frame as if they were tailored. Tyjuan's shoe game was sick. His shoulder-length dreads hung freely, and Tyjuan had one tattoo on his face.

The letters TCB were tatted under his right eye. It stood for "The Circle Boyz," the name of his neighborhood crew. His golden skin tone accented his hazel eyes and dark, thick eyebrows. His moustache was always perfectly trimmed. That made her weak. "Tyjuan, I can't come—"

"I'm not leaving until you come outside and see what I want. So, we are just gonna be here like this all night."

Hearing a noise, she jumped. She realized the sound came from the TV in her grandmother's room across the hall and her heart rate slowed. Kenya knew she should resist the desire to go downstairs and go outside, but she couldn't. Tyjuan Glover was a drug that she was feenin' for and had to have. Ever since he'd taken her virginity five months ago, he was like a band-aid on her bloody wound. The things he did to her on the basement floor in her mother's house were things she had seen on porn sites on her laptop. Things she loved, craved, and never told a soul about wanting to experience.

"Kenya, you still there? Did you hear what I just said?"

"I'm here, and yes, I heard you, boy. I'm still tryna build up my nerve to come out there. Like I said earlier, you are tryna get me killed."

"Don't even trip, potato chip. I'ma protect you from the big bad wolf."

"That's what I'm afraid of. Let me throw on some clothes. I'm coming out. But you gotta pull around the back. Go through the alley on Bryan Place and make a right. Come halfway down the alley and stop. Turn your lights out and I'll come to you. Got it?"

"I gotcha, baby girl. I'm getting in the truck now. Come on."

"Gimme ten minutes. Let me check a few things. Bye."

"I love you, Kenya."

"I love you, too . . . Bye." She disconnected the call, then crept across the hall to her grandmother's room. Peeping in her door, she saw her grandmother lying in her bed asleep with the covers over her head. Knowing her like she did, Grandma slept like the dead at night and nothing would wake her. She checked in on her little brother and sister, and they too were knocked out. Exhaling as she made her way back down the hall to her mother's old bedroom, she quickly slipped on jeans under her nightgown and put on flip flops, despite the cold weather outside. Kenya then walked downstairs and grabbed her Helly Hanson coat and put it on. Three minutes later, she was getting into the Porsche truck.

"You said you needed to see me. Well, here I am." As soon as she shut the door, she said, "What's up?"

"Can I get a hug and a kiss?" Tyjuan asked with a boyish grin.

"Of course." Kenya leaned over to hug him, but stopped short. "Wait a minute. Let me take off my coat." She and Tyjuan embraced and kissed. Kenya tried to break the kiss, but he wouldn't let her. So she just went with it. Suddenly, it dawned on her that she hadn't even brushed her teeth. For sure her breath had to stink. Again she tried to break the lip lock but failed. Finally, after several minutes, the kiss ended. Relieved, she checked her coat for the candy she'd put there earlier and found it. "So, you've seen me and damn near sucked all the breath out of my body. Can I go back inside now?"

"Not yet," Tyjuan said, straightening up, putting the car in gear and pulling down the alley.

Alarmed, she shouted, "Boy, I can't go nowhere! Where are you going?"

Tyjuan smiled. "Chill out, baby girl. I ain't going far."

They ended up three blocks over from Morris Road on Sixteenth Street in the back of the old blue clinic building. "Tyjuan, why are we back here?"

"You know why we back here. Stop the bullshit. I just wanna quickie, no bite marks, no passion marks, and no hickies. Get in the backseat."

Like an obedient child, Kenya did as told. Once there, Tyjuan unbuttoned and unzipped her jeans, then pulled them down and off. Her heartbeat raced in anticipation of what was about to happen. It was a normal occurrence for her because her body always did strange things around Tyjuan. He laid her back and pulled her panties to one side. Then Tyjuan dropped his head between her legs, and the moment his wet lips and tongue touched her pussy, Kenya completely melted and gave into the feelings of euphoria that overtook her body. By the time his tongue pressed against her clit, her legs were shaking.

"Tyjuan . . . Tyjuan . . . Wait—"

He lifted his head and looked at her. "I can't wait no more, Kenya. Your young ass got me going crazy for you. You're all I think about." With that statement, she momentarily felt like jail bait. But that feeling quickly subsided as her boyfriend dove back down in between her legs and ate her pussy like a starving third world refugee. Kenya grabbed a handful of his dreads as she simultaneously tried to wrap her legs around his head. She wanted to hold Tyjuan captive between her legs forever. A minute later, she orgasmed all over his face. "Damn, boy!"

Tyjuan lifted all the way up, raised his shirt, and removed a silver and black handgun the size of a clothes hanger. It frightened her. Seeing the look on her face, Tyjuan said, "These streets are hectic, baby girl. I can't go nowhere without this." He put the gun on the floor. Hearing his zipper come down, made her forget all about what she'd just seen. She knew what came next. Tyjuan's dick wasn't all that big compared to the men she'd seen on porn sites, but inside her it felt huge, long, and thick. As he positioned himself on top, she opened her legs wider to accommodate his body weight. He kissed her for a minute, before reaching under himself and sliding his dick into her soaking wet pussy. Wrapping her arms around his neck, she bit down on her bottom lip and squeezed Tyjuan tight.

Soft moans escaped her mouth as Tyjuan dipped into her and set her body on fire. With her heart aflutter and her hormones in flames, she whimpered like a puppy caught in a cage with a pit bull. Her legs opened wider to accommodate Tyjuan's deeper thrusts, and she caught a glimpse of the pink colored polish on her toes, just as her toes curled and ended up by her ear. With one leg pressed back, and the other touching the back of the driver seat, she gave up the ghost and orgasmed again and again.

Twenty minutes later, she was creeping back into her grandmother's house. She climbed the stairs, disrobing as she went. By the time Kenya reached her grandmother's room, she was wearing only a nightgown. Grandma was still under the covers fast asleep. She watched her chest rise and fall a few times before leaving to check on Kashon and Asia. Everything was calm in the Dickerson household. Well, not everything. Kenya's hormones were still raging. First she called Tyjuan's cell phone and confirmed their date for the movies later. She wanted to see the new *Think Like A Man* movie, but knowing Tyjuan, he'd want to see some action flick. After ending her call with Tyjuan, she got under the covers and removed her panties. She licked her fingers and slowly fingered herself. As the crescendo built and Kenya was about to cum all over her fingers, she wondered if she got her freaky side from her mother or her father.

# Chapter Four

## Shawnay

The total polarity of Antonio intrigued Shawnay. She thought this after first hearing him call the "Adhan" quietly. Then he began his morning prayer and followed it with reciting from the Holy Quran. Afterward, he ended his prayers by calling the "Taslim." How he was able to balance everything inside him impressed her and made him sexy. Antonio could be street one minute and then teach her about all the religions in the world the next minute. He was a thug, a father, a religious man, a businessman and a porn star all rolled into one. The same man she heard making his prayers every morning, had also been the same man making her scream in ecstasy most evenings. The night before, they had entered the hotel room tearing at each other's clothes.

"Wait . . ." Antonio said. "The dress, the garter, and the thigh-high stockings stay on. Just take off your heels so I can see them toes."

Then she was on the bed on all fours, her white Vera Wang wedding dress, up and settled around her waist. Her thigh-length stockings attached to a garter around each leg were still on, but her matching Victoria Secret panties lay on the floor beside the white Christian Louboutins. Antonio gripped her ass as he entered her and found a rhythm. The moisture from her pussy allowed deeper penetration, and she cried out with every thrust.

"Damn, Mrs. Felder, you got the best pussy in the world," he repeated over and over. Shawnay lay in bed and smiled as she remembered being turned over, her stocking covered feet ended up on both of Antonio's muscular shoulders as he pressed her into the bed and long dicked her with a passion and intensity that made her want to cry. He was hurting her, but making her feel so good at the same time. She came in gushes repeatly.

The memory of last night incensed her lust. Before she knew it, her hands were under the covers and all over her wet pussy. Her eyes stayed glued to Antonio's back as he now stood on the balcony and leaned on the rail. She opened her legs wide and remembered every position he'd put her in last night. And how he made her feel. A small moan escaped her mouth as she came all over her fingers, but that wasn't enough. She needed Antonio to fuck her.

Getting up, she slipped on her panties and saw her dress, stockings, garter and heels all over the floor. She smiled and walked out onto the balcony. Embracing his waist from behind, she placed small kisses on his back.

"Hey, baby," Antonio said. "Did I wake you?"

"No," she lied. "I turned over and saw you out here. What's wrong? You got something on your mind?"

"Yeah."

Shawnay let go of his waist and stood beside him. "Wanna talk about it?"

Antonio looked down at her and said, "Why not? I vowed to keep it real with you, right?"

"Right."

"Yesterday, I gotta admit, I stood on that platform and watched you come down that aisle. You were so beautiful, so sexy. I've never loved you more than at that moment. But my mind . . . my mind went to that *The Best Man* movie. The one with Taye Diggs, Morris Chestnut—"

"I know the movie, Antonio."

"Then you're familiar with the part where Morris Chestnut is at the alter waiting on Monica Calhoun, but all he can see is flashbacks of his woman having sex with Taye Diggs."

"I'm familiar with it," she admitted, knowing exactly where Antonio was headed.

"Well, that happened to me in real life, Shawnay. I couldn't get that vision of Khadafi and you outta my head."

"But yet, you married me anyway. How many times are we going to revisit this? You told me a year ago, and then reassured me weeks ago, that we could put that all behind us."

"Don't misunderstand what I'm saying. I did and I have. But that doesn't mean that I won't think about it. I have a three-year-old constant reminder of it. That ain't why I'm out here on this balcony, though, or what I was thinking about. I love you, baby, with all my heart and I'm happy. More than I ever have been in my life. Being here in Clear Water Beach, Florida, on my honeymoon with you—this is what I've always wanted. This is what I dreamed of all those years as I lay caged in various prisons all across the country. I thank Allah for the blessings he's bestowed on me, on us. Standing here peering down at this clear blue water, watching people snorkel and jet ski makes me a little sad."

"Why would that make you sad?" she asked, baffled.

"Because I'm torn inside, Shawnay. I'm here experiencing all of this, and tomorrow, you and I will board a Carnival Triumph cruise ship destined for the Carribean. But all the people I love are still in prison, in the cells that I left behind. A lot of them will never get to see any of this . . . the clear water, the jet skis, snorkels, beautiful women, the food . . . ever again. They will never get to go on a cruise or visit the Carribean Islands.

"Antonio," Shawnay said softly.

He'd heard her, but needed to express his thoughts. "They will never get married as free men or make love to their women without somebody watching out. They'll never tuck their daughters in at night. That's what I think about, Shawnay. I think about my partner Antone White, a good man, but he's doing life in the Feds and so is his codefendant, Erick Hicks. All good men that might not ever see the streets again—never see sights like this one. That's what makes me sad."

"You can't do this to yourself, Antonio. That's not your burden to bear. It's too heavy."

"It might be. But they're never far from my mind. Nehemiah, Kenny Garmagoo, and Paul Hiligh." Ameen shook his head sadly. "Joe Ebron, Kevin Bellinger, and Pat Andrews, too."

"And don't forget about Fat Bug and Trey Manning," Shawnay said. "See . . . you talk about them enough so that I know nicknames and first and last names."

Antonio continued staring straight ahead.

"One day you told me that Allah doesn't put on a person, more than he can bear. Remember that?"

"I do."

"Well, all those dudes you and I just mentioned will be okay. They have their own mountains to climb, crosses to bear. You are only one man, and you can't control time, space, and history. Didn't you also tell me that people shouldn't beat themselves up about things they can't control? Look, you're here. *We're here* and there's nothing wrong with that. You're a free man. Allah blessed you with your freedom, and there's nothing to be sad about. Do what you can to assist your friends and let the rest take care of itself."

"You're right," Antonio admitted and smiled. "I just pray the streets let me chill, and I never have to go back behind the wall. I pray I never have to be the old Antonio. I wanna live in this moment right here forever."

"I pray for the same things as well."

"While we were asleep, I got a text from Kenya. She says that all is well on the home front and that she's going to the movies later with Nadiya. Everybody was asleep, but they sent their love."

"That's good to hear, but right now I just remembered what I came out here for." Antonio's eyebrow went up. "And what's that, wifey?"

"I came out to tell my husband that his dick was required in the bedroom. I need a repeat performance of last night."

"Well, that means you gotta put the dress and stockings back on, right?"

"I wasn't talking about that part, but I'll tell you what. We'll compromise. How about I just put on the garter, stockings, and heels?"

"That's fine with me, baby."

She turned and walked into the suite, losing her panties in the process. Glancing over her shoulder, she gave Antonio a lascivious wink and picked up the garter and stockings and put them on. Last came the heels. Shawnay got up onto the bed and assumed the position.

An hour passed and Antonio snored beside a satisfied Shawnay. Her smile disappeared as something disturbing struck her. Antonio's comment about the streets letting him chill nagged at her. The thought of him going back to jail was too devastating to fathom, that she quickly pushed it out of her mind. She knew bad thoughts manifested bad actions. Damn, how Shawnay had wished that Antonio never made the statement.

# Chapter Five

## Kenya

"Where did you tell your grandmother you were going?" Tyjuan asked.

Kenya closed the door to the Porsche truck and unzipped her Ralph Lauren Ski Tech coat. She leaned over to kiss Tyjuan.

"A little bit of truth mixed with a lot of falsehood. I told her I was going to the movies, only I told her that it was with Nadiyah."

"Did you call Nadiya and tell her so she'll cover for you if your grandma calls her?"

"Duh! Of course I did. What else would I do?"

Tyjuan started the truck and pulled away from the Anacostia subway station with at least fifty pairs of eyeballs glued to the truck. "You could always just tell the truth."

"About us? Boy, you must be crazy. The last thing my father said before they left yesterday was, 'stay away from what's his name."'

"Stay away from what's his name? You telling me he don't even know my name?"

"Why would he remember? It ain't like I'm walking around broadcasting the fact that you're my boyfriend, Tyjuan. My father would—"

"Kill me," he mocked. "You already told me that about a thousand times. So, how long do you think it'll be before you broadcast to the world that you love Big Tyjuan?"

"Big Tyjuan? Boy, stop. Ain't nothing big about you."

"I can't tell. That ain't what you was screaming in my ear last night. Do I need to remind you?"

"Tyjuan, please shut up and drive. You make me sick."

"Do your parents even know that you've had sex before?"

"Are you crazy? Of course not! The only person that knows is my doctor. As long as I protect myself and don't get pregnant, she promised she'd never tell my parents. I'ma break the news to my parents one day, though. I'll be seventeen in a couple of months. They will have to respect me as a woman."

"That's what I'm talking about. Then I'll get to tap that ass in y'all's house."

"You might not ever. Not in there. The first time was the first and last time we do that in there."

"They had to know that a smooth, young nigga would come along one day and get inside them little drawers you keep buying from Target."

Playfully, Kenya punched Tyjuan on the shoulder. "My drawers don't come from no Target. I get all my panties from Nordstroms in Pentagon City, thank you."

"Oh, my bad. You got that," Tyjuan replied, then turned on some music. He selected a track by voice command and the sounds of Young Jeezy and Ne-Yo filled the truck. Tyjuan sang along to the song . . .

"She said—You ain't no good, but you feel so good . . . She said—What if I could? But I gotta leave you alone . . ."

Kenya listened to the lyrics he rapped and knew that he was talking about her. She gave Tyjuan an evil look and punched his shoulder again. He feigned pain, then burst out laughing. She changed the song to a Rihanna cut called "Take a Bow."

"I was listening to that," Tyjuan protested.

"Too bad."

About fifteen minutes later, they pulled into an empty parking spot in front of Color Me Badd tattoo parlor, and Tyjuan cut the truck off.

"I thought we were going to the movies?"

"We are. But first I wanna broadcast to the world how much I love you. Especially now that you've admitted that you hide our love."

"Hide? Tyjuan, you know I can't. You know how my parents—"

"Yeah, right, Kenya. Your parents run you. They don't run me. C'mon."

"What are you about to do? Get a tattoo?"

"That's my plan."

"Of what?"

"Of you."

Shocked, she repeated, "Of me?"

"Yeah, I just told you that I'ma let the world know how I feel about Kenya LaShawn Dickerson. Even though she gotta hide her love for me."

Before Kenya could formulate a reply, Tyjuan was out the truck and headed into the tattoo parlor. She had to skip to catch up to him.

As soon as the tattoo parlor door shut behind her, she said, "Stop playing, boy. What tattoo are you getting?"

Ignoring her, Tyjuan spoke to the fat, black chick with too many piercings who sat behind the counter. She made a call, then directed them back to a room down the hall. A short, Mexican man with tattoos all over his arms, head, and face came out of the room and motioned them inside. Kenya wondered if he had tattoos on his legs and feet as well. He looked dangerous.

"What are you tryna get today, dawg?" the Mexican asked Tyjuan.

"I'm tryna get a portrait of my girl on the left side of my chest, right over my heart."

The Mexican smiled and showed off a mouthful of platinum teeth. He looked back and forth from Tyjuan to Kenya. "That's what's up. I take it that baby right here is your girl?"

Tyjuan nodded.

"That's what's up, then, dawg. Young love. Ain't nothing like it in the world. The tat that you want ain't no problem, dawg, but I gotta tell you that your heart is not on the left side of your chest. It's actually right in the middle of your chest. I can't let you get the tat and then find out that it ain't over your heart. Feel me?"

"I feel you, slim."

"Call me Sleepy, dawg. Everybody calls me Sleepy."

"I feel you, Sleepy, but it's all good. I don't want that joint in the crease of my chest. So since shorty is my right hand and everything about her is right, put her face on my right side."

"Whatever you want, dawg. Are you getting that tat today?"

"If I can."

"I got time to do it now. You just want a portrait of her face?"

"Yeah. Just the face and maybe a little neck. Oh, and I want her whole name under the tat. Hold on." Tyjuan turned to face Kenya. "Do you think I should just get your first name or the whole name?"

Still caught between shock and disbelief, Kenya was at a loss for words.

"Put her whole name under the joint, slim," Tyjuan said to the Mexican.

"Cool. I can freehand her name, but I'ma need about thirty minutes with your girl to sketch her features. Then I'll be ready to do your tat."

"One of my men told me that you do good work. This joint is special to me, so you gotta hook it up."

"Dawg, I am the best tattoo artist in the whole DMV. I got you. Just fall back and let me do this sketch, and then I'ma show you why your man recommended me and my shop. Let me get my equipment."

Ninety minutes later, Kenya couldn't believe her eyes when Tyjuan came out of the room with his shirt off. She stood gazing at her portrait etched permanantly into his skin. Tears formed in her eyes, and her love for him skyrocketed ten levels. The connection between them forever forged in blood and ink. She wiped at her eyes and quickly pulled her iPhone out of her Prada bag. Using the camera phone, Kenya snapped several pictures of the tattoo on Tyjuan's muscular chest.

"What are you doing?" Tyjuan asked.

"What do you think I'm doing?" she asked rhetorically while typing on the phone's touch screen keyboard. "I'm putting pictures up on Facebook and on Instagram. My friends gotta see this."

"But, your mother checks your page, doesn't she?"

"Yup."

"So, you telling me that you don't care if she sees the tattoo?"

"I care, but what can she do? It's on your chest, not mine. Besides, I'm not gonna miss out on this moment to let all the groupie chicks that be sweating you know that I got you. My face is tatted on you, not theirs. They gon' really hate me now. I want everybody on Facebook to see it. And I'ma announce it on Twitter. If my mother finds out, I'ma just come clean and tell her everything."

"Everything? Like what? You faking!"

"No, I am not. I'ma tell her everything. About us, our love, me having sex, everything."

"And what about your father? You gon' tell him everything, too?"

Kenya thought about having that conversation with her father and cringed inside. *He would literally kill me.*

"Why not? That is, if I'm still breathing after I tell my mother."

*****

Between Kenya's mind wandering from the tattoo on Tyjuan's chest, to the reaction it was gonna cause on Facebook, and Tyjuan's hand inside her pants, fingering her throughout the entire movie, she didn't get the chance to really enjoy *Think Like A Man.* Kenya saw enough of it to conclude that Kevin Hart made the movie funny as hell.

As they exited the movie theater, her eyes were on her iPhone as she posted the photo of Tyjuan's tattoo on her Twitter page. So much so, that she never even saw Tyjuan collide into another dude until she heard Tyjuan's raised voice say, "You need glasses, nigga? I know you saw me walking right here."

"Nigga, fuck you and some glasses! You saw me walking, too."

The dude's caramel colored face was a mask of pure fury. His light green eyes were the prettiest shade of green that she'd ever seen on a person. He was a little taller than Tyjuan, but skinnier. His wavy hair was like well spun silk and made him look exotic.

"What's up, then?" Tyjuan bellowed.

"What's up with you, nigga! What you tryna do?"

Kenya grabbed Tyjuan's arm to get him to calm down, but he snatched away. A pretty, brown-skinned female with chinky eyes jumped in front of Tyjuan. "Tyjuan, y'all go 'head with that bullshit!" she said.

"You should be telling that to your man, with his bitch ass," Tyjuan replied.

The green-eyed dude moved the girl out of the way and was about to come at Tyjuan, when the security guard showed up right on time. "You ain't tryna see me, dawg, and you know it. You fakin' in front of that bitch," Tyjuan stated.

"Nigga, who you callin' a bitch?" the girl hissed.

"Bitch, fuck you!" Tyjuan said, before turning his attention back to the green-eyed guy. "What you tryna do, Tyger? You wanna see me outside?"

"See you outside? Tyjuan, stop all the fakin', slim."

"Faking? Yeah, I got your 'fakin' right here," Tyjuan said sternly. Without warning, Tyjuan reared back and hawk spit on Tyger.

It was as if the whole lobby gasped. Kenya stood riveted to her spot as saliva ran down Tyger's face. He tried to wipe it away, but ended up smearing it across his cheek. Then he laughed. A short, manical laugh. "I'ma kill you for that."

"Kill this dick, bitch nigga," Tyjuan responded.

Since she still had the cell phone in her hand, Kenya snapped a picture of Tyger's face and sent a Twitpic out into cyberspace. She had no clue why she took the picture, she just did. The security guard held Tyger and told Tyjuan to leave the premises before he called the police. The girl with Tyger stayed at his side, shooting daggers at Tyjuan.

Outside in the truck, Tyjuan was silent as he pulled out of the City Place Mall parking lot.

They were on Georgia Avenue, headed back to Southeast when she finally broke the silence. The quiet in the car was too loud for Kenya.

"Who was that, Tyjuan? What happened between y'all while I wasn't looking, and who was that girl that called you by name?"

"The dude was an old friend of mine named Terrell. We from different hoods, and since our hoods be beefing, we mutually stopped being friends. There's been a lot of tension in the air between them and us ever since one of their men got killed around my way. That nigga know he don't want it with me, but he jumped out there to impress that freak bitch Tashia. He saw us walking by, and he purposely acted like he wasn't paying attention and bumped me. So I pushed him, and that's when it all went south. This nigga been busting his gun a little bit, and they done gave him a nickname, and now he think he like that. That nigga's a bitch, and he and I both know it. They call him the Tyger now, and that shit is going to his head. His big homie, Fella and nem' yeasting his head up. And little do they know that they gon' get him murdered and fast, if he keep jumping out there in them waters that he ain't ready to swim in. There's a lot about me that you don't know, Kenya, and I keep that side of me away from you for a reason. I never want you to see that side of me, or know about the animal that I am. Unless I have to show you. That's why I'm lightweight glad that security muthafucka held that nigga there. Because then I would have had to open his head up in front of you, and I didn't want that."

A moment of silence passed between them.

"The bitch with him, like I said, is this freak bitch from the hood named Tashia. She been on my line for years, but I won't fuck with her and she mad. She must've said something to Tyger about me, and he wanted to impress her by jumping out there. Niggas show their asses about bitches every time they in public.

"Stupid ass nigga. Gone get himself killed about a freak bitch," Tyjuan vented and shook his head. "That nigga gonna make me put thirty in his bitch ass."

"So you don't care about the fact that he said he was gon' kill you for spitting on him?" Kenya asked, still seeing the spit rolling down Tyger's face in her mind.

"Fuck that nigga, boo! That nigga faking like shit. He don't want no smoke. He had to say something to save face in front of Tashia."

"I hear you, but you still shouldn't have spit on him, Tyjuan." The look Tyjuan gave her raised the temperature in the car to one hundred degrees.

"Whose side are you on, Kenya?"

"Why would you ask me something like that? I'm on your side, now and forever. I'm just saying that you disrespected the dude, and he might not wanna let it go. That's all. I don't want you to have to kill nobody, and I don't want nothing to happen to you. That's all."

Tyjuan's features softened. "Look, I know you're just concerned about me, and I didn't mean to imply anything bad. I'm sorry for blowing on you, but that nigga Tyger still got me kinda heated. Maybe I shouldn't have spit on him, but at the time I was so mad that I reacted without thinking, and that's what my heart told me to do. I done done it now, and I can't take it back. So if that nigga wanna beef about what I did, then we gon' have to cook it. That's just the way it goes. But I don't think he gon' do shit. That nigga know how I get down, and he know that if he jumps out there on some real live gun shit, that he gon' have to kill me and my whole team.

And that's a plate of food them niggas ain't tryna eat from. Their spoons and forks ain't big enough. Trust me on that."

Kenya leaned back in the seat and closed her eyes. She was tired, hungry, and kind of blown from the incident in the movies. "Are we still going to get something to eat?" she asked. Kenya didn't trust what Tyjuan was saying about Tyger, but she had to take his word for it, because obviously he knew better than her. She hoped . . .

# CHAPTER SIX

## KHADAFI

The texture and color of the dope on the plate was a telltale sign of its quality. Plus, Khadafi liked the fact that it was rocked up and not powdery, that was good. With latex gloves on his hands, he picked up small rocks and put them on the scale. Every time it read 1.0, he knew he had a gram. A street gram of grade heroin was worth a lot after it had been stepped on at least three times. In the penitentiary that number tripled. Khadafi dropped each gram into a small plastic sandwich bag, then twisted the ends and tied it. After cutting the excess plastic, he dropped the gram into a finger of the latex glove. He'd tear the finger off and tie it, then repeat that process with the other four remaining fingers. One more layer of plastic came next, then two small balloons. The powerful dope needed extra layers of insulation to guard against erosion once the stomach acids got to them. His fingers stiffened and cramped, but he kept on working. He'd been at the table since eight this morning cutting, weighing, and packaging dope. The long process seemed tedious and boring, but necessary. Khadafi had to maintain his ties to the good men in the penitentiaries all over the system. They needed him. "Death Before Dishonor" always.

He was trying to twist out a crook in his neck when something on the TV behind him caught his attention.

"Give a man a fish and he'll eat for a day. Teach a man to fish and he will eat for a lifetime. But if you teach a man to create an artificial shortage of fish, he'll eat steak."

He turned to see that the preson who had just said that was Jay Leno. He was on a daytime talk show discussing how he went about business. Khadafi thought about his words and was instantly transported back to 2008. He had just come home from a ten year bid. Outside of White Corner's restaurant, he was seated in the car with his uncle Marquette when he spoke those same words, but in a different way. "Ain't nothing promised to no man, nephew. The Bible say that every man shall taste death, but fuck that shit. Me and you, nephew, we gon' live forever. In these parts, ain't no motherfucker tryna give a nigga shit. I'm the same way, nephew. Don't get me wrong, I'm glad you're home and all that shit, but I ain't gonna make a bad hustler out of you. I know you tryna eat, though, feel me? I could throw you a few dollars and a fish dinner right now, but then you will only have eaten for a day. But if I show you how to fish and take you to where the fish swim, you can feed yourself for a lifetime."

That day Khadafi chose to feed himself for a lifetime. He walked—well—ran into White Corner's and killed a fish named Fat Sean Bundy and took his car keys. In the trunk of his Bentley was over three hundred grand and a couple keys of heroin. His uncle took the dope and gave him the money. Khadafi never looked back after that. He became a fisherman of men and their riches. Allowing himself a brief moment of nostalgia caused a deep wave of sadness to wash over him as he thought of his uncle. Marquette had been killed a couple months later, found dead in his Benz. "I guess it wasn't decreed for you to live forever, unc. But don't even trip, I'm living enough for the both of us," Khadafi whispered and turned back to the task at hand. After finishing the job, he counted the colorful balloons. "One hundred grams," he called out to Erykah, his man Mousey's woman.

"You finished?" she asked as she appeared.

When he first showed up at the small apartment on Galveston Street, Erykah was dressed in loose fitting cotton pajamas. That had been hours ago. Now she was dressed in leggings that looked like a second skin and a tight T-shirt that hugged her breasts perfectly. Words across the shirt read, "I got a killer pussy" and depicted a small cat. Erykah wasn't wearing panties or a bra. Her pussy print looked like a balled up pair of mittens and her nipples were as large as Tootsie Rolls. His eyes traveled down to her bare feet. They were unpolished, but pretty nontheless. His dick stiffened and the animal inside him roared. Khadafi shook his head and dropped his eyes.

"What?" she asked coyly.

"Nothing, cuz," was all he could say.

Khadafi struggled to calm the beast inside. Suddenly, he wanted to fuck shorty, and he wanted to do her dirty for what she was trying to pull. She had to know what she was doing, what she was wearing, and what it would do to him. But as bad as he wanted to do it, he couldn't. He wouldn't . . . Not to Mousey. Not like he'd done to Ameen. That's what started their beef in the first place. He couldn't let that happen again.

"Did Mousey put you down with the whole move on how to handle business?" Khadafi asked, turning back to the table and away from temptation.

"Me and Mousey been doing this shit since Atlanta. I'm good. I know what to do."

"And you don't be scared when you do that shit?"

"Them crackers don't scare me. I ain't scared of nothing or nobody."

He smiled at what he perceived to be a veiled implication about sex. Khadafi put twenty balloons a piece into five different sandwich bags and then gathered up all the utensils. He turned and tossed twenty grams to Erykah.

"Well, make sure your tough ass call me when you get back from Florida," he said as he walked past Erykah to leave.

"Uh . . . Excuse me, but ain't you forgetting something?"

He faced Erykah, noticing how pretty, pouty, and perfectly glossed her lips were. The beast inside him roared once more. He could see her lips all over his dick as he grabbed her red hair and forced all of him in her mouth. Her hands were on her hips seductively. Inviting. Enticing.

"What did I forget?" he inquired.

"The money. I can't get to Coleman without the money."

Snapping out of his reverie and quieting the beast within, he replied, "My bad, cuz." He reached into his pocket and felt a small bankroll. It wasn't enough. "Hold up, I'll be right back."

Khadafi left the apartment and went outside to the car, then popped the trunk. The bound man curled up into the fetal position had dried blood on his face and head. His eyes looked frightened. He pulled the strip of tape off his mouth.

"Khadafi, please, slim! Don't do this, slim! Let me go!"

"Marco, I told your big teeth ass not to sell no dope on my lot, didn't I?"

He nodded before saying, "I-I didn't mean—"

"You got some dope on you?" he asked the condemned man.

"No, but Khadafi, slim, don't kill me!"

"Gimmie your money. Where is it? I need it."

"In my pocket and my sock."

He searched Marco and found a thick wad of money in both places. "Don't scream and try to draw attention or I'ma kill you," he warned. "You hear me, cuz?"

Marco nodded.

"Good. I'll be back." Khadafi closed the trunk then walked back up to Erykah's apartment and knocked on the door.

"Who is it?"

"Khadafi."

The door opened and he handed Erykah both wads of cash, plus the one in his pocket. His eyes dropped to Erykah's pussy one more time. "Let me ask you something."

"Go 'head."

"Do you tell Mousey everything you do?" he asked.

"Why would I?" Erykah replied, stepping back and opening the door wider.

Khadafi knew he should've left, but he didn't. Couldn't. He guessed it was the beast in him, failing to resist the call of the wild.

An hour later, he left Erykah's apartment, tired, drained, and hungry. He picked up his cell and dialed his car lot. His man Pee-Wee answered on the second ring. "What's up, cuz? How's business looking?"

"I sold that 2008 Chevy Impala, the black joint for nine grand, cash. That was the first joint we sold. The girl and her father were here waiting on us when we opened up. That champagne DHS, the 2000 joint, that's gone. Sold it to a young nigga for sixty-five hundred. That 2004 Crown Vic gone. Another young nigga. Paid cash. I let him think he was talking me down on the price. He paid eighty-seven hundred for being too slick."

Khadafi laughed.

"No bullshit, slim. It's been jive booming. We sold that old ass Lexus and that Mazda RX8. That's about it, I think. Where that stupid nigga Marco at?"

Ignoring his question, he told Pee-Wee that he'd be at the lot the next day. Then he disconnected the call. Khadafi needed to get home and wash up before going to pick up Marnie and his daughter.

Pulling over, he got out of the Honda Accord and popped the trunk. Marco tried to speak, but Khadafi stopped him.

"Shut the fuck up and listen. If I catch your ass anywhere near my car lot again, I'ma kill you, cuz. As simple as that." He used a knife that he kept on his belt to cut his arm and ankle ties. "Now get your bitch ass out of the trunk and walk back to D.C."

Seventeen minutes later, Khadafi was home.

Inside the bathroom, he dropped his head under the shower nozzle and let the hot water sing his body a song.

Since he did his best thinking in the shower, it was a song that he loved to hear. At thirty years old, Khadafi felt like a different person. But the reality of it was that other than his hairstyle, he hadn't changed much at all. The braids were gone, but not his desire to kill, maim, and destroy shit. His hunger for money, power, and respect was still there. And his thirst to control everything at his fingertips remained. Khadafi's lust for good weed, good pussy, clothes and fly whips was also the same. But still he felt different. Letting Marco walk away with his life earlier was proof that he was softening, although the scene from the movie *Carlito's Way* kept popping up in his head. The part where Carlito, played by Al Pacino, pistol whipped a young dude named Benny Blanco, but then let him live. At the end of the movie, Benny Blanco appeared out of nowhere and killed Carlito. Would that be his fate as well?

Turning the water off and stepping out of the shower, Khadafi decided to find Marco and kill him at his earliest convenience. Better to be safe than sorry. He thought about all of his enemies for a minute. None of which were still amongst the living.

Money, Cochise Shakur, Black Woozie, Bean, Lil Cee and TJ. Then he thought about Ameen. The man who had been his biggest enemy ended up saving his life. After parting ways that night at DC Jail, Khadafi never saw or heard from him again. He guessed it was better that way because the past had a way of catching up with you, and one of them might've had a flashback and became too tempted to go at the other.

To the victor goes the spoils, and in the end, Ameen had won the ultimate prizes: his freedom, his woman, and

Khadafi's son. There wasn't a day that went past where he didn't think about Kashon, the three-year-old boy who looked just like him. Khadafi wanted to see him, be with him, love him, raise him, but instead he stayed away. For no other reason than to honor the second vow he'd made to Ameen. And keep the peace that was brokered by two women, but sealed in blood the night Ameen killed Lil Cee to protect him. Whenever he felt the sting of losing his son, he stared into the eyes of his daughter. Her eyes always made him feel better. Khadajah was his heart, his buddy, his twin. He dressed after completely drying off, then put both ten carat earrings into each ear. That act itself proved how much he had changed. Khadafi thought he would never put earrings in his ears, never cut his hair, and never walk the same streets as his enemy, yet here he was doing all the things he never thought he would.

Ten minutes later, Khadafi left the house and jumped into his new Range Rover, the 2012 sports edition. His cell-phone chirped, and he already knew the reminder beep from Marnie meant to pick her up from yoga class. All he could do was smile as he thought about her sexy, feisty, stubborn ass. She was a lot different from Kemie, but he had grown to love her. Although Khadafi could acknowledge the changes in him, he also recognized that a lot about him was still the same.

# CHAPTER SEVEN

## MARNIE

"Before we start today's session, I want you to remember that life happens. Sometimes things don't go our way. But understanding the causes of suffering can help you meet life's challenges with equanimity . . . Let's warm up, shall we . . . Come into Balasana, the child's pose, for several deep breaths . . . Okay, now press your body back into the downward dog pose. Feel your muscles stretching; let your mind and body go with it. Now work to the top of your mat and come to standing in Tadasana, the mountain pose. Hold the pose for five deep breaths . . . Feels great, huh? We should be ready to begin . . . Let's go back to downward dog . . ."

Dressed in tight black lulu leggings and a tank top to match it, she pressed her hands into the dark blue yoga mat and lifted her hips backward toward the wall. Marnie's bare feet pointed ahead and her heels touched the wall. The yoga pose wasn't meant to be sexual, but she couldn't help thinking about all the times she'd been bent over in this position by Khadafi. It was one of his favorites.

"From downward dog, go directly into flip dog," the instructor said.

She lifted her right leg and bent at the knee. With complete control, she brought her right foot to the floor, so she could flip over, landing face up. Reaching her right hand out, she touched the front of the mat, then exhaled deeply before flipping back over into a downward dog. Fluidly, she went through the plank pose, side plank, and the upward plank poses. Then onto the table top pose and the full boat pose. Her body ached a little, but overall she felt good. Marnie was thankful for her yoga time. Sometimes Khadafi and her spoiled daughter, Khadajah had a way of stressing her out. She had to find an outlet before she killed them both.

At twenty months old, Khadajah was so much like her father, Khadafi, that it was a shame. Her love for them both was a love like she'd never known or felt before. She never knew such a love existed.

Khadajah was just doing what toddlers do, but Khadafi was always testing her patience, resolve, and gangsta, and she couldn't understand why. Hadn't she proven herself already? Hadn't she been beside him through everything? Life was a funny thing. But she embraced all it threw at her and never folded or faltered. At twenty-nine years old, Marnie just wanted stability and comfortability. So she aimed to be better at everything: motherhood, friendship, lover and companion, in hopes that one day Khadafi and she would get married, have more kids, and live the way God intended, in harmony. Unfortunitely, Khadafi never got the memo.

He just didn't get it. She thought that after barely escaping a life sentence for a double murder, a near death experience the night of his release, and the birth of Khadajah would finally make the man realize that life is short and every day above ground and spent outside of prison is a wonderful day.

You can't take wonderful days for granted because they can all come to a screeching halt in the blink of an eye. Lately, all Khadafi seemed to have time for was hustling, hanging down Capers, and selling cars. Marnie was getting sick of it. His lackluster performances in bed weren't a cause for great concern. As long as he protected himself and didn't bring the streets into their home, she respected the fact that he was gonna fuck other bitches and get his dick sucked. One day he'd grow tired of the gutter snipes and butt wipes in the streets; but until then, she planned to silently play her position and pray he didn't take too long to come to his senses. One day he'd realize he has a good woman at home. One that can supply his every need and be a full-time mom to his daughter in the process. Until then, she'd just keep doing yoga . . . And waiting.

"Are you guys okay?" the instructor asked everyone.

"Yeah," the class all replied in unison.

"Good. Let's go to something more difficult. Let's go to the leg standing forward bend . . ."

Marnie thought the instructor's words fit their relationship perfectly: difficult. And she always seemed to be the one bending, being extra accommodating. Although she felt Khadafi deserved her willingness to go that extra mile, reality told her that at some point she'd have to draw a line.

*****

"Hey brotha. How you doing?" Marnie asked Khadafi as she slid into the Range Rover.

"I'm good, baby. I'm good," Khadafi said, leaning over and kissing her lips.

When he did, she smelled fresh soap, lotion, and cologne. "You look and smell good. Rough day at the car lot?"

"Naw, not really. Why you ask me that?" Khadafi queried.

"Because something must've happened. When I left you this morning, you were wearing different clothes and a different fragrance."

"I went home and took a shower. Something wrong with that?"

"Naw—not if you been out in the streets fuckin', and you gotta clean up before you pick your woman up from yoga class, it ain't." She shrugged, watching for his reaction.

Khadafi took a deep breath. "Marnie, don't start that bullshit, cuz. I don't feel like it right now. No bullshit. No matter what I do or don't do, you're gonna think I'm out here fuckin' other bitches. I'm tired of defending myself to you. Chill out with that shit."

"Chill out with what? Accusing you of fuckin' other bitches? Why should I? When I know that, that's what you do. I was once one of those bitches, remember that? Kemie was your main bitch, and I was the side whore. The only thing that's changed is my position. Kemie's gone and I'm the main bitch. I'm wifey, but you definitely got other bitches besides me. I know it and you know it. Do you! Since I can't govern your dick. But when I ask you about it, be a man and admit that you fuckin' other bitches."

"Did you call the Cadillac dealer and check on your truck?" Khadafi asked, exasperated as he pulled away from the curb.

She looked over at Khadafi, smiled and said, “Tired of picking me up already, huh?”

The look on Khadafi's face was priceless. It was one of pure irritation. She loved it when he squirmed.

“Don't even trip,” he said. “I'ma cop you something new.”

“Yeah.” Marnie closed her eyes and tried to relax. “You’re tired of picking me up. I'm getting on your nerves, huh? Too bad. But naw, I'm good. The Escalade is just fine with me. Besides, it's ready. The dude from the dealer called me earlier. You can take me to get it tomorrow morning. And you gotta go over my aunt's house to get Khadajah. Her and my mother are on Livingston Road, across from Friendship Elementary School.”

“So, you mad at me now, huh?” Khadafi asked, but Marnie didn't respond. “I ain't getting no pussy tonight either, huh?”

She opened her eyes and faced him. “You think I'ma let you off the hook that easy, you better think again. And you better believe you gon' get some pussy tonight. You gon' get a lot of pussy tonight. So I suggest that you be able to hang, because your dick will tell the story if you can't. And don't try to pop none of them mojo pills and all that other weird ass shit. I can't wait to get your ass in bed. So get ready to summon your inner Mr. Marcus, or your ass is busted.” Marnie exited the car and walked inside her aunt’s house.

After waiting thirty minutes, Khadafi watched Khadajah and Marnie exit the house. He got out and walked around to the passenger side of the truck.

“Daddy!” Khadajah screamed and reached for him.

Khadafi grabbed Khadajah from Marnie and kissed her face. Watching them made her smile. It gave her hope. It made her wanna go home and start working on a brother for Khadajah. As Khadafi strapped Khadajah into her car seat in the backseat, Marnie's thoughts went from Khadafi and making Khadajah a sibling, to the older brother she had already: Kashon.

She wondered if Khadajah would ever get the chance to meet her brother, or if Khadafi would ever get the chance to be with him. Thinking about Kashon also reminded her of something else. "Did you know that Shawnay and Ameen got married?"

"Naw, I didn't know that. When did they get married?"

"Last Saturday. I saw the marriage announcement on Facebook. They both have pages. Plus, they announced it on Twitter. I'm happy for them."

"Yeah, me too."

She looked over at Khadafi's face as he focused on the road. You couldn't tell by the look on his face, but something inside her believed Khadafi wasn't happy for them at all.

# Chapter Eight

## Kenya

After the incident at the movies on Sunday night, Tyjuan and Kenya ate at Olive Garden and then called it a night. She talked to Tyjuan everyday since that evening, but didn't see him again until Wednesday.

When she left school at 3:45 p.m., Tyjuan was sitting outside in his all white Dodge Charger bobbing his head to the music. Kenya approaching made him smile. Her heart melted, and her smile spread from ear to ear. He let the window down and said, "Kenya, I love you, baby, and I miss you. So I had to see you."

"I've been missing you too. But boy, you can't be popping up at my school. What are you doing here?"

"Coming to get you, or would you rather catch the bus and the train to Grandma's house?"

She offered no further resistance. Kenya let her bookbag fall down her shoulders. She put it and her designer purse in the backseat, then climbed into the passenger seat. Tyjuan leaned over to kiss her, but she moved away. "Not here. I don't want all these nosey ass people in my business."

Once they hit the freeway on the way to D.C., Kenya undid her seatbelt and leaned all the way over and kissed

Tyjuan before settling back into the seat. It was a little cold outside, but the sun was shining and it was a beautiful day. She was inside a car with the man she loved, and it felt good.

"Let me see your tattoo."

"Right now? While I'm driving?"

"Naw, that wouldn't be safe driving, now would it? I'll see it later."

"If you really want to, I could peel my clothes off right now . . . You know danger is my middle name."

"No thank you, and your middle name is Dewayne, not danger. Speaking of danger, have you seen that boy with the green eyes yet?"

"That nigga hangs on a street about five blocks from where I live. Of course I saw him. And he saw me. He came through the Circle one day and mugged me out, but I laughed at his bitch ass. I told you he was fakin'. That nigga hip to me."

"Where are you taking me?" Kenya asked once they passed the South Capital Street exit.

"I'm taking you to my house, but first I gotta stop and pick up a few things for my favorite girl," he said.

"And who would that be?"

"My momma!"

Kenya rolled her eyes. "Whatever!" *That lady can't stand me. I might as well prepare myself . . .*

*****

The projects where Tyjuan lived were mostly red brick tenements mixed with a few three or four-story buildings. As soon as he and Kenya walked into the house, the smell of feces and something else Kenya couldn't describe assaulted her nostrils and made her wince. It was powerful as hell. Everytime she came to Tyjuan's house, it smelled of something different each time. Whatever she was smelling now was worse than ever.

"What store did you go to, Tyjuan? The one in Delaware or something? You been gone long as shit. Did you get everything I told you to get?" Tyjuan's mother, Barbara, inquired angrily from another room in the apartment.

Tyjuan ignored her as he dropped the plastic bags filled with groceries on the floor and walked over to his one-year-old brother, Quan, who was quietly playing with a green toy truck by their dingy sofa.

Suddenly, Barbara appeared and asked with an attitude, "Did you hear what the fuck I just said to you, boy?"

"Don't you see these bags right here?" Tyjuan replied, pointing.

"Who the fuck do you think you're talking to all smart and shit?" Barbara asked.

Ignoring her again, Tyjuan picked up Quan and said, "What's up, baby boy?"

"Your motherfuckin' ass gettin' beside yourself up in here . . . Grown ass nigga actin' like you pay bills in here. You gon' ignore a muthafucka? I'ma fuck your ass up, you keep it up." Barbara walked over to the bags of groceries and rifled through them. "Where the fuck my cigarettes at, Tyjuan? Don't tell me you forgot my Newports?"

Tyjuan's face screwed up as he sniffed his brother. "Whew! What you been eatin', baby boy? Damn, Ma, why you ain't change or wash up Quan?"

"Because you just came through the door with the pampers, smart ass nigga. Put my son the fuck down. He gon' be a'ight. Where's my cigarettes?"

"Kenya, give her them cigarettes."

Obedient, she reached in her purse, grabbed the two packs of Newport one hundreds and held them out so Barbara could take them.

Barbara rolled her eyes at Kenya, walked over and snatched them out of her hand. At five feet even, she was thick boned, bordering fat, dark skinned and wearing a really bad black and blonde weave. Her clothes were tattered and dirty, her feet were bare and unkempt, and she smelled like the house. Tyjuan not only got his last name from his father, but also his good looks.

Kenya was embarrassed for him.

"Didn't I tell you about bringing this little ass girl in my house? Pervert ass nigga! Just like your damn daddy," Barbara vented as she extracted a cigarette from the pack. "How old is that girl, anyway? And don't lie."

"Kenya will be seventeen in July," Tyjuan mumbled as he wiped Quan's butt with a baby wipe and changed his pamper. "There you go, baby boy. That's better, right?" Quan giggled with glee.

Barbara struck a match and lit her cigarette, put it to her lips and inhaled. She stared at Tyjuan with an evil glare as he tickled Quan. "I don't give a fuck how old she is. Don't keep bringing your little hot ass, young bitches in my house. What you think this is? A brothel? If it is, tell me, so I can start charging your ass for the room."

"You need to act like housekeeping and clean up in here then," he replied.

"What the fuck did you just say? Huh! Say it again! Say that slick shit again." Barbara moved across the room in a flash and invaded Tyjuan's space. He towered over her by almost a foot, so she spat venemous words into his chest. "Tryna stand here and disrespect me in front of your little girlfriend. Nigga, is you crazy? Like I'm some anything ass nigga from out in the streets. You got me fucked up, Tyjuan!"

Tyjuan pushed past her, saying, "You got yourself fucked up, Ma. C'mon, Kenya."

"Nigga, fuck you!" his mother spat as Kenya followed Tyjuan down the hall to his bedroom. Without looking back, she could feel Barbara's eyes on her.

"Don't be in there all day either, nigga! I'ma need some money in a little while. And gimme some of that shit you got. I know you got it, mannish ass!"

Closing his bedroom door behind Kenya, Tyjuan locked it. Barbara could still be heard shouting on the other side of the door. Being in Tyjuan's bedroom was like being in a totally different house, as if she'd walked through a secret portal and was transported to a better place.

Tyjuan's room was warm, neatly clean, and organized. His walls were freshly painted and bare, except one large poster of Osama Bin Ladin. His closets were full of designer jeans, jackets, shirts, and sweat clothes neatly folded or hung from hangers. Stacked all around the walls were pairs of shoes and boots. Kenya read every label. Jordan's, Nike foam posites, Air Yeezy's, Prada boots, Gucci tennis shoes and countless other brands. A plastic rack attached to the wall held over thirty different hats, scarfs and other headgear.

A fifty-inch flat screen HDTV was mounted over his dresser and positioned next to a desktop computer and desk. Speakers were placed around the room for surround sound quality. A pretty, thick beige and brown comforter decorated Tyjuan's king-sized bed. His carpet was clean and the room smelled of Febreeze and Issey Miyake body wash.

Kenya unzipped and pulled off her coat, putting it on his dresser along with her purse. Tyjuan sat on the bed and removed his shoes. Then he took off his coat and sweater. Grabbing a remote from the floor, he lay across the bed.

"I don't know why you lying here getting all comfortable. You know I gotta go home."

"Call Grandma and tell her you had to stay at school for a while, but you'll be home later."

She did as Tyjuan said. A minute later, she ended the call. "I gotta be home by eight o'clock."

"Don't trip. I got you. We got three hours to chill and relax."

"Your mother doesn't like me, does she?" Kenya asked suddenly.

"My mother don't like nobody, except the nigga with the best coke. You got butters, she gone love you until you don't give her no more. Her crackhead ass gets on my nerves. I'm about to move out this joint soon anyway. Get my own spot out Maryland somewhere. That's why I'm saving all my money. My mother gon' make me flick off one day and fuck her lil' short ass up."

"Boy, don't be saying nothing like that about your mother," she scolded.

"Mother?" Tyjuan repeated and looked at Kenya with hate in his eyes. "Is that what she is? Or is that what she's supposed to be? 'Cause I can't tell. I been taking care of me and my sisters since I was eleven years old. Since my father got locked up. That lady in the living room out there ain't never did shit but run her mouth, smoke crack, and fuck strange niggas. Niggas that was all up in here molesting my little sisters when nobody was around. She don't even know who my little brother's father is. That's fucked up, and she don't do shit for him. All she cares about is cigarettes and coke. She ain't no mother to me. Never has been. You heard her just tell me, 'fuck me.' So, fuck her."

"I know how you must feel," Kenya argued, "but she's still your mother. She gave birth to you, didn't she?"

"I don't even know about that. I might be adopted. But I do know one thing, she's the reason both of my sisters are out in the streets fucked up like they is. They out there as we speak, looking for the love they never got from her. But they searching in all the wrong places. They smokin' dippers, popping pills, and trickin' niggas for clothes and shit. India is sixteen and Tijuana is fifteen and they never come home. Do you think she cares? Hell naw! All she cares about is coke. You know what? Fuck that shit. I ain't even tryna talk about that shit no more. That's not why I brought you here."

"So why did you bring me here?" she asked, already knowing the answer.

"You'll see why in a couple of minutes," Tyjuan replied and grabbed her butt.

"Tyjuan, you are too slick for me. I should've known you wanted to seduce me."

"I'ma do more than seduce you. Take your clothes off."

She untied her Nike boots and pulled them off. Her Veronica Mars socks came off next. Tyjuan tugged the sweatshirt over her head, then undid her bra and pulled it off. Being semi-nude or completely nude in front of him seemed normal to her. She stood and wiggled out of her jeans and panties. "Don't forget, I gotta be home by eight o'clock."

"How am I gonna forget that?"

Kenya sat on Tyjuan's bed and watched him undress. Her body tingled in places she never knew could tingle. Tyjuan's physique was perfect; his whole body was perfect. His dick leapt out at her as he removed his boxers, and she thought he would attempt to put it in her mouth. But she wasn't ready for all that just yet, so she lay back on the bed and scooted toward the middle. Invitingly, Kenya opened her legs and closed her eyes.

A couple seconds later, she felt Tyjuan enter her. All she could do was bite down on her lips and try not to scream.

*****

She didn't even remember exactly when she fell asleep, but she had. When Kenya opened her eyes and realized that it was already dark outside, she panicked. "Oh my gawd! What time is it?" She sat up. Tyjuan, dressed in only his boxer briefs, was puffing on a lit blunt. The whole room smelled like weed.

"Chill out, boo. It's only 7:14. You was only asleep for about an hour and something. I'ma have you home by eight. I was gon' wake you up, but you was sleeping too good. Snoring and all that shit."

"No, I wasn't! I don't even snore," Kenya replied and kicked at Tyjuan.

"You shittin' me. Who told you that you don't snore? But it's cool. I ain't turned off by that. Plus, I know I put that dick on you something wonderful. You ain't have no choice but to fall asleep and snore. It's all good."

"Yeah, whatever. You need to put that out before you have me and my clothes smelling like that weed stuff. You tryna get me killed. I knew it."

"Damn, my bad." Tyjuan put the blunt out, then he tackled and pinned her arms above her head and postioned himself on top of her. As he entered her, Kenya's last words were, "Tyjuan . . . a rubber . . ."

About twenty minutes later, she was dressed and ready to get home.

Tyjuan handed her the keys to his car. "Go ahead and get in the car, start it up, and turn the heat on. I'll be out there in a minute. I gotta take care of something right quick."

She grabbed her purse, moved through the junky, putrid smelling house one last time and headed for the door. It was quiet inside, and she wondered where Barbara and Quan had gone.

Kenya walked out on the porch and saw that the projects were alive with activity. Drug dealers and drug users were everywhere. She walked up the street to the Charger, got inside the driver's seat, and started the car up. After switching on the heat, she climbed over into the passenger seat. Still tired as hell from all the sex she'd just had, she leaned back and closed her eyes.

Upon opening her eyes, she thought about turning on some music. As she reached out to program the system, she saw Tyjuan walk out of the house and lock the door. People rushed him and money was exchanged for whatever he was selling. As he came up the street to the car, Kenya could see him preoccupied with counting the money.

Out of nowhere came a dark colored SUV. Both the passenger and driver focused on something to their left. Kenya's eyes followed them and found Tyjuan. In slow motion she watched the SUV stop and a lone gunman jumped out.

"Tyyyyjuaaannnn!" she screamed, quickly leaning over toward the steering wheel.

Just as she pressed down on the horn, the man with the gun ran up behind Tyjuan and opened fire. Helplessly, she watched Tyjuan fall to the ground and try to crawl, but the gunman was unrelenting. He stood over Tyjuan and repeatedly shot him. Tyjuan's body jerked with every penetrating bullet.

With tears in her eyes and terrifying screams stuck in her throat, Kenya watched the man run back to the SUV and get inside. The man pulled his mask off as the SUV passed by, and he turned in her direction. Through the glass, Kenya's face was visible and her left hand was still pressing the horn. Their eyes locked, and his bright green eyes were the last thing she saw before she fainted.

# CHAPTER NINE

## SHAWNAY

A little after 8:00 a.m., Shawnay's back was pressed against the wet shower wall. Her wet, curly hair fell around her shoulders and breasts. The water from the shower head sprayed rhythmically. The small shower in their cabin was cramped and not made for two people to use at once, but it was probably designed for hot, steamy, erotic moments like now.

She inhaled deeply and gave in to the feeling and wrapped her legs around Antonio's neck and gripped his baldhead. She pushed his face deeper into her swollen, soaked pussy. "Damn . . . baby! Shit . . . oooh shit . . . You gon' . . . make me . . . me . . . cum! I . . . can really . . . get . . . used to . . . this . . . early morning . . . loving! Damn!"

Antonio responded by putting his tongue inside her as far as it could go. Her body shook and exploded. This was her third orgasm of the morning, and she couldn't take much more.

"Antonio . . . Antonio . . . I . . . can't take . . . no . . . more. You win . . . baby!"

"That's right!" Antonio said as he slid up her body. "Tap out then."

Shawnay was about to give a smart reply, but as she opened her mouth, she felt Antonio's dick slide deep inside her and all she could do was whimper.

"I think the ship just docked, and I wanna see Aruba, so this won't take long," he said, long stroking her.

Again her mind formulated words for her to speak, but with the entire dick she was taking, all she could manage to say at the moment was, "Fuck me!"

*****

" . . . Located fifteen miles off the Venezuelan coast, Aruba was discovered and claimed by Spain in 1499. It fell under Dutch rule in 1636 and seceded from the Netherland Antilles in 1986 to become a separate, autonomous member of the Kingdom of the Netherlands . . ."

Shawnay tried her best to listen to the Aruban tour guide as she addressed the group that left their cruise ship to experience Aruba, but she couldn't. For some reason she couldn't keep her eyes off Antonio and her thoughts out the gutter. *Why does sex seem to be better after you're married?* Shawnay couldn't figure it out. *But hubby had me all the way out there and my nose is wide open.* She watched Antonio roam around in his linen shorts, wife beater, and white Gucci boat shoes. His body looked edible. She wanted to find a spot along the beach and jump his bones, not giving a damn who watched. As he peered into a window of a novelty store on the beach front, she walked over to him.

"Aruba is beautiful as shit, bay, but I just remembered something about this place."

"What's that?" she replied as she stood on her toes and kissed his lips.

"This is where that white girl got snatched. They never found her body or nothing, but they charged one of the locals with her murder."

"That was about five years ago, I think, but I know which case you're talking about. The girl's name was Natalie Halloway, I believe."

"Well, don't be wandering off, because this pretty ass tourist stop may be deceptive. If you disappear, I'ma kill half this island."

"Antonio, hush. Ain't nobody gon' get snatched or disappear. Chill out, brotha. I see a cafe up the way and a sign in English that says 'free Wi Fi.'" Shawnay pulled out her cell phone and looked at it before saying, "Wi Fi will give us a signal. I need to call and check on the kids. You got your cell phone?"

Antonio felt his pockets, then pulled out his Android. "Yeah, but I ain't getting no signal either. I'ma have to stop messing with T-Mobile. I ain't never got no signal."

"Verizon is the same way, but a little better. Come on."

As soon as they walked into the cafe, a phone signal popped in. Shawnay's phone alerted her to twenty missed calls. Antonio's phone did the same. She looked in his direction, then asked, "Grandma's house?"

He nodded.

Once she dialed Grandma's number, she waited for her to pick up. "Hello? Yeah . . . Wait, what! Grandma, slow down . . . What happened?"

"What's up?" Antonio asked with great concern.

Shawnay held up one finger, motioning Antonio to give her a minute.

"Is she okay? Where is she? Put her . . . Better yet, I'm on my way home."

"Shawnay, what happened?" Antonio pressed.

She covered the phone before saying, "That boy that Kenya's been messing with . . ."

"Who, Tyrone?"

"Tyjuan, baby . . . He got killed in the projects and Kenya was with him. She watched it from a car. She blacked out and had to be hospitalized."

Antonio scowled and hissed, "Didn't I tell her ass—"

"I hear you, Grandma . . . Huh? Yeah. I'll be there today, hopefully. We're leaving now. Bye." Shawnay disconnected the call and headed for the door. "We gotta get home."

"I told her little grown ass not to see that nigga!"

"Antonio, I know you told her that, baby, but she didn't listen. Kenya is okay. She's just in shock and Grandma's afraid. She said she's too old to be dealing with Kenya's nonsense. Pull yourself together and get us out of here."

Antonio snapped into action. He made a beeline for the Aruban tour guide, who was still talking to the crowd from the cruise ship.

" . . . Capital of Aruba is Orangestad and its second largest city is San Nicols. The peak of the tourist season is—"

"Excuse me," Antonio said, interrupting the lady, "I need to get to the airport. Could you tell me—"

"You are from the ship, are you not?" the lady replied.

"We are, but—"

"You cannot leave the ship, sir—"

"We can leave the ship, and we will. All I need you to do is direct us to the airport."

"But your passport . . . Customs . . . What about your luggage? Your things on board the ship?"

"I have an emergency at home, and the stuff on that ship comes last. They can mail it to me, or I can pick it up later. Now, where's the airport?"

"Reina Beatrix International Aero Puerto is five miles from here. Get a taxi over there . . ." She pointed ahead.

The customs agent in Aruba gave them a little grief, but after a thorough search and screening, they were determined to be transporting nothing but themselves back to the states, so they were allowed to board a plane to Florida.

Nine hours after talking to her grandmother, one layover and another plane,

Shawnay and Antonio exited a cab and walked through the gate at her grandmother's house.

"Chile, I'm glad you're back," Grandma said and rushed into her arms. "Kenya is . . . She won't stop crying. She needs—"

"Where she at, Grandma?" Antonio asked.

"Upstairs. In Shawnay's old room—"

Antonio turned and raced up the stairs.

"You know that chile don't much listen to me. I tell her something and she tells me anything. She lied to me . . . so bad. She was supposed to come here after school, but she called and said something . . . I don't even remember what, but I told her to be home by eight o'clock. It was after eight, and I was calling her phone, but she didn't answer. I got worried . . . You know my pressure . . .

"I got a call from Howard Hospital telling me that Kenya was there and to come and get her; she was okay. I got

Wanda to run me and the kids up there, and they told me that she was in shock and had fainted. That girl hollered and screamed all night, and that's when I started calling you. This morning is when she finally calmed down long enough to tell me what happened to that boy she was seeing."

"Grandma, let me go upstairs and check on Kenya." Shawnay walked upstairs to her old room and heard Kenya and Antonio in a heated debate.

"I heard what you said, but didn't I tell your ass specifically not to go to the projects? Huh? Didn't I tell you to stay away from that nigga! Didn't I!"

"Daddy, please!" Kenya exclaimed, and then looked up at her mother as she walked in the door. Her eyes pleaded for help. "Ma . . ."

Shawnay walked over and hugged her.

Kenya's eyes were red and puffy, and her hair disheveled. She looked a lot older than her sixteen years. A clear hospital armband rigidly dangled from her wrist. She crumbled in her mother's embrace and cried.

"Go ahead and cry, baby. Get it all out. Crying is good," Shawnay said as she consoled her. She looked up at Antonio, who stared at her with an evil scowl, but she threw one of concern and patience right back.

After a few minutes, Kenya's cries subsided. "Tell me what happened," she requested softly.

"I . . . I . . . was with . . . Tyjuan," Kenya started, but continued to sniffle, "at his house . . ."

"At his house? You were at his house? By yourself?" Antonio queried.

"His mother . . . Barbara was there."

Shawnay heard Antonio exhale.

" . . . But at some point, she left. I fell asleep in his bed."

Antonio paced the floor. He stopped suddenly. "His mother wasn't there . . . You fell asleep in his bed . . . Kenya . . . Did you . . . Were you?"

With her eyes focused on her hands in her lap, Kenya nodded and said, "Yes . . . I did. I was . . . We were . . . You know what I mean."

"Naw, I don't know what you mean, Kenya. Spell it out for me. You were what!"

"I had sex with Tyjuan," Kenya confessed, looking up at Anonio, who was visibly hurt. "There, I said it. Is that all you care about? Tyjuan is dead . . . And all you . . . care . . ."

Antonio cursed, balled up his fist, and then smacked his head with both palms.

Kenya watched her father pace the floor like a caged lion in a zoo. She could see how hurt he was, and she seemed to revel in the fact that she could hurt him deeply. With her eyes now glued to Antonio, she continued, "And it wasn't the first time. We've been having sex for the last five months. He loved me and I love him."

Antonio quickly turned and came toward Kenya. "Shut your mouth! Shut your goddamn mouth right now before I—"

"Antonio, please calm down." Shawnay intervened. "Don't you see how messed up she already is? You threatening her ain't—"

"Do *not* interrupt me when I'm talking to my daughter!" Antonio spat before turning his attention back to Kenya.

"You don't know anything about love. You're only sixteen. What you did was out of rebellion and lust, not love."

"Kenya, let's get back to that part later," her mother interjected. "You were with Tyjuan, then what happened?"

Kenya turned and faced the window. Then she told Shawnay what happened. Although she tried her best to comfort Kenya, she was inconsolable. Shawnay's heart went out to her. After a long, quiet pause, Kenya looked up and dried her eyes.

"He saw me, Ma. Right before I blacked out, he saw me."

"Who saw you, baby?"

"The dude from the movies. The one that killed Tyjuan."

"What dude from what movies?"

"After you and Daddy left, the next day I went to the movies with Tyjuan. He got a tattoo of me on his chest—"

"The dude went and got a tattoo of you on his chest?" Antonio asked.

Kenya nodded before saying, "Since I couldn't tell anybody about us, he said he would. He said he wanted the world to know that he loved me. The tattoo artist sketched my face and put it on Tyjuan's chest. Then we went to the movies to see *Think Like A Man.* After the movie was over and we were leaving, Tyjuan got into it with some dude he knew." Kenya retold the incident that escalated between Tyjuan and Tyger at the theater.

"'I stay strapped and I never slip. Tyger ain't gon' do nothing to me.' That's what Tyjuan said," she continued.

"And that dude from the movies is the one who killed Tyjuan?" Shawnay asked.

"The same one. While they were in the movies arguing, I had my cell phone out, so I took a picture of the dude. He didn't know it, but I did. Maybe it was because I was mesmerized by his eyes. I have never seen eyes like his before. They were the light-greenest eyes I'd ever seen. After the dude shot Tyjuan, he got back in the SUV and it drove past me. He pulled off the mask, then looked right at me. Our eyes locked for a moment. It was him. I'm sure of it. His eyes won't leave my head."

# CHAPTER TEN

## AMEEN

That's when you blacked out?" Shawnay asked.

"Yeah. The next thing I know, the car was surrounded by people and police. They thought I was shot. I got out the car and saw Tyjuan's body still lying in the street, but there was a white sheet draped over him. I lost it. I was hysterical. They put me in an ambulance. At the hospital, the police questioned me."

"The police questioned you? What did you tell them?"

"I told them what I saw, Daddy. What was I supposed to tell them?"

"Did you tell them about the dude with the green eyes?"

"I don't remember . . . Maybe I did. Maybe not," Kenya replied.

He turned and smacked the wall. "Shit! Fuck! Damn! Damn! Damn!"

"Antonio, what the hell is the matter with you?" Shawnay asked.

"She might've told the police about the green-eyed dude. If they lock him up and charge him with murder, that makes Kenya an eyewitness. Fuck!"

"And?"

"She can't be no witness. I'ma have to get Rudy to check and see what they have. If she did name the dude, they can't use it in court. She's a minor and she had no parental guidance there. She was illegally interrogated," he reasoned, still pacing the bedroom floor.

All eyes were on him as he talked out loud, more to himself than to them. "She didn't have a lawyer there. She can take her statement back, if she made any."

"Take her statement back?"

"Take my statement back?" Kenya repeated.

"Why would she have to take her statement back?" Shawnay inquired.

"Yeah . . . Why would I do that?" Kenya followed.

"Because you didn't know what you were doing. You can recant whatever you said, and you will recant. That way they can't make you testify in open court."

"But Daddy, why wouldn't I tell people what I saw? Recant for what?"

"Because I ain't raising no damn rat, that's why! I ain't gon' have nobody running around in the joint talking about, 'Ameen's daughter told on me. Ameen let his daughter rat me out.' That's not gonna happen."

"Hold on . . . Wait a minute . . . Wait a minute," Shawnay spoke up. "This ain't about you and your fragile sensibilities. This ain't about your wounded pride and ego. This is about our daughter and what she feels she needs to do to help her heal to get closure."

"Closure? Ain't nothing she can do to bring that boy back. Her closure is in the sad, irrefutable fact of him being gone. Getting on a witness stand and getting the dude that did it fifty years in prison ain't closure. Becoming a rat ain't healing. And it damn sure ain't closure."

"I think you are taking this too far. First of all, we don't know what Kenya told the police. Second of all, if she did tell them what she saw and who did it, how does that make her a rat?"

"Because that's what rats do, they squeal. And I ain't raising no rats. Simple as that."

"Antonio, Kenya is not held to your street code and standards. She's not a part of your twisted loyalties and 'Death Before Dishonor.' That doesn't apply to her. That's your life, not hers."

"She's governed by the code vicariously through me. Just like you are. That's why I told you not to accept that jury duty months ago. My family is not going to be put in harm's way because the cops want to solve a case and secure a conviction. My daughter ain't getting on nobody's stand and telling nothing. Whatever happens to the green-eyed dude will have to happen without her assistance. She didn't see anything."

"But she did see something. You can't change that."

"Why are you both standing here talking about me as if I'm not sitting here?" Kenya asked meekly.

Her dad ignored her. "She was traumatized. She was afraid. She made a mistake. She didn't see who killed that boy. Even if she did see him. That's it and that's all. I am the head of this family. It's my job to protect y'all and that's what I'm doing. So, I say no. She can't get on no stand and tell. My daughter ain't gon' be labeled as a rat. I'm sorry about what happened to the young dude. I didn't want him with Kenya. Why? Because I saw the 'me' in him.

"I saw the streets in him. I noticed him carrying a gun the first time we met. My trained eye spotted that. I knew what he was about, but I didn't wish death on him. Right now, I'm hurting because my daughter is hurting. Every tear she cries stabs at my heart like a knife. That's why I didn't want him to be around her. I knew this could happen. It happened, and we can't change it. Telling on the dude who did it won't change anything. That's not the answer. The streets have a way of dealing with its own problems. Tyjuan has friends that will give the green-eyed dude his just due. His crew will handle it for you. Let them do what they need to do."

"But what if they don't?" Kenya asked, her eyes filling with tears again.

"What if they don't what, baby?" her dad asked.

"What if the streets or Tyjuan's friends don't handle it? Then who'll get justice for Tyjuan? Who'll make sure that Tyger gets what he deserves?"

"I'm going to check on Asia and Kay Kay and give 'em both a kiss." With no answer to her question, Ameen decided it was time to leave. He had spoken and that was that.

# Chapter Eleven

## Kenya

Kenya put down the book she was reading entitled, *Letters to a Young Sister* and wondered if Hill Harper could tell her how to heal her broken heart. How to resurrect the dead or how to turn back the hands of time. She wondered if he could tell her how to pick up the pieces of her life and go on when the person she loved with all her heart was now gone. Clicking on her iPod, the first song to come on was Miguel's "Adorn You." A shiver ran through her body because that was one of Tyjuan's favorites. He sang it to her often.

She walked over to the dresser and stared at herself in the mirror. Her eyes were different. Puffy. Older. They weren't the eyes of a sixteen-year-old girl on the cusp of womanhood.

The gown she wore was the one she'd worn the night she slipped out of her grandmother's house to make love to Tyjuan in the car. It still smelled of him, Issey Miyake, his favorite.

Pulling the gown over her head, she cocked her head to one side and found the spot above her breast where she'd gotten a tattoo of her own. One of Tyjuan's face. So that they'd be together forever. Kenya pulled the bobby pin out of her hair and it fell loosely down her back. It was the way her mother wore her hair. Kenya's honey-brown complexion seemed to glow, to radiate. She stood there, all 5-feet 2-inches and 120 pounds and cried her eyes out. Lately, that was all she seemed to do.

Grabbing her breasts, she squeezed them together the way Tyjuan loved to do and imagined his lips and tongue on them. She remembered his touch as she lowered her hand to her panties, finding her sex. Playing in the wetness, she imagined Tyjuan there doing the same. Kenya could feel his hands in her, on her. Could smell him. The light purple polish on her toes was his favorite. Her left hand caressed her dark brown nipples that hardened under her touch, the way they did for Tyjuan. Tears fell down her cheeks and landed on her breasts, but she didn't care to wipe them away. Her eyes dropped to her flat belly. She rubbed it and silently prayed that a part of Tyjuan was growing inside of her.

Kenya recalled how panic stricken she was the day Tyjuan failed to pull himself out of her, the day he died, but he calmed her nerves as always and made her forget his blunder. She had forgotten it too, until now.

Fervently, she prayed his seed found an egg and created a new life within her. One that she would always have to remind her of him. A baby and a tattoo.

Ever since the chaotic scene in the bedroom at her grandmother's house five days ago, she'd been cooped up in her parent's house like a caged bird. No school, no nothing. Her father grounded her and forbid her to leave the house, even if it was on fire, and she believed him. She knew how hurt and disappointed he was in her, and it pained her to see him upset. Kenya loved her father with all her heart, but one day, he'd have to realize and accept the fact that she wasn't his little girl anymore. She continued to rub all over her body erotically and thought, *I'm a woman now.*

*****

"Kenya, have you seen my laptop?"

She shot daggers at her little sister, Asia. "How I'ma see your laptop, Asia, and I been in my room all day, every day? You should learn to keep up with your stuff better anyway." The microwave beeped and she went to get her chicken pot pie out.

"You ain't gotta be mean to me. I ain't done nothing to you," Asia snapped and left the kitchen.

Kenya spotted the *Washington Post* newspaper on the table. Blowing the pot pie to cool it off, she flipped through the paper to the Metro section. Instantly, she went to the obituaries and sure enough, Tyjuan's was there.

Reflective, she stared at the color photo in the paper and then rubbed it. The photo was one that she'd never seen before, a smiling Tyjuan with cornrows. He appeared to be in his early teens, before they met. His multicolored Solbiato shirt drew attention. She smiled. Tyjuan stayed fly. Under the photo read the words:

*Tyjuan Dewayne Glover 6/12/94 - 2/18/13*

*Suddenly on Wednesday, February 18, 2013. Beloved son of Tyrone Glover and Barbara Copeland, loving brother of India, Tiajuana, and Tyquan. Also surviving are his maternal grandmother, Marjorie Copeland, a paternal grandfather, Ronald D. Glover, and a host of other relatives and friends. Friends are invited to visit on Tuesday, Febuary 24 from 1:00 p.m. until the time of the service at 3:00 p.m. at the Allen Chapel AME Church, 2498 Alabama Avenue, S.E. Reverend Michael Bailey, Pastor. Interment, Harmony Cemetery. Arrangements by Pope Funeral Home.*

Until she felt the wet shirt sticking to her chest, she didn't realize she was crying again. Still, she studied Tyjuan's photo and lost herself in memories. A tugging on her shirt caused her to look down into the face of her little brother, Kay Kay, who had his arms out requesting to be picked up. When she picked him up, he wiped at her wet eyes, then hugged her. Kenya couldn't love a person more at that moment. Before she could say a word, Kay Kay turned in her lap and put his finger in her pot pie.

"Hot!" he said and snatched his finger back, blowing on it.

She couldn't help but laugh as she kissed his little fingers and blew on them. "That's what your little bad butt gets. Don't you know better than to just stick your fingers in people's food? Huh, little boy? Answer me."

Kashon smiled a smile that made her day instantly better. "Yes! Too hot!" Kashon said once again.

"Yeah, it is too hot," she said. *Just like my love for Tyjuan, and this terrible pain I feel ever since the dude with the green eyes killed him.*

*****

The half-eaten pot pie sat on the dresser as Kenya scrolled through her phone at all the texts she'd saved from Tyjuan. Then she scrolled through their photos. Her parents' raised voices could be heard all throughout the house as they argued down the hall. It seemed like, lately, that's all they did. She couldn't help feeling responsible for their shortened honeymoon. After a while, their voices quieted and she smiled.

*Make up sex.*"They are probably in there humping," Kenya said. "Nasty asses." She couldn't picture her parents having sex. Her father making her mother feel all of the wonderful things that Tyjuan made her feel. The thought of them having oral sex made her wanna hurl. Shaking those thoughts from her mind, the green-eyed dude, Tyger invaded her head. Did he know how much he'd ruined her life and how much he'd changed her? Anger filled her when she saw him again, after he shot Tyjuan. After he got in that SUV and took off his mask. After he looked her right in the eyes as the SUV drove past. Every day she wished him death—wished him a slow, torturous death in the streets or in prison. Whichever came first.

The detective who tried to talk to her at the hospital, whose name she thought was Winslow, had been calling the house nonstop lately. Something inside Kenya wanted to call him and tell him everything, from what happened at the movies to everything she saw when Tyger killed Tyjuan. The temptation was great, but all she could hear was her father's voice telling her that he wasn't raising no rats. "Let the streets handle it," her father's voice echoed in her head.

She picked up her cell phone and thought again about contacting the police, but then her fingers dialed someone else.

"Nadiyah!"

"Kenya . . . Hey girl. Are you okay?"

"I'm not okay, Nadiyah. I'm in a lot of pain, but I'll survive, I guess."

"Your voice sounds different. Scratchy almost."

"I've been crying a lot, but I'm good. Really, I am. I just gotta learn how to deal with what happened."

"I feel you, girl. I still can't believe this shit. I been crying too. You know I loved me some Tyjuan Glover. Everybody did. That nigga was the shit with a capital S. Bitches at school been crying and acting crazy, like he was their man and shit. They got a makeshift memorial in front of his old locker and everything, girl."

"For real!"

"Hell yeah! You know I ain't gon' bullshit about nothing like that. Before he dropped out of school, Tyjuan was Mr. Eastern High School. He was the flyest nigga there, hands down. He birthed a small crop of baby Tyjuan's around there, but none of them niggas could quite get it right."

Kenya laughed. "You crazy, girl."

"Naw, bitch, I'm real. That's why you love me so much."

*Let the streets handle it . . .*

"I wonder what his friends been saying about Tyjuan's death."

"Saying? Kenya, them niggas ain't been saying shit. They been riding around shooting shit up. All up and down Benning Road. Last I heard, they thought some Benning Park niggas did it."

*A dude with green eyes named Tyger did it.* Instead of saying that, she replied, "Is that right?"

"Yeah, girl. And let me tell you this . . . Tyjuan's sisters, India and Tia, them little young bitches done went crazy. They were already out there, but now with Tyjuan gone, them bitches live in the streets. They fuckin' niggas out of both pants legs. Believe me when I tell you that they getting their brains fucked out. Joey, Ericky, and Don P had them bitches at the Embassy Suites making fuck movies. They disrespecting Tyjuan's memory like a motherfucka . . . It's sad, girl. And his mother, Ms. Barbara be walking up and down Drake Place talking to herself. She look bad. And she strung out on that shit. I wonder who be—"

"Are you still going to the funeral tomorrow?" Kenya asked.

"Girl, you know I am. Why?"

"I'm not supposed to go, but I want to, to say my final good-byes to him."

"You're not supposed to go? Why not?"

"My father says that niggas might act crazy and start shooting up the funeral. Besides,

I'm grounded. You know how Antonio 'Ameen' Felder and my mother are. They don't understand me at all."

"So, what are you gonna do?"

"I don't know," she told her honestly. "I'm thinking about sneaking out. My mother will be at work, my father has to get ready to open his store, and Asia will be in school, so she won't be able to tell on me. Kay Kay will be at my great grandmother's house, so I won't be stuck watching him. The service is from one to three. I can go and then just hurry up back here. I just gotta go. I can't let nothing stop me from saying good-bye to Tyjuan. So, can you come and get me?"

"Of course, I can."

"Well, let me pick out an outfit. I'ma call you back in the morning." Kenya's mind was made up. If her parents found out she went to Tyjuan's funeral, she'd just deal with the consequences later.

*****

Clutching her Michael Kors bag tightly to her side, she walked into the church with Nadiyah. A lady dressed in a white dress handed out obituaries with Tyjuan's face and other photos in them. She put hers in her purse to look at later. Cries and screams permeated her being as they pulsed inside the large packed church. Kenya had never been to a funeral before, but she knew to get in the line that snaked around Tyjuan's casket. She followed Nadiyah and surveyed her surroundings.

Women were screaming and asking God why at the top of their lungs. Some even fainted, and the women in white dresses had to tend to them. She saw several of Tyjuan's friends inside the church dressed in casual clothes and matching T-shirts with "We Miss You T-Dawg" on them. Tyjuan's smiling face was emblazoned across every shirt. Little kids cried while music played in the background. Tyjuan's funeral had an old church revival feel to it. Someone prayed out loud and wished death on the people responsible for Tyjuan's death.

As Kenya made her way to the front of the church, she spotted Tyjuan's mother, Barbara, dressed in all black. Her hair was immaculately coifed. Her solemn expression fell on Tyjuan's casket. In her arms, Tyjuan's baby brother, Tyquan stirred, but appeared to be asleep. He was dressed in black as well. Beside Barbara sat Tyjuan's sisters, who at one year apart, could be mistaken for twins.

One sister sat stoically and stared at the floor, while the other cried openly, her grief almost palpable. Other people lined the pew that Barbara sat on with her children, but

Kenya couldn't place them. All were Tyjuan's relatives, she guessed. Before she knew it, she was at Tyjuan's casket.

Kenya felt like a stranger sneaking a peek at a celebrity as opposed to a girlfriend seeing her boyfriend for the last time. Tyjuan's dreads were perfectly twisted and encased his head like a halo. He looked as if he were sleeping. A white Louis Vuitton button up shirt with a single black stripe in it fit his upper body as if it were tailored. Black linen slacks completed his outfit.

For the final time, Kenya stopped and reached for Tyjuan's hand that lay on top of the other across his stomach. He was cold and hard. Tears clouded her vision, but she stayed there at the casket and dropped her head onto him. Her tears stained his shirt, but she didn't care. She touched his chest, right where she knew his tattoo of her was. Then suddenly, firm hands prodded her forward. The ladies in white had come to move her along.

The pastor stepped onto the podium and stood at the lecturn. He tapped the mic once, then gave a nod. He looked across the room at the attendees before speaking. "A gun fires, a bullet is sent forth, and a person stands in its way. That person may die. The death of the person . . . I say the death of the person, y'all," he preached, "is the consequence of another person pulling the trigger of a loaded gun. Words are that way too. They go forth and wound another person. The wounding is the consequence of damaging words. Yet other words go forth too . . . spiritual words, and a person accepts Christ. And we must have faith that this young brother, Tyjuan Glover, accepted Christ in his life. When we accept Christ, we are given eternal life. This does not prevent the death of the body, but it does assure us true life with him in heaven forever."

Kenya sat in back of the church and listened to what the pastor said. She hoped that what he said was true and that she'd get to see Tyjuan again in heaven, if there is such a place. She wasn't so sure. Kenya had read about heaven in her mother's Bible and a place called Paradise in her father's Quran, but neither book offered her comfort or true solace. Nothing stopped her pain and suffering.

"Death is no respecter of persons. It is the greatest equalizer here on earth. The rich, the poor, the wise, the foolish, the great, the weak . . . All will die. But there is a way to have something waiting for you in heaven."

After the pastor finished speaking, people sang songs. Then others read poems and finally Tyjuan's casket was closed. Kenya's eyes stayed glued to that flower draped casket that would hold the remains of her heart for eternity. As the latches were locked into place and the reality of the situation hit her again, she closed her eyes and prayed.

A couple of minutes later, Kenya was strapped into the passenger's seat of Nadiyah's Acura with tears still in her eyes. Nadiyah didn't say a word as she drove. Kenya guessed that Nadiyah must've known that she just needed to sit there, cry, and remember Tyjuan. She held the obituary and thought about every day that she'd spent with Tyjuan. Suddenly, Nadiyah broke the silence.

"I gotta stop for gas, Kenya. Plus, I want some gum."

Kenya nodded and leaned back in her seat.

A few minutes later, the car pulled into a gas station. "You want me to get you something?" Nadiyah asked as she got out the car.

"I'm good. But thank you anyway."

Kenya's thoughts raced back to Tyjuan. A second or two later, a movement to her right caught her attention. She turned and looked out the window, only to see that a person dressed in black had run up. Then, as if watching a DVD movie, he raised something in his hand.

Kenya saw a flash of light and then nothing.

# CHAPTER TWELVE

## TERRELL "TYGER" HOLLOWAY

Tyger watched the window of the Acura shatter and blood splattered all over the driver's side of the car. Stepping up on the car a little more, he fired a few more rounds into the girl to make sure she was dead. He could hear someone screaming on the side of him, but he was oblivious to the noise. Tunnel vision. All he saw was the pretty young girl possibly on the witness stand telling nine white people and three blacks that he committed a murder on F Street a week ago.

Snapping out of the zone, his adrenaline pumped like he was infused with a case of Five Hour Energy drinks. Tyger raced back to the Maxima and jumped in. "Pull off!" he told his cousin Choppa. His heart rate didn't slow until they were way outside of D.C. and on the Maryland side. By then he pulled off the mask and exhaled as his eyes scouted the area quickly. They were still on Pennsylvania Avenue, and the surroundings started to become familiar. They were in the city of Forestville.

"Pull off the main street right here by Walter's Lane. There's a McDonald's in the little shopping center. Go there," Tyger told Choppa.

At McDonald's, he pulled off the black Hugo Boss hoody, balled it up and threw it, along with the mask, in the dumpster behind the fast food restaurant. Quickly, Tyger dismantled the .40 caliber Smith & Wesson, tossing the barrel and chamber, but keeping the body in his pocket.

Walking back to the Maxima, he pulled out a gray hoody and a gray Northface ski vest and put it on. He also switched his shoes from black Nike Foam Posites to gray New Balance 990's. Carrying the Nike Foams, he went inside McDonald's and ordered a chicken sandwich, fries, and a coke. Minutes later, Tyger was walking out the McDonald's eating fries. Inside the bag with the food was the body of the Smith & Wesson.

Casually, he walked down the sidewalk of the shopping center until he reached the CVS drug store. With the Nike Foam Posites in one hand and the McDonald's bag in the other, he walked into the store and checked for a trash can. He found one in the back and tossed the shoes into the trash can before walking out the store.

At the end of the sidewalk was a dry cleaners. Tyger walked behind it and threw the McDonald's bag as far as he could into the nearby woods. Then he unzipped his pants, pulled out his dick, and pissed all over his hands up to his wrists. The first thing the police did with a murder suspect caught the day of a killing was test his hands for gunpowder residue. Urine was the most effective way of getting rid of that evidence. At least that's what his big homie, Fella told him. After pissing on his gun hand, he went back to McDonald's and washed his hands in the restroom.

Tyger walk over to Choppa, who was sitting in the Maxima, and explained, "The cops are probably looking for a nigga with a dark colored baseball cap driving a dark colored Maxima. Take that hat off and get your ass in the passenger seat."

"Damn, moe, you talkin' to a nigga jive harsh, ain't you?" Choppa replied, as he did exactly what was asked of him.

Tyger slid into the driver's seat and started up the car. "Stop being so sensitive, nigga. Tonight we celebrating, but first we gotta get back to Southeast and get rid of this car.

*****

Thirty minutes later, Tyger lay across his aunt's bed at her house on Burns Place. The murder he committed was all over every news station. Silently he prayed that Choppa wasn't outside running his mouth to niggas on the strip about what he'd done. He hoped that taking his younger cousin on both missions wouldn't come back to haunt him later. The pink weed he'd smoked had him in a reflective state. Tyger lay on his back with his hands behind his head, staring at the ceiling. About five roaches walked casually across the ceiling like they didn't have a care in the world. The life of a roach had to be a pretty good life until it got killed. He wished that his life could be so simple, but it wasn't.

All his life, things had been messed up. Both of Tyger's parents were crackheads. His father ended up going on a robbery caper when he was ten and got smoked. As for his mother, she got locked up so many times for petty shit that finally, the courts had had enough. They gave her a rack of time for possession of cocaine and sent her to the Feds. While she was in Danbury, Connecticut doing her time, she met some nigga, whom, when she got out, she married and made a new life with in Connecticut. She literally said 'fuck Tyger' and the family she left behind in D.C., so the streets raised him. The streets and his big homies.

They were the ones who had always told him that he needed to toughen up. They called him soft and all kinds of other names because he wasn't as hard and couldn't fight as well as they could. His big homies called Tyger a pretty boy because all the girls loved his good looks and his eyes. The girls went crazy about his eyes, a trait he inherited from his father. Tyger always tried to prove to everybody that he was more than a pretty boy, but his efforts always failed. Well, until he started carrying and busting his guns.

Tyger became the secret weapon because nobody ever suspected him. He was soft, a sucker, the pretty nigga, Terrell. But the dudes closest to him knew the animal instinct inside him and how tenacious he could be as he stalked his prey. They nicknamed him 'The Tiger' at seventeen years old. He liked the nickname, so it stuck. He just changed the spelling and told everybody his name was Tyger with a "Y" instead of an "I."

Information is important in life, and oftentimes knowledge is the key to life. The misinformed man with no knowledge makes mistakes, and sometimes those mistakes can be fatal. That's something that he learned young, but evidently, his old friend Tyjuan hadn't. He still believed Tyger was just a pretty boy, a sucker nigga that could be punked and carried like a bitch. He had no clue. He was misinformed. So he had to teach him.

The night Tyjuan spit in his face at the movies was the night Tyger knew another lesson would have to be taught. Tyjuan had to learn that men didn't spit on other men, especially the dangerous ones, and live. Like his man Beanie Sigel rapped in a song, "Try to get out the streets, haters will draw you back/like an automatic weapon, they pull you back/load something in the brain, just to see you snap."

Well, Tyger did snap and nailed his ass to the pavement in his own hood, twenty feet away from his front door. Also in front of his girlfriend.

Now, that part he regretted.

When he pulled off the mask after jumping into the truck, he turned and locked eyes with the pretty young girl who was with Tyjuan at the movies. Tyger couldn't believe it. He couldn't do anything but shake his head as the truck he was in drove down F Street. He knew she'd seen him. They looked right at each other. She had to have known who he was. She had to have remembered him as the dude from the movies that Tyjuan spit on. She heard Tyger threaten to kill him. The whole City Place movie lobby heard him say that. The look in the young girl's eyes screamed recognition. And she had just watched him kill her boyfriend, or whatever Tyjuan was to her. All of that concocted a recipe for disaster. Tyger knew five minutes after killing Tyjuan that he had to kill the girl.

Since he didn't know her, or where to begin to look for her, he just sat back and waited . . . And hoped. Hoped that Tyjuan had only told her his nickname. Because if he had, then it would take the police a minute to find out Tyger's true identity. The fact was, he really didn't know what, if anything, Tyquan had told her. But he couldn't chance her describing him and being the reason that he went to prison on a body and never came home. So she had to go.

He figured since she was with Tyjuan on both occasions when he'd seen him, that she would also attend his funeral. And he could catch her there and kill her. It was a gamble either way he looked at it, so he played the odds. When Tyger went to Alabama Avenue, on the other side of Southeast to the church where the service was being held, he expected to find the girl. And he did. He spotted her coming out of the church with another girl he knew named Nadiyah.

"Terrell! Tashia is down here," his aunt hollered upstairs, breaking his thoughts.

"Send her up here! I'm in your room, Aunt Linda," Tyger hollered back.

At first he thought he was gonna have to kill both girls. He didn't want to, but he wasn't going to hesitate if he had to. But then lady luck smiled at him. Nadiyah pulled into the Amoco gas station and got out the car.

Tashia Parker knocked once on the door, and then came into the bedroom. Tyger sat up on the bed and put his feet on the floor.

"Whassup, T?"

"You, nigga," she replied. "I want some weed and dick, in that order. But before we do that, I need you to slide these two pills into my ass. They make me the freakiest."

Tyger looked at Tashia's banging ass body and smiled. "I think I can handle that for you. Gimme the pills." He needed her as much sexually as she wanted him. Tyger needed her to fuck him into oblivion, to make him forget that he'd killed an innocent girl. He felt a pinch of guilt rising, but that animal instinct in him strangled the emotion, like a Tyger does its prey.

# CHAPTER THIRTEEN

## AMEEN

"Aye, ock, the salat just came in. You tryna offer, or you gon' wait?" Furquan asked.

Just as Ameen turned to respond, his watch called the Adhan, signaling it was time for prayer. He glanced at his watch: 4:50 p.m. Ameen wondered where the whole day had gone as he looked at the rest of the mannequins that he had to dress.

"You go ahead, ock. I'ma finish these mannequins, and then I'ma pray."

Furqan nodded, dropped the stack of sweatpants on the shelf, and disappeared into the back of the store. Ameen fastened the lightweight tan cargo shorts onto the mannequin and added a multi-colored ISO couture shirt.

Pride swelled up inside Ameen as he stared at the outfit. His designs were finally on display for the world to see. He felt like he had actually accomplished something. The idea of designing clothes and opening a store came to him while locked up in prison. But then his appeal happened and he was released, and that idea became a reality.

Ameen got the money from Shawnay, who did a good job at saving and investing the money Khadafi had given her more than four years ago. He tried to never even think of what went on after he brought her money. The fact that he was fucking Shawnay then, was negative energy that Ameen had to resist if his life and marriage were going to have a fighting chance.

Ameen took the money and enrolled in a sewing class, bought sewing machines, threads, fabrics, patterns, embroidery machines and all the utensils and accessories needed to design and make clothes. He lost a lot of money, ruining clothes until he finally got the hang of it and did his thing.

Initially the clothes were going to be centered around his belief in the street code of silence: Omerta. He sat and designed the logo himself. LTO (Live The Omerta). But then something dawned on him. He sat in a chair one day and realized that the Omerta was dead. The way it was in the streets, the most notorious rats ever, were deeply entrenched in the hoods, doing business with and dictating to the good men. Only the dudes in the joint still cared about the Omerta. And Ameen. But he couldn't do business with himself, so he had to switch the game up.

Ameen created another logo. One of a man standing in the beginning position of the prayer, with his hands at his ears. The name of the clothes became I.S.O (Islamic Sportswear Originals). He opened a business bank account, went through hell getting the proper licenses and permits. Then he made deals with a few vendors, and eventually found a store front property in a shopping center off of Walker Mills Road in District Heights, Maryland. That had all been about three months ago, and he was finally ready. Ready to make his mark on society.

As planned, he timed his grand opening to coincide with spring. The reaction to the clothes on his website was good, and he expected the clothing to be successful. Inside the shop, Ameen moved from mannequin to mannequin and put a variety of colorful outfits together. The young generation that he liked to refer to as the 'BET Generation' loved a lot of color in their clothes. Finally finished, it was time for prayer. Just as he was about to go in the back and pray, his cell phone vibrated on the counter. He was going to ignore it, but decided to see who the caller was.

It was Shawnay.

"Hey, baby. I was just—"

"Antonio . . . This is Sheila. I'm calling from work. Shawnay—she can't come to the phone—"

"She can't come to the phone? Why not," he asked as a sickening feeling crept into the pit of his stomach. "What's wrong with her?"

"She's . . . uhhh . . . She's being looked at. The police called her . . . They . . . uhhh . . . ummm . . . Sothething happened to your daughter. Something's wrong with Kenya, Antonio."

Momentarily his heart stopped. "What's wrong with Kenya?"

"She—she . . . She got shot at a gas station. It's been all over the news."

"A gas station? Naw . . . That's a mistake. Kenya is at home, grounded. Kenya is—"

"Kenya's not at home, Antonio, and she's not okay. There's no mistake. The police called Shawnay and told her. Kenya's dead. Somebody killed her."

The cell phone slipped from his hands. Ameen dropped to his knees.

*****

"Before we go in, Mr. Felder, let me just say that I am sorry that this happened to your daughter. My name is Detective Corey Winslow, and I am the one who's been calling your house lately. I understand your reasons for not wanting to deal with the cops, but we were trying to avoid— Listen, I am going to do everything possible to catch this motherfucka and put him behind bars. I just need a little cooperation from you and your family. I am also assigned to the Tyjuan Glover murder case. I was on the scene at F Street when your daughter was discovered inside the Dodge Charger that belonged to Glover. I spoke to Kenya for a little at the hospital, but I didn't get much from her because of her traumatized state. I believe—especially now—that she knew the killer. I believe that, that person went to Tyjuan Glover's funeral looking for her. She was—"

"I want to see my daughter."

"Mr. Felder, it's not a pretty sight in there. Your daughter was . . ."

Ameen walked past the detective and entered the room. There was a lone white man dressed in a white lab coat standing beside a metal table. On that table lay a body, a small one, covered with a white sheet. The look on his face told the story.

"This is the victim's father," the detective said from behind him. "He's here to identify the body."

The white man nodded his assent and then looked at Ameen. "Are you sure you want to see her?"

Ameen nodded.

"Okay," he replied, before pulling the white sheet back slowly.

He took one look at his child and turned away. It was her. There was no mistake. His daughter was gone forever and only her bullet riddled, lifeless shell remained. What had been beautiful in life was now scarred, damaged, and ugly in death. Kenya's kind, gentle, and loving spirit was departed.

Devastated, he dropped his head and wept. The pain was great, almost too heavy to hold up. His body threatened to collapse due to the weight of it. When his knees buckled, he knew he needed to sit down, but he couldn't. He wouldn't. Suddenly, Ameen couldn't breathe. It felt like his lungs were inside of a vise being squeezed. He had to get out of there before he released his rage.

"Mr. Felder! Mr. Felder!" he heard the detective call out to him, but he kept walking until he reached the parking lot. Then Ameen ran. Just took off running away from the coroner's building. Away from the fact that his oldest child was back there. Cold and alone in death, lying on a metal gurney. He ran away from time. Tried to run from the reality of it all.

Ameen ran past bus stops and people waiting for buses. He ran past a high school, past stores and cars. His breath was constricted a little, and his chest was on fire, but he kept running. Although his legs ached, he ran. Tears flowed as he ran. By the time he stopped running, due to sheer exhaustion, he was at the Safeway grocery store on Seventeenth Street in Northeast. Ameen sat down on the curb and put his face in his hands and cried as people moved all around him.

The walk back to the medical examiner's office on E Street took him about forty-five minutes. His car was in the parking lot there, so he had to go back. Ameen was in bad shape. Completely devastated. Angry and in a state of disbelief, he was numb. Inside the car, he sat defeated, ignoring his cell phone as it vibrated. He didn't know what to say to anyone. What to do. Where to go, or how to go on. What was he going to say to Asia and Kay Kay about their sister? How do you explain life and death to children who've never experienced loss? How could they go on as a family, living with grief everyday? Knowing that one of them was missing and would never return? What would he say to Shawnay to comfort her? How could he comfort her? Especially when he couldn't comfort himself.

When the cell phone vibrated again beside him, he checked the screen. Shawnay. He didn't want to answer it, but he knew he had to.

"I'm sorry, baby," Ameen blurted. "They killed my baby. She's gone . . . She's gone. I couldn't protect her." He broke down crying again.

"Antonio, don't you dare blame yourself for what happened. Do you hear me? Don't you do this to yourself or to me. There was nothing that either one of us could've done to save Kenya. No matter what we did or said, she was gonna do what she wanted to do. We did all we could, short of chaining her to the bed or locking her up. She was grounded, but she left the house anyway . . . It's not your fault. You have to believe that. I don't want you to . . . Wait. Let me get off this phone. I'm not supposed to be on it while in this hospital—"

"Are you okay? Your friend who called said that—"

"I'm not okay, but right now me and the kids are at Hadley Hospital waiting to hear something about my grandmother. When she found out about Kenya, she had a heart attack. Let me go . . . I love you."

Ameen disconnected the call and dropped the phone. Here he was crying like a baby and his wife seemed stronger than he was. He respected her more right then than at any time in his life.

After he wiped his eyes and took several deep breaths to clear his head, the realization of Kenya being gone was still crushing, and he wanted to mourn his daughter, but that would have to wait. What he needed at the moment was retribution. Ameen needed blood. Craved it like a vampire. He pulled himself together and drove home.

The house was quiet and somber as if it knew what had happened. Ameen undressed as he walked up the stairs. In the bedroom, he exchanged his clothes for more comfortable, loose fitting, black ones. He put on black socks, black fatigue cargo pants, a thick black wool shirt, and a black sweatshirt with black Nike boots. Then he walked downstairs to the basement and turned on the light. In the back corner were bags of clothes and plastic bins with all kinds of stuff in them. Inside one of those bins was a small metal lockbox. He pulled at the marked bin, dug inside it under all the clothes until he found it.

Ameen rubbed the black lockbox as he remembered the vow he made to himself when he last held it. Also, he remembered the vow he made to Allah. After he unlocked the box, and gazed at the small cache of weapons, he pulled out a small, compact HK submachine gun that spit fifty rounds before requiring a reload. The Sig Sauer .45 with the sound suppressor attachment came out of the box too. Since he didn't know who the green-eyed dude Tyger was, he'd settle for whoever was outside on his block.

*****

*In the car, Tyjuan told me that the dude's name was Tyger, and he was from the Avenue,* Kenya's words replayed in Ameen's head over and over as he drove to Alabama Avenue on the side of town where Shawnay used to live. He thought about the beef at the movies that started everything and cursed under his breath. Damned if he hadn't told Kenya that the young dude she liked was trouble, but she hadn't listened. He knew of Tyjuan being from "The Circle" and Tyger being from "The Avenue" and the history those two neighborhoods had. It was always bad blood between them like the Hatfields and McCoys.

As he drove to the destination, he realized he had no particular plan of action. All he had was time, motive, desire, and the tools to bring about destruction. Ameen knew what obstacles he was up against, but he didn't care. He had zero fear and gave no thought to his own life, but only the one that was now gone and the one that he wanted to take. Had to take. And until he succeeded in taking that life, or death took him, the whole Avenue would feel his pain.

At 8:19 p.m., he turned onto Forty-sixth Street and drove down to Alabama Avenue. The block between F and G streets was where dudes were known to congregate. He cruised by and mentally counted at least fifteen people in one crowd by the wall. All eyes were on the Lexus as he went by. They were alert eyes, but even alert eyes could be surprised. Southeast projects were all filled with cuts and alleys behind and throughout them, and he knew an alley ran behind Alabama all the way down to Texas Avenue. Getting through the alley unseen would be the biggest challenge, but it wasn't insurmountable.

Parking the Lex' on Texas Avenue, he hopped out with a small, drawstring bag slung over his shoulder. Casually, he walked up E Street, then hit the alley.

Now fully dark outside, Ameen prayed the alley was clear. He knew he was directly behind the houses on Alabama Avenue. As he counted houses, he visualized exactly where he'd seen the crowd of people standing. Scanning the area, he didn't see a soul. His luck held. So far, so good.

He climbed a small fence and then ducked down inside someone's yard, curious about being seen or heard. Yet, nothing happened. He breathed easily. The yard had a fence that stopped directly at the house. There was a small space between the house and a tenement right next to it. Ameen hugged the wall and skulked his way to the opening at the end of the house. He held his breath and peeped out onto the street.

Exhaling, he smiled. The crowd he saw as he rode down the Avenue was still there, about twenty feet away from where he now stood. Putting his back flat against the wall of the house, he opened the bag and pulled out the weapons, then dropped the bag on the ground. Ameen placed the HK in his right hand and the .45 in his left. Looking into the sky, he mouthed a silent prayer to Allah. The night sky seemed menacing and added to his vengeful mood. With thoughts of Kenya's cold body lying on that cold gurney in the morgue, Ameen dashed out of the cut and stood on the small wall that stopped at the sidewalk. From an elevated position, he indiscriminately opened fire on the crowd. People ran and scattered as others collapsed on the sidewalk and out in the street. He never stopped firing the HK. Everything moving, he shot at it. Then he hopped off the wall and tried to find green eyes.

One dude pleaded for his life as he lay mortally wounded. He wasn't the man that Ameen had come for; his eyes were the wrong color. Nevertheless, he raised the four-fifth and took his life anyway.

As he stepped over each fallen body, he surveyed the scene. Some eyes were already closed; their bodies devoid of life. He didn't have time to stop and check eye colors, so he kept moving. Every person that breathed, he pumped a silenced hollow point into their brain. Adrenaline pumping, Ameen felt like the Terminator. Suddenly satisfied with the carnage and death he'd brought to Alabama Avenue, he turned and ran back the way he'd come, stopping to pick up the bag as he went. Before leaving the alley, he stopped long enough to put both guns back into the bag.

Sirens could be heard in the distance. Ameen's war with the person that killed his daughter had officially begun. He raised a hand to his face to remove his mask and felt nothing but skin. Shaking his head, he muttered, "Shit!"

He exited the alley and jogged back to his car and pulled off. Absorbed completely in the desire to kill, Ameen had forgotten to put on the mask.

*****

After changing clothes in the basement, he walked upstairs to find Shawnay sitting at the dining room table with a bottle of Remy Martin within her grasp and a glass filled with brown liquid in her hand. It was the first time he had ever seen Shawnay drink any type of liquor. As he approached the table, her eyes found his. They were bloodshot red and swollen with tears.

Before he could speak, Shawnay said, "Ten days ago we got married, and it was by far the best day of my entire life. Now today is the worst day of my life. Today, my oldest child was murdered in the street, gunned down like an animal, and as a result of that, my grandmother left this world. Grandma died forty-five minutes ago, Antonio."

# CHAPTER FOURTEEN

## DETECTIVE MAURICE TOLLIVER

Last night in D.C. was a bloody one. D.C. Police were called to the 4300 block of Alabama Avenue in Southeast last night after witnesses reported hearing multiple gunshots in the vicinity. Responding to the scene, authorities discovered several people with gunshot wounds. According to a source close to the D.C. Police Department, seven were pronounced dead at the scene. Four victims were transported to various hospitals around the city. No identities have been provided to the public."

"We have to notify each next of kin, and then we will release the identities to the media," a homocide official said.

"An eye witness reports that a lone gunman appeared out of the darkness and surprised a crowd as he opened fire on them. Witnesses also reported that the gunman then walked amongst the fallen victims and executed people. A vague description was given to police, but as of yet there are no suspects in custody.

"A teenage girl slain early yesterday afternoon at an Amoco gas station on Pennsylvania Avenue in Southeast has been identified as sixteen-year-old Kenya Dickerson. The teenager was shot and killed as she sat in a car while a friend paid for gas. Authorities believe that Kenya Dickerson was killed because of her connection to a young man named Tyjuan Glover, who was killed seven days ago on F Street in Benning Heights, a few blocks away from the scene of the mass murder of seven people.

"Police have also identified the body of a man found decapitated on Wayne place in Southeast four days ago. The man's head was found several feet away from his

body in a dark colored gym bag with a basketball. The man was identifed as thirty-year-old Quincey Mitchell. Authorities believe Quincey Mitchell was killed because of the statements he made in the murder case of twenty-nine-year-old Jerome Stroud. The murder . . ."

The sound of the house phone ringing caused Moe Tolliver to look up from his iPad where he was reading the morning edition of the *Washington Post* online. The caller was insistent and persistent in reaching him. Since he had been ignoring the phone all morning, he put down his venti pumpkin spice latte from Starbucks and walked across the living room to get the phone.

"Hello?"

"Tolliver?"

"Speaking."

"It's me, Moe. Greg Dunlap. How you been, buddy?"

Moe ran his hand through the unruly, thick curls on his head and sighed.

"I'm good, Cap. What happened now?"

"A lot has happened, Moe, that's why I'm calling. This place ain't been the same since you left. I'm surrounded by the greatest minds in the world who can't catch a cold during flu season."

"I'm sorry to hear that, Captain, but what does that have to do with me?"

"It's been what, a year since you resigned?"

"Yeah, about that."

"Well, listen to me, Moe. You know me, right?"

"Yeah," he replied.

"Okay, so you know that I ain't never been one to beg or grovel. I ain't never had to kiss nobody's ass in my life. Hell, that's why I'm only a captain after being in the department for thirty-five years. But I'm wearing lip gloss, Moe, and my lips are puckered. I need you back, Moe. You've been on your self-imposed sabbatical long enough, buddy. I never realized how important you were around here until you quit. I've been sitting back waiting for you to come to your senses and come back to work, but now I see that you're either really done with police work, or you're just plain stubborn. I tend to lean towards the latter. Have you been keeping up with the news lately?"

"Actually, I was just reading the paper online when you inter—" He caught himself before politely saying, "when you called."

"So you know about what happened yesterday?"

"The crowd that was fired on and the deaths of seven people?"

"The Alabama Avenue thing. Naw, not that, Moe. We've identified every person killed on Alabama Avenue, and somebody did the world a favor. I hate to say this—and I'd never repeat it in public—but the big guy upstairs finally got it right. All seven of them guys were drug dealers, gang bangers, and murderers. Apparently, there's a war going on between the Avenue and Simple City again. I'm not talking about that, Moe. I'm talking about Kenya Dickerson."

"The sixteen-year-old girl killed at the gas station?"

"Exactly. She was a good kid, Moe. She didn't deserve to be gunned down like that."

"Nobody deserves to be gunned down like that."

"Hey, save the sound bites for the media, Moe, and give me a fuckin' break here, okay?" You know what I mean. She wasn't a part of the streets. The fuckin' First Lady is rumored to be attending her funeral. That's why I called you. I need my best man on this job. I know that the Fuller case where Emily Perez and that other girl—"

"Latasha Allison, Cap. Her name was Latasha Allison. A mother of two."

"Yeah, right, okay. I know that, that case and the way it evolved put a bug up your ass. But Moe, that happens to all the great detectives. We all have our Rebecca cases—"

"Rebecca case?"

"Yeah. That's what it's called. A Rebecca case. Don't fuckin' ask me why it's called that, but it is. It's the one case that got away. Like a woman you've always wanted but couldn't have, it's the one case that you couldn't solve. Every detective has one or two. I damn sure got mine. I just try to never think about it. That's what you gotta do. File it in the back of your mind and just keep going. I accepted your resignation without a word back then, Moe, but you know like I know, that you're not a quitter. I know you were under a lot of pressure to close that Fuller case with all them damn murders. And Fuller getting acquitted pushed you overboard. You weren't the only cop affected by that case. We all were. We're still affected by it. Do you think Emily Perez would agree with you quitting the force for good?"

Moe ran a hand down his face and then noticed a mustard stain on his shirt. It was the same shirt that he'd washed and wore over and over again. He looked at his navy boxer shorts and bare feet, then around the living room. His life was off track and he knew it. Briefly, Moe remembered Emily Perez and how happy she'd been to marry her husband, Reuben. Then he asked himself silently, *What would she want me to do?*

"Cap, it's . . . it's been over a year that I've been away . . . I can't—"

"You can't what, Moe? Get back up on the horse and ride it again after you fell off a few times? Nonsense, kid. You can still ride that horse. You just gotta believe it in your heart and get back on it. Coming back won't be easy at first, but once you get back out on the streets, the old you will appear in a flash. You don't have to give me an answer right now, but think about everything that I've said. Then call me in a day or two with an answer. Okay?"

"I'll do that, Cap. Whatever decision I make, you'll be the first to know."

"That's great, Moe, but you remember this: we gotta get the motherfucker that killed that teenage girl. And the trail is getting colder by the second."

"I'll remember that, Captain. Thanks for calling."

Putting the phone back on the base, Moe stared down at it while replaying everything that Captain Dunlap had said. He walked across the living room and sat down in his favorite chair. As he grabbed the iPad and set about to finish reading the *Post*, he put it down again. Call it nostalgia, but Moe remembered how good life was before quitting the force. He was doing something he loved and spending nights with the woman he loved. Balancing work and a social life had come easy to him then. But after he quit the job, maintaining a healthy relationship with Dollicia became hard. Moe's 'Rebecca case,' as the captain called it, dogged his body and soul eveyday. And the deaths of Emily Perez and Latasha Allison wouldn't leave him alone. They haunted his dreams like no other.

Falling into a deep depression, Moe became a different person. Dollicia said Moe was a stranger to her before she left him for good. He was crushed by her abandonment, but yet he understood her decision. Even he didn't want to be around himself. After that, he'd simply sit around and wallow in self pity. The Captain's words sparked something inside him and gave him a new perspective. Suddenly, he felt as if the dark cloud that hung over him for months was leaving. Going back to work was starting to sound better and better as he thought about it. Maybe it was time for him to rise from the dead. Just like Lazarus had.

# CHAPTER FIFTEEN

## TYGER

Tyger thought about all seven homeboys that died on the Avenue and felt tears roll down his cheeks. Inhaling the strawberry kush, he tried to make the potent exotic weed dull his senses, but it failed. He was still in too much pain. The grief threatened to overwhelm him. To lose one childhood friend was devastating enough, but to lose seven friends at once was cataclysmic and life altering. Even more so when you know that something you did was the direct cause of those deaths. When Tyger made the conscious decision to kill Tyjuan, he knew there would be repercussions. But never in his wildest dreams did he imagine that the Circle would retaliate to that magnitude. He saw them riding through and letting off a few shots, but killing seven people in cold blood? Naw, he didn't see that one coming. And he guessed that's why he felt so fucked up on the inside.

Wiping tears from his eyes, he thought about how crazy life could be. The fact that a shot of pussy had saved his life was sobering, despite the effects of the weed. Tyger was headed to the Avenue yesterday right before Tashia popped up and changed the rest of his day and night. They had unfinished business, she said. The things she did to him that day and for half the night came to mind and his dick stirred in his pants. Without even knowing it, she had saved his life. Even though nobody in the room was going to say it aloud, he knew that people blamed him for the deaths of their men. They knew like he knew that the retaliation was a result of what Tyger did on F Street when he killed Tyjuan. They all knew he killed him. So, they also knew he was the intended target last night and that others had died in his place.

When he awoke this morning to the bad news about his men, Tyger's heart broke and went out to the other four people still in the hospital fighting for their lives. He vowed that their pain, suffering, and deaths wouldn't go unpunished. As he looked around the room through red eyes and fogs of weed smoke, he saw that all the faces looked like his, somber and filled with tears. Suddenly, a knock on the door broke the eerie silence and startled him. Since he was nearest to the door, he rose from his seat and went to answer it. His homies, Fella, D-Roc, and Blue walked in dressed for war.

"What the fuck happened out there last night?" Fella exploded as soon as the door closed behind them. Everybody in the room dropped their heads, so Tyger spoke up. "Somebody came through shooting." If looks could kill, he would've been dead.

"I already know that, stupid ass nigga. I'm tryna hear something I don't know. Like who did it?"

"I wasn't out there," he mumbled and exhaled weed smoke.

"What did you just say, Tyger?"

"I said I wasn't out there."

"That's what I thought you said," Fella said, walking over and standing directly in front of him. "I'm like five minutes off of ya ass, slim, so I suggest you shut the fuck up and let somebody that was on the Avenue last night talk."

Deep inside Tyger fumed at his big homie's lack of respect, but he knew not to publicly challenge Fella. He was a made nigga in the hood, and Tyger's weight wasn't up enough to go against him. So he chilled and kept quiet.

"We was outside standing in front of Levi and nem' house, drinking, smoking, and chilling like we always do," Spock explained, breaking the silence. "Then the dude came from outta the cut . . ."

"You saw him?" D-Roc asked from his position on the wall by the kitchen. "The muthafucker that did this . . . You saw the nigga?"

Spock nodded.

"And you didn't recognize him?"

"Naw," Spock replied while shaking his head.

"What did he look like?"

"I only saw him for a second or two. He just appeared and got to busting that choppa at us and I broke. I don't know the dude from nowhere, never seen him before in my life. He was about my complexion, and he had a baldhead."

"One muthafucka," Fella asked. "Just one muthafucka?"

"That's all I saw." Spock turned to the dude sitting to his right. "What about you, Bird? It was only one nigga, right?"

Jay Bird was the youngest dude in the room at sixteen years old, but he was the most vicious nigga with a gun in hand that they knew. "One dude, brown skin, baldhead, just like Spock said. Dressed in all black. I saw him for a second before I got outta there myself."

"I can't believe this shit!" Fella bellowed. "One nigga, seven dead, and nobody busted back at the nigga?"

"You know how the cops been coming through the spot. Wasn't nobody out there strapped. Niggas wasn't tryna catch no gun charge on a humble. All the guns were inside TC's Excursion."

"Nobody recognized the shooter. So that tells me that somebody sent him," D-Roc added.

Fella paced the living room floor before saying, "I figured that out already, but what I don't know is: who sent him? Them niggas ain't never put nobody up to shoot for them before, so why now? Which leads me to believe that it could've been somebody other than them Circle niggas."

"Dawg," D-Roc said and took the floor, "you my nigga and all that, but you know what it is, and you keep tryna act like you don't see what's right in your fuckin' face. We just had this conversation in the car, and I told you why it gotta be them niggas. Was you listening to me, or was the sound of your heart beating too fast? It had to be them. Even if this is a little unlike them, they brought in a nigga and put him on us.

"They sent that dude. They figured out that Tyger killed Tyjuan and they hit back. Simple as that. That shit ain't hard to see. On some real live shit, dawg, this is the dead give away. The dude that came through the block appeared and disappeared with no problem. And what does that tell us? It tells us that he had help. You know like I know that you gotta be from around our way to navigate the cuts and alleys. An outsider would get lost and get killed. The dude had to know when to strike.

"Why? Because he knew the cops been around a lot, and that nobody outside was

probably strapped. All of what I just said is enough for me to know that Squirt and nem' sent the dude. When Lil Rob got killed in the Circle months ago, you told us to let it go because you wasn't convinced that niggas in the Circle would jump out there like that. And we listened to you. We swallowed our anger and thirst for retribution, but now this shit is getting outta hand. If we let this go, dawg, we gonna have all kinds of niggas coming through the Avenue thinking they can get at us and we won't respond. Fuck that! If we don't hit the Circle, we might as well pack up and move. Either that, or bend over and take some dick because niggas gonna know we pussy. I ain't leaving my hood, and I damn sure ain't taking no dick, so I know what I'm gonna do. With or without you, dawg. With or without you."

Fella looked D-Roc in the eyes and then glanced over at Blue. "If we do this, ain't no turning back from it. It's gonna be like '96 all over again. A whole lotta muthafuckas gonna die."

"A whole lotta muthafuckas just died. Last night we lost seven. It's time to even up the numbers," D-Roc said.

"Blue? What about you?" Fella asked.

Daniel "Blue" Nelson was an old head. Recently released from the pen, Blue had been home for only thirty days, but his murder game was legendary in the hood. His word would basically make all the difference in the world. If he said, "go," they'd go and if he said to, "hold up," they'd hold up.

"It is what it is. You know how I get down."

"Does everybody else here feel like D?" Fella asked.

Everybody present nodded, including Tyger. He was ready to kill. His homeboy's blood called out for vengeance.

"A'ight then, if this is what y'all want, so be it. Blue, you fall back and I'll let you know when I need you. D-Roc, you take whoever you want and y'all go through the Circle. I'ma take Tyger and go after Squirt. Kill the head and the body will fall. Let's do it."

Three hours later, Fella and Tyger sat in a stolen Dodge Magnum across the street from a white and beige brick townhouse on Michelle Drive in Landover, Maryland. "Tell me again what happened."

"What happened with what? The Avenue?"

"Naw," Fella replied. "What happened with you and Tyjuan?"

Tyger sat back in the passeneger seat and fingered the loaded Highpoint 9-millimeter in his lap. He thought back to the night of the movies and started there.

"That nigga spit in my face. He hawk spit—some green shit on me. That fucked me up the most. I told Tyjuan I was gonna kill him. I caught him three days later when he wasn't expecting it. He was walking up the block, counting money. I jumped out the truck and fucked him around. All head shit. As we were leaving, I was pulling off my mask when I saw her."

"Saw her, who?"

"The girl, the pretty ass young girl that was with Tyjuan that night at the movies. She was in his car, pressing down on the horn. That's what drew my attention to the car. We locked eyes, and I knew that she recognized me. That's why I had to get her. I didn't wanna hit shorty; I *had* to hit shorty. It was that, or do a million years in jail. She knew who I was from the movies, and for all I know, she was probably already talking to the cops about the murder. I ain't never killed no bitch, slim, and I gotta admit it's a little different. But like I said, she had to go. I kinda figured that she'd come to Tyjuan's funeral and that I'd catch here there. Me and Choppa spotted her and her buddy in a car, followed them, and I crushed her."

"Slim, do you think it's wise to put Choppa in all your business like that? I mean, I know y'all first cousins and all that shit, but niggas don't see none of that family shit when them people get on their ass. What if he gives you up under pressure?"

"Big Boy, with the girl gone, there's no witness and no case. Choppa would rather die than cross me like that. But I respect what you're saying."

"That's what's up then. I guess you did what you had to do. I ain't mad at you. Although ain't nobody gon' get no money during war. Good men are gonna die and niggas is gon' go to jail. This beef is gonna change everything we know, and all I can do is keep asking myself is it worth it. So, let me ask you again, despite the fact that our men got hit—and keep in mind that we don't really know who did it. Do you think it's worth it?"

"Seven of my friends died last night, and another four are barely clinging to life. Even if the Circle niggas didn't do it, they 'bout to pay for it like they did. It's worth it to me."

Fella closed his eyes and appeared to be asleep. For a long time he didn't say a word. Then his cell phone vibrated. He answered it. "Talk to me."

"We hit 'em. Ten minutes ago. Walked through and fucked it up," the caller said.

"A'ight. Later." Fella turned and faced Tyger. "That was Roc. They just hit the Circle. In the next five to ten minutes, that door right there is gonna open and slim should be coming out."

"Are you sure about that?" he asked, palms sweaty. Tyger was ready to kill in the memory of his fallen comrades.

"Positive. Big Squirt should've already got the call telling him what just happened in his hood. In a few minutes, he'll come out. Watch."

For a minute Tyger lay back and thought about what Fella just said. Then just as he started to doubt his words, the front door to 7819 opened and out rushed his target. He locked eyes with Fella and smiled.

"Go get him."

Sliding from the Magnum, Tyger crept around a car and made his way toward the Porsche truck. The evening sky was clear, but it was dark. Perspiration ran down the inside of his sweatshirt, and he noticed how unusually warm it was. A cell phone glued to Squirt's ear would prove to be his undoing. He neither heard nor saw Tyger approach. He slid up on him from the rear and called his name. Squirt stopped in his tracks and turned to face him, his cell phone now at his side. Their eyes locked and he recognized Tyger. Death was upon him and he knew it. Tyger raised the gun and fired. Big Squirt was dead before his body hit the ground. But Tyger still ran up and gave him head shots. When he got back to the Magnum and slid into the passenger seat, he couldn't resist asking Fella one question. "How did you know that Squirt was in that house and that he would come out when he did?"

"Squirt ran the hood. He had to make an appearance after the Circle got hit. A good general knows he has to corral the troops, keep morale up, and strategize a retaliation move. It's what I would've done. And I knew he was in the house because I been fuckin' his wife for years."

With that said, Fella smiled again and pulled the car away from the curb.

# CHAPTER SIXTEEN

## KHADAFI

After speaking with Mechanic Mike about a malfunctioning Northstar computer chip in a Cadillac, Khadafi left the garage and walked across the car lot, surveying the space. Something inside him smiled at the sight. The cars he had assembled for sale were all pretty good ones, and his lot looked respectable. Who would've thought that an outlaw would one day change his life and become a legit businessman? Although, he still moved drugs on the side, the car lot was his primary hustle. Taking the steps that led to the trailer, two at a time, he stopped in his tracks. The sliding panel door was open. He knew he hadn't left it that way. He never left it like that. His eyes darted around the lot to see if he could spot Pee-Wee's Benz anywhere, because he was the only other person with a key to the door. He didn't see the Benz at all. Somebody was inside the trailer, and he didn't have a clue as to who it could be. Reaching into his waist band, Khadafi pulled the chrome Desert Eagle .45 out and hid it beside his leg. He opened the door some more and stepped inside the trailer. Even though the lights were out, there was enough sun shining through the windows to illuminate the room. He could make out the shape of a person sitting in the chair that sat across from his desk. Loudly, he chambered a round into the barrel of the .45.

"Assalaamu Alaikum, ock," a voice said.

Khadafi recognized it instantly. That made him grip the butt of the gun even tighter.

"I gave you the greeting, ock. That should tell you that I come in peace," Ameen said, without moving an inch. "So, you can put the gun up—unless you are gonna kill me."

*How the hell did he get in? Why is he here?* Khadafi shook his head and put away the gun. He walked around Ameen and sat in the chair behind the desk. "Cuz, you can't be sneaking up on a nigga like that. You know I'm a paranoid schizophrenic, and I usually shoot first and ask questions later. Wa Laikum assalaam. I heard that you and Shawnay got married. Congratulations."

"Thanks, ock. This should be the happiest time of my life, but it's not. Some niggas in Southeast ruined it for me. I'm supposed to be on my honeymoon, but instead I'm about to bury a child."

Khadafi's eyes dropped to Ameen's lap where he checked to see if he was holding a gun. He wasn't. His eyes were closed, and he was dressed in all black, just as he was the last time he had seen him. Several questions came to mind as he finally digested what Ameen had just said. "What did you just say! You gotta bury a child?"

"Yeah, ock. That's what I said. I still can't believe it, but it's true. Somebody killed my daughter." Ameen's voice broke and he broke down in tears.

In all his years of knowing Ameen, he had never seen him cry, get weak, or appear vulnerable. Khadafi shot straight up in his seat. He couldn't believe what he just heard.

"They killed my baby. They killed my baby . . ."

He didn't know what to do or say. Although he knew the pain of loss firsthand, he couldn't imagine what it must feel like to lose a child. Khadafi kept quiet and waited for Ameen to continue talking. After a while he did.

"My daughter came home one day with a dude she wanted me and her mother to meet. I could tell she was digging the lil dude jive hard. In my mind, Kenya would always be the little girl I left when I went to prison back in the day. Even though I saw a young woman before my eyes, my heart saw a little girl. As soon as I saw the dude I knew what he was about.

"His whole swag told the story. One of them Lil Wayne wannabe type niggas. Young, dumb nigga who wore his pants too tight and had the nerve to be packing a big ass gun the day I met him. The clip had to be an extended one because the goofy joint stuck out too far. It was easy to notice, and the kid didn't even recognize that. I was hot about that alone, and him having my baby with him almost made me lose it.

"I took shorty outside and politely, but forcefully told him to stay the fuck away from my daughter and that if I caught him with her again that I was gonna get with him. Then I found out he was eighteen years old, and all I saw was this grown ass man fuckin' my baby. Which he was by the way, I just didn't know it then. Had I known that then, I would've killed shorty. That's what crushes me the most now. If I would've killed shorty like I wanted to, this would've never happened." Ameen stopped to wipe tears from his eyes.

"I thought that after I talked to my daughter and hollered at the dude, that maybe I got through to 'em both. But I didn't. What I did was run her into his arms even more and cause my baby to sneak around and lie to me and her mother. After I got married, I made Kenya promise me that she wouldn't see the lil dude, but she did. She promised me . . . Looked me right in the eyes and lied. Some shit happened with the dude while we were gone. To make a long story short, what Tyjuan did got him and my daughter killed." Ameen retold how the beef started between Tyger and Tyjuan at the movie theater.

"It seems like a dream to me. I'm still telling myself this has to be a dream, that I'm gonna eventually wake up from. And I pray to Allah that I wake up soon because this nightmare has been going on for too long and it's too vivid. I'd rather wake up back in prison, never having gotten married and never having experienced any of the things that I've experienced if that would bring my daughter back. I'd trade everything and anything to bring her back, ock."

Khadafi sat riveted to the chair and watched Ameen going through a sea of emotion and didn't know what to do or say. Then the obvious came to mind. "Cuz, where these niggas at? You know how I get down. Say the word and they dead. Everybody. Anybody can get it. Where the green-eyed dude . . . What's his name? Tyger? Where him and his men at?"

Ameen used his shirt sleeve to wipe his eyes and nose. Then he said, "They from Alabama Avenue . . . but I been there already. Their whole neighborhood been on the news fucking with me."

"Hold on, cuz. You not saying . . . that was you! You the one who went through there and put that work in like that?"

Ameen nodded. "I was looking for Tyger and didn't see him, so I charged my daughter's death to everybody out there. My last count was like seven dead, a few others injured. I went through there right after I left the morgue identifying Kenya."

"You might've got the dude, cuz."

"I didn't. I watched the news. They released the names of the dead. Kenya told me that Tyjuan said the dude Tyger's real name was Terrell. Wasn't nobody killed by that name. But nonetheless, I'ma get him. I'ma go back through there every day until I get him. That's why I'm here. I need you, ock. I can't trust nobody in the world on something like this but you. I know you, and I know what you made of.

"I know if you get caught, or we get caught, that you ain't gon' snitch. I know your gun game is mean, and you gon' rock and roll however it may come. That's what I need, and I came to ask you to help me punish those that had a hand in the death of my daughter."

"Cuz, fuck what we been through in the past. I owe you my life and all that comes with it. None of this"—Khadafi gestured, waving his hand around the office they sat in—"would be possible without the sacrifice you made and what you did for me the night I got released from the jail. So, how could I say no?"

"I respect that, ock, and I appreciate it. All you gotta do is watch my back, and I'ma put the work in—"

"Watch your back while you work? Stop that, cuz. You know good and damn well that I ain't no sideline kinda nigga. I ain't tryna play if I can't get in the game. I'ma body them niggas, straight like that. I'ma watch your back while you watch mine, and we gon' rock like that."

"I feel that. But I'ma little blinded by pain and vengeance, so I might not make a good watch-out man. I'ma try my best though. On this mission, we gon' have to get creative. These niggas ain't gon' give me the opportunities that I just had. Now that they know I'm coming, they'll be a little harder to get. Like the song says: we might have to dress up like ladies to burn 'em with dirty 380's . . ."

"No matter what it is, I'm with you, cuz. Like I'm stuck to the clothes you're wearing. When you call me, I'm coming."

Ameen stood up and stretched. "I just had a thought. Do you know anybody from around there? On the Avenue?"

Khadafi leaned back in the chair and pondered Ameen's question. "That weed got my memory fucked up, cuz. Yeah, I know a few dudes around there. As a matter of fact, they are the main niggas around there. D-Roc, Fella, Ced, Pretty B. Why? What's up?"

Reaching into his pocket, Ameen extracted a cell phone. He tossed it to Khadafi, who caught the cell phone and quizzically glanced at the screen. A photo served as the screen saver. A face lit up the four-inch screen. The man in the photo was brown-skinned with the lightest green eyes he had ever seen.

"Tyger?" Khadafi questioned.

Ameen nodded. "That's him. Kenya took that picture the night he got into it with Tyjuan at the movies. I almost forgot about it until yesterday. I picked up her possessions from the police, and they gave me her phone. I remembered Kenya's words and scrolled through her album. There he was, in living color. That's the face I see in my dreams, ock. This is what I'm thinking now, though. You get in touch with one of them dudes you know, and you tell 'em that I'ma come through there everyday and kill everybody I see until I get Tyger and everybody else that had a hand in killing my daughter. Tell 'em I'ma keep killing and killing until my thirst for blood is quenched. If they don't want that to happen, they can hand over Tyger, and I'll be content with just him. He's the main one that I want.

"I kill him and all the bloodshed stops. One life for the lives of many. Sorta like a sacrifice. Tell them that and see what they say. If they say no, then they all become food in the food chain and I'll kill them too. It's just a matter of when I kill them. It makes no difference to me at all. Tell them this can play out any way they like. Pay for extra funerals and cry extra tears or not. It's their choice.

"I just thought I'd try things the semi-peaceful way first, before I get cranked up, but if that doesn't work, it's on and poppin'. Their mothers, fathers, kids, dogs, cats, everybody becomes a target. If you get in touch with one of 'em, make sure they understand that. Try to get to one of them as soon as possible, and I hope to hear from you in a few days. If I don't, then I'ma assume they did something to you, and then I'ma really kill everybody they know. You feel me, ock?"

"I feel you, cuz. I feel you."

# CHAPTER SEVENTEEN

## KHADAFI

Khadafi smelled murder in the air from the time Ameen revealed his hand and asked for his assistance. He left the car lot not too long after he watched Ameen's Lexus disappear into traffic. He needed to call Marnie and speak to his daughter Khadajah before he could bounce. After hanging up with them, he thought about Ameen and everything he said about wishing his whole life up until this day had been just a bad dream and how he'd gladly trade his marriage and everything, just to have his daughter back. That was some deep shit.

But he felt those sentiments one hundred and fifty percent because if something happened to Khadajah, he'd trade in everything for her life too. Khadafi thought about Shawnay and what she must be going through, the grief she had to feel. Anger rose and his blood simmered. When that happened, he knew someone was about to die. The animal inside him howled and screamed for food and blood. His palms started to itch, and his index finger got twitchy. The gun inside his waist got heavy and begged for relief. Putting all eight rounds in someone's head would lighten its load. He turned on some music to quiet the voices in his head.

". . . avoid the cage, but you can't avoid the grave/ when you live by the sword, you die by the sword . . ."

That evening, Khadafi drove through the city, his mind in a fog. All the photos he'd seen of Ameen's daughter as a kid came to mind. Then the actual times that he'd met Kenya replayed themselves in his head. Still, he couldn't believe someone had killed that beautiful young girl.

He remembered thinking how much Kenya looked just like Shawnay when he first saw her in person, and then tears welled up in his eyes. Thoughts of his son, Kashon, and the bond he probably had with his big sister added to the sadness. Khadafi thought about Ameen's younger daughter, Asia, and the pain she must feel. Before he knew it, he was cruising down Alabama Avenue. The street was relatively empty except a few people lounging on porches. Just as he was about to bust a U-turn and go back the way he'd come, he saw a familiar face. He blew the horn and lowered the window. "Tashia Parker, what's up?"

Her face showed no signs of recognition. "Who is that?"

"Dirty Redds from down Capers."

"Heeey boy!" Tashia sprinted off the porch and got into full groupie mode. "I thought you were still locked up. What you doing around here and these niggas out here beefing hard as shit with each other. Killing like shit. You ain't heard?"

"Naw, I haven't heard. Who they beefing with?"

"The Circle, who else? These niggas out here killing each other ninety goin' north. That's why it ain't nobody out here and can't nobody get no money. The police been riding through here all day. What's up with your red ass, though? What brings you through this neck of the woods?"

"I'm looking for a few good men that be out here. I need to holla at them."

"Who is a few good men?"

"D-Roc, Fella, and Ced. You know 'em?"

"Who don't know them niggas, although I can't stand none of 'em. Ced locked up over the jail. On some old ass bodies. Benji and Ronnie T. telling on him. D-Roc big nose ass probably somewhere smoking a dippa. Fella probably around somewhere."

He reached into his pocket and produced a wad of bills. Peeling off five 100s, he passed them through the window to Tashia. Her eyes lit up like a Christmas tree.

"I need to get in touch with D-Roc or Fella. Can you get a message to one of them?"

"Yeah, probably Fella," Tashia said and quickly pocketed the money."What you want me to tell him?"

"Tell him that Kha—Dirty Redds from down Capers tryna holla at him and that it's super important. Give him my number. Put this number in your cell phone." He gave Tashia his cell phone number. "Tell him to get at me ASAP. Tell him we need to rap, and it has something to do with all his current troubles. You got that?"

"You need to holla at him ASAP. It's important and about his current troubles. Give him your number to call you. I got it."

"And when all is said and done, I'm tryna come and scoop you for some rest and pleasure. Just like back in the day, if you know what I mean."

"I know exactly what you mean, nasty ass boy. But you got that, just holla."

"I will, and Tashia, just make sure he calls. I gotta few more big faces for you if he does."

"Nigga, he'll be calling you today and so will I. Is this your Range Rover?"

He didn't even bother to dignify Tashia's question with a response. He simply rolled up the window and pulled off.

*****

Not even two hours later, Khadafi's cell phone chirped and a number came across the screen that he didn't recognize. "What's good?" he said, answering the call.

"Dirty Redds?"

He recognized the voice instantly, although he hadn't heard it in years. "Fella, what's good, cuz?"

"Ain't shit, slim. Long time, huh?"

"Yeah, but you know how that goes."

"I got your message, slim. What's really good? You said it was important and pertaining to some current troubles that you believe I have."

"You know how these jacks is. I ain't gon' say much on it. I need to holla at you in person. I come in peace, and I got some news that you can use."

"Slim, I ain't gon' bullshit you and act like this whole set up ain't suspicious to me. But I'ma gambler, and I wanna hear what you gotta say."

"C'mon, cuz, you actin' like you and me had beef before or something. It's suspicious because I'm tryna wire my man up to some shit. That's foul, cuz."

"You know the rules that govern the streets: trust no one. I haven't heard nothin' from you in about ten years, and out of the blue I get word to holla at you and that it's important. You tellin' me that you wouldn't think the same thing?"

"Well, now that you put it that way, I feel you."

"And you haven't exactly been on your church boy shit in the last few years. I heard you call yourself something different now, but you been in the streets putting it in and getting money. Either way, it's all good. Where you tryna meet at to talk?"

"You the one that's acting like I'm the enemy. You tell me. You set the time and the spot."

"What you doing right now?" Fella asked.

"Nothing important, you tryna meet now?"

"Why not? Meet me at the Wendy's on Nannie Helen Burrough in thirty minutes."

"I'll be there, cuz. I'm out."

*****

When Khadafi pulled into the Wendy's parking lot, he saw a couple cars parked that had dudes sitting in them, and knew they were with Fella. Smiling to himself, he parked the Range Rover. Under his shirt, the Desert Eagle was idling and waiting to throw up all on a muthafucka if need be. So he wasn't alone either. Khadafi spotted Fella as soon as he walked into the restaurant. He'd gained a little weight, but overall he hadn't changed much. Fella was dressed in all black, and from the looks of it, he was wearing a bulletproof vest. He couldn't blame him for that. At the table where he sat, Khadafi pulled out a chair and sat down. He reached across the table and gave Fella some dap. "You look like life has been treating you good, cuz."

"What's so important that I need to hear? We can kick the bobos later on. What's good?"

"I respect that, cuz. No small talk, huh? You always been an impatient nigga." Khadafi reached into his pocket and extracted the cell phone that he'd gotten from Ameen. He powered it up and passed it across the table to Fella.

Fella picked the phone up and stared at the screen. "What's this supposed to be?"

"A teenage girl named Kenya took that picture one night at the movies. Right after her boyfriend and youngin' in that picture had a little scuffle. Youngin'"—he tapped the photo on the screen—"got spit on, and he threatened the dude that spit on him. The dude I'm referring to is named Tyjuan. A coupla days later, youngin' on the screen goes to the Circle and kills Tyjuan. The teenage girl, his girlfriend, witnesses the murder from his car. She locks eyes with him and remembers him as the dude from the movies. She tells her family but nobody else. A week later she goes to Tyjuan's funeral to pay her respects. The day of the funeral, she ends up dead. What I forgot to mention is that she remembers the dude had light green eyes, and Tyjuan called him Tyger. After the girl's death, naturally, her family puts one and one together and comes up with the fact that she was killed to silence her about what she witnessed. But she never told the cops what she saw. So, her family feels that she was killed unjustly and they want blood. Tyger's. They know youngin' is from your hood and a few other things about him. That's why I'm here to relay the message to you."

A scowl crossed Fella's face. "That's what you came here to tell me? *That's* the news that I can use? That the girl's people want my lil man? Who the f—slim, are you for real? You serious? You wasted my time to tell me some sucka ass shit like that?"

Khadafi kept his composure and spoke slowly, respectfully. "I called you here, cuz, to avoid further bloodshed. I called you here thinking you would listen to an old friend. I called you here to hopefully talk you into finding a peaceful way to resolve this, and that way you won't have to lose any more of your men."

"Lose any more of my men? Further bloodshed? Slim, are you high? What the fuck are you talkin' about? What are you saying?"

"On the strength that I know you and D-Roc and I respect y'all niggas, I put this meeting together. I figured that maybe I could diplomatically deal with this situation. The girl's family is tryna see youngin' one way or another, and they don't care about anybody that gets in the way. I'm the one that decided on the strength of you and D-Roc that I would try to see if nobody else other than youngin' had to die."

"Nobody else? What do you mean by nobody else?"

"Who do you think put that work in on the Avenue a coupla days ago?"

Fella's face went ashen. Then he recovered and growled, "You telling me that, that was the teenage girl's people that hit my hood the other night?"

Now that Khadafi had Fella's attention, he went in for the kill. "Yeah. One dude, all black, no mask, a Heckler & Koch and a handgun. Hit everybody he saw, then walked around and killed everybody that fell with shots to the head with the handgun. Seven people total. Check it out with your people, then ask yourself how else would I know all that."

"We thought that—"

"It was the niggas from the Circle, and then y'all went and retaliated, we know that. Y'all thought it was about Tyjuan. It wasn't."

Suddenly, Fella pulled a gun and put it on the table, barrel aimed directly at Khadafi. "What's to stop me from killing you right now, slim? And sending a message of my own to shorty's people?"

Right then Khadafi made up his mind that no matter what happened, whether Ameen got Tyger or not, that he was going to kill Fella. He smiled one of his best smiles and said, "Like I said earlier, I'm just relaying a message, cuz. But you can do what you want. If you think that killing me is gonna stop what's about to happen, then by all means go ahead and kill me. All the niggas I done killed, do you really think I'm afraid of death? I ain't never scared. Go 'head and do what you gotta do. But just know the streets ain't gon' be safe for nobody if you miss, or if I pull this cannon that I got on me before you get a clean shot off."

Fella must've read his eyes and saw that the same thing that lived in his eyes also lived inside Khadafi's eyes. So there was no intimidating him. He put the gun away and smiled to lessen the tension. "You say these people want my young nigga, Tyger, huh? And if we hand him over, all the bloodshed stops?"

"I was told that if you give up youngin' free and clear, that they have no other beef with your hood. But if you choose not to give him up, then somebody you know is gonna die every day until they find and kill Tyger. I was told that if the gloves come off, everybody is fair game, everybody is a target. Old people, kids, mothers, fathers, pets, everybody. Anybody."

"Is that right?" Fella asked.

Khadafi threw up both hands in a sign of mock surrender. "Just repeating what I was told. Word for word."

"Well, I tell you what, *message boy*. You tell your folks that I said that we don't give up our own for nobody. And just remember that you gotta bring ass to get ass. We ready for whatever and thanks for the heads up. Because now, you and your folks are the hunted ones."

"Damn, cuz, I always thought you were the smart one, but now I see that I was wrong and that the one with the brains must be D-Roc." He stood up to leave after he put Kenya's cell phone back in his pocket. "How you gon' hunt an enemy that you can't see and don't know. That's crazy."

"Everything that's done in the dark will come to the light eventually. And when it does . . ." Fella rose from his seat as well. "Oh . . . and one more thing . . . the next time you and I meet, it's gonna be from opposite ends of a smoking barrel. That's my word."

"That's your word? I feel you, cuz, and I'll remember that. You take care."

*****

Khadafi waited until he was back in Southeast before calling Ameen."What's up, cuz? Can you talk?"

"Yeah, ock, what's good? Did you holla at them dudes?"

"Yeah, I got in touch with one of 'em, and pretty much, I think that he spoke for the both of them. The dude Fella that run the hood, he won't listen to reason. He mad about all his men that got hit on the Avenue. Cuz was real hostile. From the moment I mentioned Kenya, his disposition changed, so that tells me he knows about the incident. And he didn't deny the fact that Tyger killed Kenya. You definitely barking up the right tree. I told him we wanted Tyger and Tyger alone, but he said they never give up their men. He got mad and pulled a hammer on me and everything. Called me a message boy twice. I just left him about twenty minutes ago."

"Oh yeah? Well, don't even trip. You tried it the peaceful way and he said fuck you. Now we do it the gangsta way and I'ma say fuck him. In a few days, ock, I bury my daughter. With a heavy heart, a lotta tears, and a ton of regret. It will be the hardest thing I ever did in my life, but I'ma get through it. For no other reason than to make a whole lotta other people feel my pain."

"I feel you, cuz, and I'm with you until the wheels fall off."

"I know that, and I appreciate you tryna talk to the dude, but all niggas these days understand is violence. Just like in the pen . . ." *Time to go to war.*

# CHAPTER EIGHTEEN

## SHAWNAY

All niggas these days understand is violence. Just like in the pen . . . What's that, ock? You got that. And one more thing before I go . . . always protect your family. Because I couldn't protect mine . . ."

Shawnay felt like a thief creeping in the night as she leaned on the wall and listened to Antonio's call. He paced the kitchen floor like a matador awaiting his only chance to kill the bull. He paced and talked and his pain was visible. His expression was heartbreaking. *Who was he talking to?* The comment about not being able to protect his family wouldn't leave her mind. Her heart was also broken, and to see her husband in pain because he blamed himself for Kenya's death was even more hurtful.

She watched as Antonio finally broke down into a heap on the floor and cried. As bad as she wanted to go to him, to reach out to him, to wrap her arms around him, she didn't. Couldn't. She had to let him have his moment. And she didn't want him to know she'd been there the whole time. Tears fell down her face as she slowly tipped back up the stairs to the bedroom. "You gotta be strong for your family," a voice inside her said. "Hold it all together." Shawnay wiped her eyes and told herself that her conscience was right, and she had to be the strong one, or else the whole family would suffer. So, she took two deep breaths and sat back down in front of the laptop on the desk. She scrolled through all the flash drives and memory cards in search of photos of Kenya that she wanted to include in her obituary. Deciding to go through the photos later, she started typing the words that would go inside the obituary, her heart aching with every word typed.

*Kenya LaShawn Dickerson was born on July 9, 1996, to her proud parents, Antonio and Shawnay Felder. She attended D.C. public schools until high school, where she attended Eisenhower Sr. High in Arlington, Virginia, where she excelled in dance, computers, academics, and other areas of the performing arts. At the time of her passing, she was on the honor roll as a straight A student. Known to her family as Kenya or Yah-Yah, she was sweet, considerate, beautiful, and an intelligent teenager who loved to laugh, cook, read, text her friends and stay on her computer for hours. She loved to talk on the phone, spend time with her family, and collect Dora the Explorer socks.*

*She often spoke of exploring the world herself one day. Unfortunately, Kenya's life was tragically cut short on February 24, 2013. She leaves to mourn her passing, her parents, one sister, Asia Renee Dickerson; one brother, Kashon Tariq Dickerson; two aunts, one uncle, and a host of other relatives and friends.*

"Ma," Asia said as she swept into the room wearing her favorite pajamas and holding her brother on one hip. "Kay Kay won't go to sleep. He keeps asking for Kenya, and I don't know what to tell him."

Shawnay got up and grabbed her son. Seeing his gorgeous, big brown eyes brought a light to her soul that outshined everything that was dark inside. She kissed his little nose and lips.

"Stop it, Mommy!" Kay Kay shrieked and giggled.

"Time for your little butt to go to bed," she said in a stern voice.

"No, Mommy, I want Kenya to tell me a story."

Her voice broke as she said, "She can't, baby. Kenya went to heaven to be with God and Grandma."

"I wanna go! Can I go to heaven too, Mommy?"

Tears started up then. "One day, baby, but Mommy doesn't want you to go now. You can go when you get old, okay?"

"Was Kenya and Grandma old?"

"Grandma was, but Kenya wasn't. God wanted Kenya to be with him, so he called Kenya home to heaven."

Kay Kay's eyes filled with tears. "But why?"

"Because God needed another angel, and he chose Kenya. Do you know what angels do?"

Kashon shook his head.

"Angels watch over us and make sure that we're okay. Kenya will watch over us from heaven. Her and Grandma."

"I wanna go with Kenya!" he screamed and started hollering.

Shawnay hugged him close and cried with him. Asia hugged them both and she cried as well.

"We're gonna get through this," she said to her children as much as to herself. "We are gonna be okay. Don't cry."

"I miss her, Ma," Asia said. "I miss Kenya so much. I want her back, Ma. I want my sister back. Tell God to send her back."

"I can't do that, baby. God won't do that. We'll all just have to wait until we get to heaven to see Kenya again."

"If God won't give me my sister back, then I don't like God, Ma. I hate him!"

"Don't say that, baby. God took Kenya because he needed her more than we do. Don't hate God for that." She tried to explain things to Asia, but she wasn't trying to hear anything. Shawnay watched her lie across the bed and bawl her eyes out. She wanted to go to her, but Kashon was in her arms and in tears, and for some reason, she couldn't move. Kashon's cries grew louder in her ears as if he was determined to cry louder than his sister.

This all overwhelmed her. She looked up and saw Antonio standing in the doorway. His eyes found hers and then quickly looked away. Without a word, he turned and walked away.

After putting the kids to bed and staying to make sure they went to sleep, she searched the house for her husband and found him in the basement. He sat in the dark on an old brown leather recliner they put there months ago. Shawnay stood on the stairs by the light switch and debated whether she should turn on the lights. Antonio made that decision for her.

"Leave the light off, Shawnay. I like the dark better right now."

"Is that because you'd rather not face me? Am I hard to look at now?"

"This ain't about you and you know that."

"Well, what is it about, Antonio? We're supposed to be a team, remember? Why are you shutting me out?"

"I'm not shutting you out. I'm here—"

"You're here, but I still feel alone."

"I'm tryna find a way to deal with . . ."

"With what, Antonio? Can't you say it?"

"I can't say it because I still can't believe it."

She walked in the dark to approach her husband. "You can say it. You have to say it, because if you don't, the pain and grief will eat you up inside. I just spent thirty minutes upstairs figuring that out. We have to accept what has happened as God's will and deal with it. Me, you, and the kids, we all have to find a way to deal with it and then heal. Kenya wouldn't want us to fall apart like this."

"Kenya would want to still be here, alive and on her way to accomplishing her goals. If she had, had a choice. That's what's so hard for me to deal with. The fact that somebody took that choice away from her. I still can't believe this happened to me, to us." He let silence loom for a few seconds.

"I saw my baby on that table in the morgue, and my first instinct was to cover her and shield her as if she was still here. I wanted to lie there beside her and wrap my arms around her and tell her how sorry I am that this happened to her. I wanted to tell her how helpless I feel. I can't stop thinking about how cold she must be and how alone she must feel. I wanna tell her that I'm sorry for failing her and not protecting her."

Tears fell down her face two at a time. Shawnay grabbed her husband's face and said, "You listen to me and you hear me. This is not your fault. You didn't fail anybody. How many times must I tell you that? You are not Superman.

You're *not* God. You can't be at two places at once. I cannot—will not stand here and allow you to beat yourself up about this. We both told Kenya to stop seeing Tyjuan. And after he died, we both told her it was best that she not attend his funeral. We grounded her. We talked to her and explained ourselves to her. We threatened her. We did everything short of taking her outside and chaining her to that tree out back. She didn't listen, Antonio. She defied us and it got her . . ." She released him from her grasp. "This is not your fault. It's not Kenya's fault. She didn't ask to be—"

After a brief pause, Antonio finished her sentence. ". . . Killed. She didn't ask to be killed. Is that what you were trying to say, but couldn't? See what I mean? It's hard to say even for you. Our baby was killed, Shawnay, and nothing we do or say can change that. A muthafucka out there killed my sixteen year old—"

"Antonio—please—" She laced her fingers together.

"Please what, Shawnay? It's the truth." Antonio grabbed her hands and held them tight. "And I'ma make it right."

"How, Antonio? By going back to prison and leaving us alone again? Is that your idea of making it right? Huh?"

"I gotta do something. For Kenya and for me."

"Didn't you just tell me—hold on, I need to see your face." Shawnay gently broke their connecting hands. She found the light switch along the wall, then hit the light. She walked back over to Antonio."You just told me that this ain't about me. Well, it ain't about you either. This is about our daughter."

"I gotta do something," Antonio repeated.

"You already did something. Wasn't that enough?" If her eyes were accusing, Antonio's eyes were questioning, curious.

"You don't think I know, huh? You *really* don't give me much credit, I see." She placed her left hand on her hip.

"Know what? Credit for what?" Antonio asked.

"Antonio, you're my husband and my best friend. I have loved you since the first moment I saw you years ago. I've been around you since I was fourteen years old. In the last eighteen years, I've grown to know more about you than ever before. Those people that were killed on Alabama Avenue the day Kenya was killed—you killed them."

"You're mistaken—that wasn't me. You saying anything right now." His eyes stared straight through her.

"Am I? Witnesses said that a lone gunman dressed in all black, shot all those people out there that night. One man killed all those people. One man, Antonio."

"I didn't kill anybody—"

Suddenly, her face contorted into a scowl. "You gon' sit here and fucking lie to me when I know that you did it!" she bellowed. "Did the vows that we just took include us lying to one another? I thought our motto to each other was no faking, no games, and no lies at any time? Didn't we agree to that?"

"Yeah, but—"

"Yeah, but, nothing. That's what we agreed on and that's what you need to stick to. I know what you did, Antonio. I know it was you." She went into her pocket and pulled out a nylon mask. "You dropped this in our bedroom as you changed your clothes. Did you forget that I'm the one who does the laundry around here? I saw the black cargo pants, hoodie, and socks in the washer that night. I moved your muddy Nike boots from beside the machine, and I knew that they weren't there earlier that day. I noticed all the stuff you moved around down here, and I knew you'd been in that locker of yours. So, do you still wanna sit there and tell me that you didn't do anything?"

Antonio dropped his head in defeat.

"How could you, Antonio? What if you had been caught that night?"

"It is what it is, Shawnay, and I am who I am." For a few seconds he closed his eyes and then opened them. "I told you that the last time you visited me at D.C. jail. Remember? I told you that violence begets violence and that's all I know. I meant that. I told you that if someone hurts me, I lash out to hurt them more and harder. I lash out to destroy, to kill. That's me, bay. That's who your husband is. If I should go back to prison for killing those who killed my daughter, then so be it. I did it for my daughter." He shrugged.

Antonio's words stabbed Shawnay deep like a knife to the gut. She was hurt, offended, and devastated by the harsh, callous, and cavalier way that he cast the rest of his family off. He came off cruel, vicious, and uncaring. "So be it, huh? So be it. So the rest of us—me, Asia, and Kay Kay don't mean shit to you, huh?"

"How can you ask me that? Y'all mean the world to me."

She reared her head back. "Oh my God! How can you be so hypocritical like that? We mean everything to you, but you'd hurt us all by jeopardizing yourself—to be killed or given another life sentence. That shit don't add up." She thought about his earlier phone conversation. "You gotta stop this, Antonio. Let it end with what you did already."

"I can't do that, Shawnay. I gotta do it to make Kenya's death even out."

"What!"

"You heard me. Kenya needs me—"

"*We* need you! *I* need you. Kenya is gone, Antonio, and she ain't coming back no matter how many people you kill, so you can never make it right. Kenya is gone, but we are still here. We need you to stay here, but if you—" Her tears started again.

"Nothing is gonna happen to me." He nodded. "Only those who stand against me."

"How do you know that?" she shouted venomously. "Are you God now, too?"

"Naw, I'm Ameen. I'm Antonio Felder. That's all I can be. And to ask me not to kill the people responsible for my daughter's death is asking me to be someone else. I have to kill the green-eyed dude and whoever was with him the day he chose to take away from me someone who wasn't his to take. You may not understand me now, but one day you will. If I don't kill the green-eyed dude, it will eat me alive, and I will be no good to you either way. No matter what you say to try and soothe my aching heart, I failed Kenya, but I won't fail to bring justice to the people that killed her. You have to trust me on this and respect my decision." Drained and exasperated, Shawnay's hurt ran deep. "You can't keep killing in her name, Antonio. Where does it stop? When will it end?"

"I'll stop when the green-eyed dude and everybody involved is dead." Antonio's words and defiant tone weighed heavy on her mind. Her words were falling on deaf ears. Continuing the conversation would be fruitless. Shawnay's body sagged from exhaustion, and all she could think about was a long, hot bath and a warm bed.

"When I first moved here from Fifty-sixth Street, I was running away from you, the memory of you, and the people you sent to kill me. I lived in complete fear every day for months. I was nervous whenever someone approached me, or I answered my own front door." She released a long sigh.

"I always believed that one day someone would show up to finish the job that the man with the beard didn't. But over time, I stopped worrying about the things I couldn't control. I decided to let go and let God handle it. I had to be strong for the kids, you know . . . When I told myself that, my fears waned and my nightmares lessened. I was no longer afraid of every sound that went bump in the night. And then suddenly I was glad I moved away from D.C. I was glad to be in Arlington. I was away from the past and it felt good.

"Unfortunately, now I realize that Arlington wasn't far enough. I can't go back to those days when I lived in fear, Antonio. Not for you, not for anyone. I won't regress back to being afraid. I can't. I won't. And that's what I'd be doing if I allow myself to stay in this situation. Never knowing when the cops are gonna kick in the door to arrest you, or knock on it to tell me that you've been killed. I can't live my life wondering if the people that you kill—if their relatives will hunt you and then kill all of us in the process. I have to protect what family I have left since you have so little regard for us."

"That's not true, Shawnay," Antonio replied.

"What makes the people that you kill any different from our Kenya? What makes you different from their parents? What if they decide to kill in their child's name as well? How many people would die then?"

He knew she wouldn't understand his state of mind no matter how many ways he tried to explain it to her. Therefore, he kept silent.

"If you continue to let your puffed up pride, narcissism, and ego cause you to continue killing in my daughter's name, I'm leaving you. I'm leaving Arlington, and I'm taking the kids with me. I have already lost my child and my grandmother. I'll be goddamned if I'm gonna stand by and wait to lose you. And this time when I move, I'ma make sure that it's far, far away. So, the ball is in your court, Antonio. You decide. You decide what's most important to you. Continuing your self-imposed war to honor the memory of the child that you don't have, or keeping the ones that you do have."

With that said, she turned, leaving the basement and an ultimatum for Antonio.

# Chapter Nineteen

## Detective Tolliver

Monday, March 2nd

"How's it hanging, Moe?"

"Hey, look, it's Moe T!"

"Good to see you, Moe."

"Welcome back, Tolliver. Missed you!"

Moe smiled from ear to ear and waved at all the cops that he'd worked with for years, but hadn't seen or spoken to in over a year, as he made his way to the Captain's office. He tapped on the door and peeped in.

"Come on in, Moe. All the commotion out there, I figured it was you."

"What did you do, Cap? Make an announcement?" Moe asked as he sat down in an old fashioned cloth office chair that Captain Dunlap refused to part with.

Captain Dunlap blushed. "Well, I might've told a person or two that you wanted back in."

"The moment we hung up the phone the other day, you knew, didn't you? You knew I'd come back. Am I that predictable?"

"It's not about being predictable, Moe. It's about being a good detective and a great one. The good ones do just enough to crack the case, and then rest on their laurels. A great one feeds off a good case, chases it. They love to solve riddles. It's in the blood. You are one of the great ones, Moe. You're a hunter by nature. And you don't stop until you've solved the case. But like I told you on the phone, every great detective has his Rebecca case and you have yours. You know that. I know that. Accept it and move on. The great ones always do. Hey, I'm not yanking your chain here."

Moe suppressed a grin.

"You know me, right? Working under my command for over ten years, right? When I say something I mean it, and I don't throw around accolades too often. But I always knew you were different, kid. You never talked a good game, you changed it. When you resigned last year, I wanted to tell you not to, but I had to let you recover. I knew how hard you were taking Emily Perez's murder. Her's and the mother of two that got killed with her. I knew how bad you wanted Luther Fuller, and to see him acquitted in court . . . I knew how bad it hurt you. So, I let you go, but I always knew that one day I'd talk you into coming back. I was just waiting for the right spark. That came in the form of a sixteen-year-old girl getting murdered at a gas station. Kenya Dickerson's case is not a spark, though. It's a fire. And if we don't lock up the bastards who did it, that fire threatens to consume us all. But why you, you ask? For all the reasons I just gave you. I've got people in here who've passed all the tests that you did, some with much higher scores, but they can't go out in them streets and pick up a criminal caught on tape. They can't do what you do."

"Okay, Cap, I'm sold. Lighten up on the flattery. I'm starting to feel like the fatted calf being fed on his way to slaughter."

"In a way, you are," the captain joked. "You're just too smart to take the bait."

"And what exactly does that mean?"

"One day I'll explain it to you, Moe." Captain Dunlap stood up behind his desk

and reached out his hand. "Welcome back, kid. I'm glad you listen to reason."

Moe stood up and grasped the captain's hand and pumped it. "Glad that you called me. I was getting bored outta my skull."

Captain Dunlap reached into a drawer and produced a badge and a police issued weapon, then pushed it across the desk. "Scarsborough in Personnel already started the paperwork, so go down there and sign it. There's a kid already on the Dickerson case by the name of Winslow. Corey Winslow, remember him?"

"About my height and complexion, slim build, curly hair. I remember him. Good kid. Smart."

"That's his problem. Good, but not great. Too much of a ladies man, if you ask me. If he spent more time chasing bad guys instead of chasing tail, he'd be a pretty good detective. You take lead."

"I work alone, Cap. You know that."

"Still the lone wolf, huh, Moe? I can respect that, but you've been gone awhile. Let the kid walk you through the case for a couple days, and then I'll reassign him. No biggie. He already knows that the case is yours."

"Does he? Like I said earlier, you already knew I'd come back. I'm predictable."

"No, Moe, you're like me, a natural hunter. It's in your blood. By the way, the Dickerson girl's funeral is in a couple of days. I want you to go. Scope out the scene and run off the riff raff. I don't want no fireworks popping off. That family's been through enough. Now, get the fuck out."

Moe walked out of the Captain's office with a smile on his face. It felt good to be back. He was determined to solve the Kenya Dickerson murder.

*****

Corey Winslow double parked the Impala on F Street. Moe stepped out the car and felt the cold, crisp air smack him in the face. He buttoned up his jacket and flipped his collar up, then he pulled his hat down over his ears and rubbed his hands together to warm them.

"The key to finding out who killed Kenya Dickerson lies inside the enigma of who killed Tyjuan Glover. "He pointed to a spot beside the sidewalk. "An SUV pulled up here and a lone gunman jumps out. He walks up behind Glover and shoots him. Kenya Dickerson watches from the Charger. A witness reported hearing a horn blast. I believe that, that was Dickerson trying to alert Glover that someone was behind him. She failed. Apparently, Kenya Dickerson passed out and was found moments later inside the Dodge. She came to and became hysterical. She was transported to Howard for observation. Come on, we got other places to go."

In the car, Winslow told Moe all about his interviews with Tyjuan Glover's mother, Barbara Copeland. "She's on drugs. That was obvious to me. She didn't know where her two teenage daughters were. Tyjuan's father, Tyrone Glover is incarcerated. I checked the computer, and he's listed as being in a federal penitentiary in Inez, Kentucky. Big Sandra or something like that. Nobody knows of any reason that somebody would want to kill Tyjuan. None of his buddies in the Circle would talk to me. You know how that goes . . . Tolliver?"

He turned to face Winslow. "Yeah!"

"Why did you quit the department? We heard something, but I'm just curious if it's true."

"What did you hear?"

"We heard that it was stress-related and that you became unglued about the deaths of Emily Perez and Latasha Allison. Then we heard that you were forced out because of the Luther Fuller case and the fact that he got off after killing all those people."

"Probably a little bit of both, but I wasn't pushed out. I quit before I could be. I heard the whispers. I needed a break. Now I'm back."

They pulled into the police impound at Blue Plains and walked down a row of cars until they got to a black Acura.

"The passenger side window shattered on impact. Glass fragments were embedded in the face and neck of the victim. The car is owned by Regina Benton, but driven mostly by her daughter Nadiyah. You can see one single bullet hole in the passenger door. That bullet and four others found their mark inside of Kenya Dickerson. According to forensics, she must've tried to duck down because a couple bullets missed her completely and embedded themselves in the driver side door. But other bullets found her head and neck. Powder burns at the entry wounds suggest that the killer was close, maybe a foot away or less when he opened fire. We found shell casings for nine bullets, but we believe that at least ten shots were fired. Caliber of the bullets were 9-millimeter, copper jackets."

Moe wrote down everything Detective Winslow said in his notebook. Back in the car, things became silent as they both probably envisioned the sixteen-year-old girl's last moments alive.

Ten minutes later, they pulled into the Amoco gas station off Martin Luther King Avenue. There, he walked Moe through the scene.

"Nadiyah Benton says she picked up Kenya Dickerson from her home on North Glebe Road in Arlington, Virginia. From there they drove to Allen Chapel A.M.E. Church in the 2400 block of Alabama Avenue, where Tyjuan Glover's funeral was being held . . ."

"What's Nadiyah's relation to Kenya Dickerson?" Moe asked as he surveyed the gas station and noticed the exits on two different sides. The perfect place to commit a murder.

"Kenya and Nadiyah were best friends. Kenya Dickerson grew up on Fifty-sixth Street

in the residential part of the neighborhood. She went to Fletcher Johnson with Nadiyah

and Tyjuan Glover. A few years ago, Kenya Dickerson's mother moved the family to Arlington. Glover and Benton stayed at Eastern High School, while Kenya Dickerson transferred to Eisenhower High in Arlington. Although separated, Nadiyah and Kenya remained close.

Winslow retold the events that happened on the twenty-fourth, the day of Tyjuan's funeral. From the time Kenya first called Nadiyah for a ride to Tyjuan Glover's funeral, to the point after the funeral when Nadiyah decided to stop for gas. "The killer followed . . . well, the person who was driving the car must've followed them to this gas station . . . The perps parked right back there. According to a witness, it pulled in a minute after the Acura."

"You said perps . . . the killer wasn't driving the car?"

"No. According to the witness who saw everything, a cashier, and Nadiyah Benton, the killer ran back to a dark colored Nissan Maxima after shooting Kenya Dickerson. He got into the passenger seat before the Maxima sped off."

"No description of the killer?"

"Nothing we could use to put out an alert. Dressed in all black wearing a black mask. Between five-ten and six-feet tall. Medium build. That's it." Winslow added the witness accounts from Nadiyah Benton and the cashier, Joanne Poindexter, who called the cops. They heard gunshots and saw the guy run to a dark Nissan Maxima. "That's the official version of what happened, but now let me give you the unofficial version. Here goes . . .

"Something happened between somebody and Tyjuan Glover. When, I'm not sure. On the eighteenth, Tyjuan and Kenya leave his house. Somebody guns Tyjuan down as Kenya watches. The horn blast alerts the killer to somebody in the car. The killer recognizes Kenya as he or she leaves the scene. Kenya faints and goes to the hospital. There, I tried to talk to her, but she wasn't making sense. She was traumatized and incoherent. I remember something about the *Think Like a Man* movie and somebody with green eyes. That's it. Doctors ran me away before I could finish. I tried to talk to her a few days later, but her father blocked me. Referred me to the family lawyer, a Rudy Sabino. I did speak to Shawnay Dickerson, that's Kenya's mother, briefly, but basically got nowhere. Without Kenya, I had jack to go on, except what the witnesses on F Street told me. Which was basically nothing. Whoever killed Tyjuan Glover also knew Kenya Dickerson."

"How old was Tyjuan Glover?"

"Glover was eighteen. He had a birthday coming up. He was two years older than Kenya. She also had a birthday coming up in July. They went to school together and grew up in the same circles. I believe the person who killed Tyjuan knew that Kenya could identify him. He guessed that Kenya would attend the funeral. The perp saw her and Nadiyah Benton. When they left, the perp did too. Followed the Acura to this gas station and waited until Nadiyah left the car. He runs up to the Acura and kills Kenya. The same day, somebody, either related to Tyjuan Glover or Kenya Dickerson, goes to Alabama Avenue with the belief that the killer hangs there. That person surprises a crowd of people and kills seven. The next day, dudes from Alabama Ave go to the Circle where Glover was from and retaliate, killing five. All the recent murders, starting with Tyjuan Glover are related."

"Your hypothesis is duly noted, Winslow. Is there anything else that I need to know?" Moe asked.

"Yeah, one more thing. I told you that I tried to talk to Kenya Dickerson, but her father blocked me. Well, after she was killed, the father showed up to I.D. the body. He said maybe two words to me. He was dressed in a sweatshirt that read 'Live the Omerta,' and he struck me as a street-wise dude. He had the coldest eyes I'd ever seen in my life. I've been around some tough muthafuckas in my life, but for some reason, that guy scared me, Tolliver. If I were you, I'd watch him."

*****

The Kenya Dickerson murder played itself out in Moe's head as if he'd watched it in person. He wanted to solve the case, needed to solve it. That evening as he ate dinner at home, he reread all his notes. Key points of the investigation got his internal juices flowing, and he couldn't think of anything else as he cleaned up the house. Even as he lay down, he was still asking himself questions. Then before he knew it, he fell asleep and dreamed of a faceless boy blasting an innocent young girl sitting inside a car mourning the loss of her first love. The shooting was so vivid, that Moe sat straight up trying to catch his breath.

# Chapter Twenty

## Ameen

"Thanks for coming through, ock," Ameen said, breaking the embrace with Khadafi. "And you called at a good time because I needed to get out of there for a minute or two."

"I gotta pay my respects, cuz. I started to come inside, but decided it would be better for me to stay away. I figured that things would get a little awkward with Shawnay and Kashon being in there. And my presence would be a dead giveaway about me and you communicating. Everybody will probably be better off in the blind about that. What do you think?"

"I agree with everything you just said."

"How are you holding up?"

"I'm holding," Ameen replied and steered Khadafi over to his truck. "Like I said earlier, I needed a breath of fresh air. But considering the fact that I just offered the Janaza prayer for my daughter, I'm doing about as good as can be. I'd be a lot better if I could bury her knowing that the green-eyed dude was dead. But he will be in due time. I guarantee you that. My heart is hurting so bad, ock. I can't even describe the pain."

"I know the pain, cuz. Trust me, I do. My mother, my uncle, and Kemie, I know the pain you speak of. I live with it everyday."

"You feel me, then. I wanna cry and cry, but I gotta be strong for my family. Shawnay's family is in there. They came from North Carolina to be here and their faces convey two things to me: hurt and disdain. They don't understand why Kenya is being eulogized inside a Masjid by Muslims, when her mother raised them Christian. Shawnay explained it to everybody and now they look at me with disdain in their eyes. But fuck 'em, ock. She was my baby, my little girl. They can all get together and worry about Ms. Dickerson, Shawnay's grandmother."

"Worry about her for what? She sick?" Khadafi asked.

"Sick is an understatement. She died of a heart attack the same day Kenya got shot."

"Damn, cuz! I didn't know that. I know that Shawnay is crushed."

"Yeah, she's fucked up bad. Her grandmother's funeral is tomorrow. And on top of all that, Shawnay knows about what I did."

"What you did? What did you do?"

"She knows about the work I put in on Alabama Avenue."

"Get the fuck outta here, cuz! How could Shawnay know that and nobody in the world besides us knows?"

"She watches too much of that CSI shit, I guess. But she put it all together and I admitted it. She threatened to leave me and take the kids if I don't give up my vendetta. I tried to explain to her why I have to keep killing, but she ain't seeing things my way. She don't understand and she's afraid."

"Afraid of what?"

"Afraid that something will happen to me. Afraid that I'll go back to prison. Afraid that the body trail will lead to our front door, and somebody other than the cops will kick the door in and want blood. She has every right to feel afraid, but I got every right to avenge my daughter's death. So I can't stop killing until Tyger and his men are dead. You feel me?"

"One hundred and ten percent."

"Good. So from now on, I have to be more discreet. Now, I'ma do everything outta my store. That's where we'll meet, talk, and plan from now on."

"Got you. Give me all the info on the store and I'm there. Just call me when you ready to move. In the meantime, I gotta bitch I need to fuck to get a line on Fella and Tyger."

"That's whats up. What's her name again?"

"Tashia, the whore's name is Tashia."

# CHAPTER TWENTY-ONE

## DETECTIVE TOLLIVER

After grabbing a bite to eat and making a few calls from his desk, it was time for Detective Moe Tolliver to hit the streets. So much had happened in the Benning Heights area over the last few weeks that he wanted to canvas the neighborhoods and see what he could find. It didn't take him long to get to Simple City and Alabama Avenue, and once there, it was plain to see that the recent onslaught of murders there were affecting drug sales and life in general. The two neighborhoods were basically deserted at a little after ten in the morning. Moe decided then to make the short trek to Eastern Senior High School to talk to a witness. Winslow's notes were detailed, but Moe kinda felt that he hadn't asked the right questions, therefore, not getting the right answers. He needed to ask Nadiyah Benton the right questions, so he double parked his truck in front of Eastern and went inside. At the front office, a pretty, mature woman accosted him and asked, "May I help you, sir?"

Pulling out his credentials and passing them to her, he replied, "You can. One of your students witnessed a murder about five days ago, and I couldn't catch her at home. It's imperative that I speak to Nadiyah Benton. So, if she's here today, I need to speak to her."

"Nadiyah? I know Nadiyah. A witness . . . you must be talking about Kenya Dickerson . . ."

He nodded.

". . . She went here, too. Before transferring to the school out in Arlington. That's so sad what happened to that beautiful child. She was very charismatic and bright. The principal cried when we first heard the news. I do believe that Nadiyah is here today. Let me check . . . by the way, my name is Linda Porham." She walked into another room, but returned a few minutes later. "She's in American History. Her teacher is sending her down here now. Would you like to use the conference room next door?"

"Yes, ma'am. Thank you."

Nadiyah Benton turned out to be a gorgeous, young lady that looked exactly like Reverend Run's daughter, Angela Simmons. She sat in a chair across from him wearing a puzzled look.

"Nadiyah, my name is Moe Tolliver. I'm a detective investigating the murder of Kenya Dickerson. You talked to another detective, but I need you to talk to me. Tell me everything that happened on the twenty-fourth."

After explaining everything that had happened from the time she picked up Kenya Dickerson up until the murder and talking to the cops, Nadiyah started crying. Moe let her cry for a few moments before proceeding.

"Are you okay, Nadiyah?"

"I'm good. Just incredibly sad, that's all. I feel responsible somehow. Maybe if I would've never stopped for gas . . ."

"Nonsense! Nothing you could've done or didn't do would've stopped Kenya's murderer from killing her. We believe she was killed because she knew who Tyjuan's murderer was. We believe she saw him and that person feared being identified. Did Kenya talk to you about Tyjuan's murder?"

"She did, but she never mentioned knowing who did it. If she knew who did it, she never told me anything."

"Okay, let me switch gears for a minute then. Do you know anybody who would want to hurt Kenya?"

"Everybody loved Kenya."

"No enemies. Male or female?"

"Not that I know of. Enemies, no. Haters, yes. If that means anything."

"Haters? Why would she have haters?"

"Why? Lots of reasons. She was beautiful, she was fly as hell, and Kenya had a body like a video vixen. But the main reason was because of Tyjuan."

"Tyjuan Glover?"

"Yeah. Tyjuan was a big deal to a lot of people around here and in our neighborhood. All the girls wanted him. He was fly and caked up. An up and coming hood star. Chicks went bananas whenever Tyjuan came around. But Tyjuan loved Kenya and never failed to let it be known, so all the girls hated Kenya for that."

Moe digested what he'd just been told. Tyjuan Glover was a chick magnet and he had money, which meant he was a hustler. *Was he killed because of a drug deal gone bad? And how did Kenya fit into the equation?* "Tell me something about Kenya that only a good friend would know."

Nadiyah closed her eyes. "There's not much to tell. Kenya was Kenya. She was sweet and thoughtful. She'd surprise people with gifts. She was somewhat spoiled. Her mother bought her whatever she wanted. Her father too, but he just got out of prison about a year or so ago. Kenya was outgoing and friendly, a fun person to be around. She was super intelligent and a computer geek, I mean to the point of being a hacker.

"But she was the average teenager. Loved to talk on the phone, text, Skype, go on Facebook and Twitter. She hated drugs, cigarettes, and people that hurt little kids. Tyjuan was her first and only boyfriend, and she loved him wholeheartedly. He was all she talked about, especially after the tattoo . . ."

"What tattoo?"

"The tattoo. Tyjuan was frustrated because Kenya couldn't tell her parents about them. Her father hated Tyjuan and forbid her to see him, but she didn't listen. Tyjuan went and got a tattoo of Kenya's face on his chest because he wanted the world to know that he loved Kenya. As a matter of fact . . . I have a photo of it on my phone." Pulling out her cell phone, Nadiyah went to Instagram and pulled up several photos, the infamous tattoo being one of them. She handed him the phone to scroll through the pictures himself.

He stared at the photos and a thought crossed his mind. *Was Kenya carrying a phone the day she died? If so, had it been searched for photos?* He made a mental note to check when he got back to the station.

"He must've really loved her."

"He did," Nadiyah said. "Tyjuan loved Kenya a lot. Their love was real. Something that we all pray for. That's what's so sad about it. I can't shake the thought that maybe their deaths had something to do with what happened the night Tyjuan got the tattoo."

"What happened that night, Nadiyah?"

"They went to the movies afterwards. Tyjuan got into a scuffle with a dude with green eyes."

"Green eyes?" Moe repeated.

Nadiyah nodded. "That's what Kenya called him. Green Eyes. She told me Tyjuan spit on dude and security had to separate them. What else happened, I don't know. Kenya didn't go into detail. She just told me that she worried about Tyjuan. I never thought anything of it until a few days ago."

Moe wrote down everything Nadiyah said. "You never told the other detective about this movie incident?"

"I'm not sure. He talked to me while I was still traumatized. I don't know what I told him."

"Do you know what movie theater this happened at?"

"Uh . . . let me think. I know it wasn't the one here in the city. Nobody who lives in D.C. goes to the movies in D.C. Movie theaters in D.C. are too ghetto."

"Not even Union Station?"

"That's the ghettoest one . . . I'm gonna have to go with City Place Mall. Knowing Kenya like I did. They went to City Place."

"And this all happened when?" he asked.

"The night she posted the pictures on Instagram and Twitter. I believe it was the fifteenth. Tyjuan got killed three days later on the eighteenth. The date should be on the pictures on the phone!"

The key to solving Kenya's murder was solving Tyjuan's murder. Detective Winslow had been on point. Both murders were connected. "Nadiyah, you live in the Simple City area, right?"

"Across Benning Road on Fiftieth Street, in the private homes."

"So you know a lot of the same people that Tyjuan knew, right?"

"I guess so. Eastgate and Hampton East are right across the street from Simple City. Everybody in both neighborhoods went to school together and basically moved in the same circles. We all went to the same house parties, go-gos and rec centers, so yeah, I believe we knew a lot of the same people."

"Do you know any dudes with green eyes? Somebody that Tyjuan would be beefing with?"

"Green eyes? I know two people with green eyes. Marcus from Potomac Gardens, but he be down the Market on the avenue and Tyger. Tyger be on Alabama Avenue."

"Do you know Marcus or Tyger's whole name?"

"Um . . . naw. Marcus ain't from around our way. Tyger's first name is Terrell, but I don't know his last name."

He put away the notepad and handed Nadiyah back her cell phone. "Thank you for talking to me, Nadiyah. You've been a real help to me. I'm sorry about Kenya, but rest assured, I'ma catch the piece of shit that killed her. Here, take my card and call me if you think of anything or hear anything that might help me. Okay?"

Nadiyah accepted the card and put it in her purse. "I will. Do you know why Kenya's parents closed her wake and funeral to the public?"

"Didn't know that they did. Maybe they have some security concerns. I can find out for you."

"Naw, that's okay. I wanna remember my girl the way she was."

"I understand. Thank you for talking to me, Nadiyah. You take care of yourself." Moe wanted to dance his way out of there, but instead he kept his composure. He was steps away from catching Kenya's shooter. Certainty tingled throughout his body.

*****

The homegoing service for Kenya Dickerson was held at a small Masjid in Herndon, Virginia. The obituary in the local paper asked that only family members attend. The service was listed as private. Moe pulled his truck into a space on Cypress Street, down a ways from the entrance to Masjid Al-Nur. Again he stared at the photo of Kenya Dickerson inside the *Washinton Post* and then remembered the photo that Nadiyah Benton showed him. What a waste of human life. The teenage girl was too beautiful to die so young. From his truck he watched as cars and trucks pulled up and parked and people went inside the Masjid. Then a beautiful platinum colored Range Rover Sport, the 2013 model pulled up and double parked. Moe was about to turn his head, until the driver got out. Then he stopped beside the Range Rover and straightened out his clothes. The face looked familiar, but the eyes were hidden behind a pair of designer Aviator sunglasses. Moe's face was damn near glued to the windshield as he struggled to get closer to see the man better. He was stylishly dressed and holding a phone, a black cell phone. His hand went up to his glasses and pulled them away from his eyes. The man turned and looked up at the Masjid. Moe couldn't believe his eyes, and his blood ran cold, nearly stopping his heart momentarily. *It couldn't be. How could it be possible?* Like a blast from Moe's sordid past, he recognized the man. Gone were his cornrows and individual plaits, but there was no mistake. The sun shined bright on his face as he put the cell phone to his ear. The man Moe was looking at was Khadafi.

A few minutes later, a man who appeared to be a little shorter, with a complexion like coffee, a baldhead and a beard, exited the Masjid. He was dressed in black slacks, a black shirt and jacket and black shoes. He walked down the steps of the Masjid, met Khadafi on the sidewalk, and embraced him.

*Who in the hell is Khadafi meeting?* Moe wondered.

# Chapter Twenty-Two

## Khadafi

Khadafi turned to embrace Ameen again. "Cuz, I'ma go 'head and bounce. Set up the overplay for the underplay."

"Assalaamu Alaikum, ock. I'll be in touch."

"You do that," he replied. Khadafi walked to the Range and hopped inside and drove back to D.C. with murder on his mind. All he could hear was Fella's voice inside his head.

*". . . and one more thing . . . The next time you and I meet, it's gonna be at the opposite ends of a smoking barrel. That's my word."*

"That's your word, huh?" Khadafi said aloud.

Fellano Jasper was the new face of his enemy, and he planned to eradicate him just like he'd done to all of his previous enemies. All except one. TJ. Still thinking about TJ and everything they'd done together, everything they'd said to one another, and finally about what he'd done to Khadafi personally, his destination became set, as if his mind were a navigational device.

Minutes later, he pulled into the Central Treatment Facility (CTF) parking lot and parked beside a gray Ford Fusion. In his pocket was an identification card in the name of an anonymous dude that he copped from a chick he knew at the

DMV. Khadafi pulled that ID out and passed it through the window of the visitor's booth in CTF's lobby. A female CO passed him papers to fill out. Khadafi filled out the proper forms and passed them back to the CO. In return she gave him a laminated visitor's pass that he clipped onto his shirt.

The elevator chimed as the doors opened. He stepped into the elevator and pushed two. On the second floor, he walked into a spacious visiting room and sat down in a brown leather and wooden seat that faced a table. Several tables and seats like the one he occupied adorned the room.

About ten minutes later, the woman he'd come to visit strolled in looking fit, healthy, and well groomed. At the sight of Khadafi, her eyes lit up. Her smile stretched from ear to ear. He stood and welcomed her into his arms. They embraced. Then kissed. An opened mouth kiss. Khadafi pushed five balloons of heroin into her mouth with his tongue.

"Bay One, you look good, baby," he said as he sat down.

Bay One sat across from him, and he realized she'd finally swallowed all five balloons. "I feel good. You look good too, nigga, with your fine, red ass. Marnie better be glad that I'm on pussy, because if I was on dick, I'd be tryna get yours."

"I'll be sure to tell her what you said. What's good with you?"

"I'm just laying back in my style, waiting to see what these people gon' do with me. I couldn't go to trial because I did what I did in front of a cop."

"Oh yeah? I didn't know that part."

Bay One closed her eyes as if reliving the day she shot and killed TJ. "Yeah, the detective, I forgot his name—was there to arrest TJ, but I didn't find that out 'til afterwards. I had been riding around looking for TJ for days. I got the call from Wayne Wayne telling me that TJ was coming to his apartment and then another call saying that he was there. Wayne Wayne and nem' knew TJ had killed Reesie, Dawn, and Esha and they wanted me to kill TJ. I never knew the detective was out there until he walked up after I'd already shot TJ once. As I stood over him, the cop walked up with his gun drawn and told me not to kill him. He told me to put my gun down, but I couldn't do it. I had to finish what I started. For Esha, for Reesie, for Dawn . . ."

"And for Kemie," he added.

"Kemie? But . . ."

"TJ was the one who shot Kemie. I found that out before I went to jail. That's why I tried to kill him the day he left Esha's. I sat in the car that day and watched TJ walk into Esha's front door. Then he left out the back way."

"Hold on . . . go back, how did you know TJ shot Kemie?"

"I gotta be straight up with you right now and tell you what really happened. And you gotta take all of this to your grave. You agree to that?"

"I would never betray you. I'd rather die than violate your trust. Talk."

"When I came home after doing the ten year bid, me and Kemie hooked back up. You know all about her beef with Marnie, right?"

Bay One nodded.

"Kemie was fucking with Marnie's boyfriend or some shit like that."

"Yeah," Bay One said, lowering her gaze. "I kinda knew that."

"Marnie stepped to me one day on some 'get back at Kemie' shit. Offering to give me the pussy, and at first I thought it was a set up, orchestrated by Kemie to test me. I said as much to Marnie, and that's when she told me how cruddy Kemie had been carrying it while I was in prison. About Kemie fucking her man *and* Bean and Omar. She told me about some other niggas, including a dude named Phil, but I couldn't get past what she said about Bean and Omar. You know them niggas were my men. I was crushed to hear that my men fucked my girl."

Bay One closed her eyes and shook her head. "You should've been." She opened her eyes and focused on Khadafi.

"Even while I was doing a bid, I still claimed Kemie as mine. I loved her with all my heart and all my men knew that. So naturally I was devastated by the news that they crossed me. I was going through a rack of other shit that had my mind fucked up, like when Marquette got killed. So I killed Bean, Bay One. I killed Bean and Omar. For treason. They crossed me, so I killed them."

Bay One's eyes watered, but they never left his.

"The only person I told was Marnie. And that was the day Marnie told me that Kemie was back fucking with the dude named Phil, after I'd come home the second time. I was hurt by Kemie's betrayal, but my heart would never allow me to hurt her, even though I wanted to on several occassions. Instead, me and TJ kidnapped Phil and brought him to

Capers, where I forced Kemie to kill him. They found his body in a vacant house in 501."

"Damn, Khadafi!" Bay one commented.

"After that, I told Marnie I wanted to be with Kemie and Kemie only. Unbeknownst to me, Marnie went and cried on Reesie's shoulders, and she also told her about me killing Bean and Omar. Then for some reason, Reesie told TJ."

"That's what messed up things between you and TJ."

"Yeah. TJ must've felt I wasn't to be trusted, or he just wanted to avenge Bean and Omar. He probably killed Reesie somewhere around that time. Later on, he followed Kemie and he shot her." A long paused loomed between them.

"That's when I told Marnie to contact you and tell you everything," Khadafi said.

Tears escaped Bay One's eyes. "Did I ever thank you for that?"

"No need to. Did I ever thank you for killing TJ when I couldn't?"

"No need to. I did it for everybody, but especially for my baby, Esha. I miss her, Khadafi. I miss the shit outta Esha."

"We all do. You were saying you couldn't go to trial because the detective witnessed the murder."

Bay One wiped her eyes and then dried her palms on her pants. "Yeah. I had to cop. Since the cops knew that TJ was responsible for killing a lot of people, they talked the U.S. Attorney into letting me cop to manslaughter. I did that about five months ago. I'm just waiting to be sentenced. The lawyer you sent to see me says I'm only facing a max of ten years, but that the judge may try to enhance me because of my priors. She may or may not do it. I go back to court in three weeks, on March 20th."

"Well, make sure you call me at least once a week. I wanna make sure you go out to the Feds with enough pack to lock the pound down for a year. I'ma come back and give you the kiss of life every time I can. You need anything else or want me to do anything?"

"Naw, I'm good. You done, done enough for me as it is. I 'preciate it."

"That shit ain't shit." He rose and hugged Bay One again. "Just holla when you ready to see me again."

Before Khadafi could break their embrace, Bay One reached down and palmed his dick and balls. It caught him off guard, so he jumped. "Can I get another one of them kisses before you go?"

He pushed Bay One's hand away. Then he smiled and said, "Go head with that bullshit, Bay One. I'll see you at the next visit. I'm out."

On the elevator, he thought about everything he told Bay One and the things he had purposely left out. Some things were oftentimes better left unsaid.

*****

Khadafi walked out of CTF and jumped into the Range. His cell phone automatically sensed that he was in the truck. The cell phone and its voice integration system kicked in, and he heard a voice come out the car speakers, asking whom he would like to call.

"Call the hood rat whore," he said as he started the truck.

"Calling the hood rat whore . . . connecting . . ."

A few seconds later, a female voice said, "Hello?"

"Tashia?"

"This me. Dirty Redds?"

"Yeah, but I don't like to be called Dirty Redds no more, cuz. That was my juvenile name. Now that I'm grown and sexy, everybody calls me Khadafi. Say it with me . . . Khadafi."

"Khadafi. I got it. You can call yourself whatever you want, but what took you so long to call me?"

"I was caught up, but I'm free now. You free?"

"Free as a bird," Tashia replied.

"Good. I'm on my way to get you. Where are you?" Khadafi was almost anxious to get as much info from her about Fella and Tyger as she could possibly offer or be forced to offer.

# CHAPTER TWENTY-THREE

## DETECTIVE TOLLIVER

Moe watched the silver Range Rover exit the parking lot, tempted to follow it, but he didn't. In his lap sat some information he needed. He would have to work for the rest. Seeing Khadafi today after not even thinking about him for months had thrown off his equilibruim. He could focus on nothing else. After following him to CTF where his truck now idled, he made a few calls and was now awaiting a few answers. Just seeing Khadafi made his skin crawl. He was his nemesis, his adversary, his most cunning and treacherous opponent. *What was Khadafi's connection to Kenya Dickerson, and who was the man that embraced him outside of the masjid?* The vibrating cell phone got his attention. He answered the call. "Moe Tolliver."

"Moe, it's me. Reese. I ran the license plate you gave me, and the truck is registered to a business called Imperial Autos. I dug a little deeper and learned that Imperial Autos is owned by Mary Henderson."

*Mary Henderson . . . Khadafi's aunt. Sister to Marquette and Margaret Henderson, Khadafi's uncle and mother.* "Thanks a lot, Reese. I owe you one, buddy."

"You owe me more than one, but who's counting, huh? Take it easy, big guy."

Disconnecting that call, Moe dialed Corey Winslow back. This time he answered his cell phone on the second ring. "Detective Winslow, it's me. Moe Tolliver."

"What's up, Tolliver? Did I miss something in the report I gave?"

"Naw, buddy. Your report was thorough and detailed. I just need to ask you a few questions. You gotta minute?"

"Yeah, shoot. What do you need to know?"

"You told me you tried talking to Kenya Dickerson again about the Tyjuan Glover murder, days after it, and you got blocked by her father, right?"

"Yeah. That's right."

"Tell me that you got his name."

"I did . . . Hold on . . . Let me see if I still have my notes. Okay, here it is. Yeah, Kenya Dickerson's father is Antonio Felder."

"Antonio Felder." Moe repeated the name as he wrote it down. "And you got the chance to talk to him, right? In person?"

"Yeah, at the morgue. He identified the body."

"Describe him for me, please," he asked.

"About 5-feet-11 or 6-feet. Solidly built, appeared to be muscular. Maybe 200 to 220-pounds, brown-skinned, medium complexion, baldhead, and a beard."

"All right, buddy. That's all I needed. Thanks again, kid."

"Don't mention it. Just catch the bastards that killed that girl."

"I'm on it. Take care." He disconnected that call and made another. Then he dialed Priscilla Prescott, a no nonsense detective who had been in the department almost as long as Moe. "Hey Priscilla, how you?"

"I'm good, Moe. And you?"

"I'm great, baby. Just glad to be back at work."

"I can dig it. Everybody needs about a year away from this shit. And it ain't getting no easier. Them muthafuckas at the union and the asshole Mayor . . ."

He had to cut Priscilla off before she got too deep into her spiel, or she'd have him wrapped up complaining about the system for hours. "Not to cut you off, Priscilla, but pretty lady, I'm pressed for time. I gotta name I need you to run, and let me know what comes out of NCIC. The name is Antonio Felder, spelled F-E-L-D-E-R. No middle name known. I need whatever you have on him and I need a photo."

"Gotcha, Moe. Give me about ten or fifteen minutes, and I'll call you back. If I gotta photo, I'll text it to you. Good enough?"

"That's great, Priscilla. Thank you." He stared at the brown brick facade of the Central Treatment Facility and wondered who Khadafi had just visited. Suddenly, to kill some time he got out of the truck and walked the short distance to the entrance. At the visitor's booth, Moe flashed his badge to the female CO.

"Good afternoon, ma'am. My name is Detective Maurice Tolliver, and I'm investigating a murder. I followed a suspect here about forty-five minutes ago and watched him enter the building. I need to know who he just visited."

"Don't you need a warrant for that type of information?" the CO asked.

"Technically, no. But I could get one if you'd like me to," he replied.

The woman smiled. "Naw, no need. Just pulling your chain. Let me check the book. What was the man's name?"

"Kha—Luther Fuller."

"Luther Fuller? I don't have a Luther Fuller logged in as visiting anyone. Are you sure that, that's his name?"

"I'm postive. He was dressed in blue jeans, a dark shirt, and an expensive looking jacket, wearing—"

"Aviator sunglasses, a diamond in both ears, a low haircut, shadow beard and a ruddy brown complexion. Freckles across his cheeks and nose."

Moe nodded. "That's him. He left about ten minutes ago."

"He was here, but his name . . . well his ID didn't say Luther Fuller, it read Daytwon Player with this address." She turned the book around for him to see.

He read the info on the page, then traced a line across to the inmate that he visited. Seeing the name, he smiled. Bayonna Lake. Khadafi, using a fake ID, had come to visit Bay One. "Thank you so much, CO Franklin. I appreciate you."

"Anytime, baby. Anytime."

Outside in the parking lot, his phone vibrated with the icon for a text message. He pressed the button and a picture appeared on his screen. The photo was an earlier mugshot of Antonio Felder, when he had hair, but it was him nonetheless. He was the baldheaded man that exited the masjid and embraced Khadafi. Next came the phone call from Priscilla Prescott.

"It's me, Moe. You got the photo, right?"

"I got it, Priscilla."

"Good. Antonio Felder is thirty-five years old, date of birth 6/7/78. Height: 5'11", weight: 200 pounds. Black hair, dark brown eyes, medium complexion, no tattoos that we know of. Born and raised in the Disrict of Columbia, been arrested twice here. Once as a juvenile in 1993 and once as an adult for first degree murder, that was April of 2000. He was convicted and sentenced to 50 years. He was released after an appeal in 2011. Owns and operates a clothing store. Has an address for Fourteenth Place in Southeast Washington. You want it?"

"Naw, it's probably no good anyway because I believe he now lives in Arlington, Virginia with his wife and kids. That's all I need. Thank you, Priscilla. The next time I'm at Municipal, lunch is on me."

"I'ma hold you to that, Moe. Bye."

Moe climbed into the cab of the F-150 and leaned back for a minute. Both Khadafi and Antonio Felder had been released from prison in the last year or so. *What was their connection to one another? Had they been cell mates? Had they done time together?* The murders on Alabama Avenue came to mind.Witnesses said that a lone gunman, dressed in all black surprised the crowd and opened fire on them. The same day that Kenya Dickerson was killed. The exact same day. *Were the murders committed on Alabama Avenue in direct retaliation for Kenya Dickerson and not Tyjuan Glover, as everybody assumed? Was the lone gunman Kenya's father, Antonio Felder? Or was it Khadafi? Sent by*

*Antonio Felder*. Moe decided it was worth digging into to find the answers he sought.Then something else hit him, and he again turned to face CTF's brown brick facade.

Something that United States Attorney, Anne Sloan, who tried Khadafi's double murder, said to him a couple months ago came to mind. He had bumped into her at the Municipal Building while downtown. Quickly, he snatched up his cell phone and dialed her number. She answered on the third ring.

"Anne Sloan."

"Hey, Anne. This is Detective Moe Tolliver."

"Hey, you. I heard you were back on the force."

"Yeah. I couldn't stay away. That's why I'm calling, Anne. I'm investigationg some murders in the Simple City area, and I need some help. The last time we spoke, you told me that Ronald Brisbane was in D.C. and willing to snitch on everybody he knew to get his freedom. Is he still in town?"

"Uhhh . . . I believe so. Let me check the database right quick." He heard fingers pecking on a keyboard quickly. "Yeah, he's still in town. He's at CTF on the fourth floor, also known as the Witness Protection Floor."

Inwardly, he yelped with delight, but outwardly he said, "Thanks, Anne. Can anybody visit him, or does it have to be someone specific?"

"Anybody can visit him. He's only obligated to talk to us and the FBI, nobody else. So if he refuses to talk, you can't make him. Am I clear?"

"Crystal clear. Thanks again, Anne. Good-bye."

* * * * *

"Not you again, officer. Did you leave something behind?" the female CO named D. Franklin asked.

"Naw, but it's good to see you again," Moe flirted. "Seriously though, I need to visit an inmate on your fourth floor."

"Name?"

"Ronald Brisbane."

After conferring with her computer, CO Franklin said, "G4A. Here. Fill these papers out."

Moe did as requested, hoping Ronald Brisbane would give him an important lead.

Ronald "Ronnie T" Brisbane was a thirty-three-year-old murderer who was well known in the streets of D.C. After being sentenced to sixty-eight years in prison and getting stabbed a few times on the prison yard, he decided he wanted to get out of prison, thereby becoming one of the most vicious rats D.C. had ever seen, besides Rayful Edmonds. Moe had, had the opportunity to question Ronnie T on several occasions about murders that happened in the Hillside/Benning Park area, but back then he would never talk. As he sat and waited for him to make a grand entrance into the small, cramped visiting room that smelled like an abrasive scouring powder and urine, he wondered if he'd talk to him now.

A few minutes later, Ronnie T walked into the room wearing royal blue pants and a matching shirt with slip-on deck shoes. He hadn't changed physically, but he looked different, older. Moe stood up, reached out and shook his hand. "Ronnie T, what's good, slim? Rough time in the Feds, huh?"

"Fuck you, Tolliver! What you want with me?"

"Come on, Ronnie. You act like I'm the enemy. I'm here to help you."

"Help me how?" Ronnie asked indignantly.

"I happen to be real buddy buddy with the U.S. Attorney's office right now. With a little word from me, that can help you give a few more years back, and I can always write a letter to your judge about the substantial cooperation you've given to law enforcement. How's that for starters?"

"What do you want, Tolliver?"

"Information. What else?"

"About who, Michael Wanson?"

"Pretty B is already doing numbers in the Feds. Why would I waste my time with information on him? Have you heard about the new beef in your old neighborhood?"

"How could I not hear about it?"

"Who's running things in the Circle now?"

"It was Big Squirt and Scoop, but Squirt just got killed, and nobody has heard from

Scoop."

He pulled out a notepad and scribbled the names down. "And Alabama Avenue?"

"That would be D-Roc and Fella."

"D-Roc and Fella . . . Would you happen to know their government names?"

"Yeah, we all grew up together. D-Roc is Darius Queen and Fella is Fellano Jasper."

Moe pulled a picture of Tyjuan Glover and passed it to Ronnie T. "Do you recognize him?"

"Naw," Ronnie T replied and slid the photo back to him.

"His name is Tyjuan . . ."

". . . Glover. I know *of* him, but he was a kid when I last roamed the streets. I know his mother and father, though. You investigating his murder?"

He nodded. "Do you know anything about it?"

"Naw. I just heard about it and the fact that the Avenue and the Circle is now beefing behind it. I heard about his girlfriend getting killed after the funeral. Somebody must've believed she could finger them for the boy's murder."

"That's the conclusion I came to myself. And you don't know who committed either of those murders?"

Ronnie shook his head.

"Well, let me ask you this. Do you know anybody that hangs on the Avenue with light green eyes?"

"I do. A youngsta I been hearing about lately. He been in the hood putting his work in and his name jive ringing. I know his family, too, but youngin' ain't but nineteen or twenty. His name is Terrell, but the streets call him Tyger. He hangs out with his cousin Choppa a lot. But they all take orders from D-Roc and Fella."

Moe wrote down the names Terrell, Tyger, and Choppa. It was the second time in a matter of days that he'd heard two of the names mentioned. Tyger was certainly a person of interest. He pulled out his cell phone and an old picture that he carried of Khadafi and showed Ronnie T the photo of Khadafi first. "You know him?"

In seconds, recognition flickered in Ronnie's eyes. "Of course, I know Dirty Redds. I was on the juvenile tier at D.C. jail with him years ago. He goes by Khadafi now. He's somewhat lengendary in the pens because of the way he killed some rat nigga named Keith Barnett. They say he used a homemade axe and chopped the dude's body up, then scraped all the meat off the bones on some Hannibal Lector shit. He went home and put his murder game down heavy. I know him. Why? What's up with him? You think he killed Tyjuan and the young girl?"

"I'm still tryna figure all this out, but he's definitely somebody that I'm looking at. You were in a few penitentiarys in the Feds, right?"

"Yeah."

"Do you know this guy?" He slid his cell phone to Ronnie T.

"He looks familiar. What's his name?"

"His name is Antonio Felder."

"Antonio . . . Antonio Felder. I'm hip to him. His name in prison is Ameen. He was with Khadafi on that murder I just told you about. The story is that Ameen took the murder beef to free Khadafi and some other dudes. Then they fell out and started beefing about something. They say Ameen tried to kill Khadafi."

"Are you sure about that?" Moe asked Ronnie, remembering the two men embracing outside of the masjid.

"None of what I said can be proven, but that's what I heard."

Moe rose out of the chair. "Well, that's my time, Ronnie T. You've been a big help, and I promise to let the Attorney's office know."

"Thanks, Tolliver. And when you talk to U.S. Attorney Sloan, tell her that I know all the crooked cops that's bringing in drugs, cell phones, and weapons to inmates, and I'm tryna tell her all about it."

# CHAPTER TWENTY-FOUR

## KHADAFI

The sign over the entrance to the building read 3600 Ely Place. Khadafi checked the text message on his phone and saw that the two addresses were one and the same. "Call the hood rat whore," he said into the phone, and seconds later, Tashia picked up.

"Hello?"

"I'm outside."

"A'ight. I'm coming out now."

Ending the call, he put the phone back in the case attached to his belt.

A few minutes later, the door to the building opened and out stepped Tashia, looking good as hell. Her whole look for the night was totally different from the one she displayed three nights ago when he'd first scooped her and rode around with her. Her hair was done up differently, looking fly. He liked the color because it matched her eyes and kind of reminded him of Kemie.

She was dressed in a thick peacoat styled trench that hugged her every curve. Visible inside the coat was a low cut shirt that dipped toward her ample breasts. A pair of knee-high leather boots with a nice-sized heel rounded out the outfit. No matter how negatively Khadafi thought about a bitch like Tashia, he couldn't deny she was a bad muthafucka.

Climbing into the Range, Tashia reached over and embraced him. He hugged her back and got a whiff of some type of body spray or perfume that smelled good as shit. His dick got like rock instantly. “You killing 'em, cuz. I like the outfit.”

“You do? That's what's up. You look good, too.”

He smiled. “I always look good.”

“A’ight then, conceited, red ass nigga. That's the last time I compliment you.”

“Yeah, right. You gon’ be complimenting me a lot tonight, especially after I get that ass somewhere and make you scream.”

“Scream? Ha . . . boy, please. I haven't screamed since I was thirteen, and my boyfriend broke this pussy in. But I like your confidence. You gon’ need it.”

“Girl, stop!” he exclaimed as he pulled out of the parking lot. “Where do you wanna go first?”

“That's up to you. At first I was thinking about a good meal and a show of some kind, that's why I put on some clothes. But now that you done took me there, talking about I'ma be screaming and shit, I'm sidetracked. I can't think about nothing but us fucking. On some real live shit, I'm ready to say fuck my hair and fuck these clothes and tell you to get a room and let's see who's going to be screaming. I'm one of them bitches that love a challenge. Plus, I wanna see what you done learned over the years.

“I know that while you was in jail you probably read a whole lotta books on how to please a woman.”

"I did. You make the call."

"Did you get some loud?" Tashia asked.

Khadafi reached into his pocket and pulled out a sandwich bag filled with blueberry kush and tossed the weed into Tashia's lap. She picked up the bag, opened it, and smelled it. "Good gracious, boy! This that shit right here. Gawd damn . . . look at it. And it smell so fruity. I don't know whether I should eat it or smoke it. Did you get the pills, too?"

From his pants pocket, he pulled a small Ziploc bag. Inside it were two pills. "Two mollies on deck. I told you I got you."

"Well, fuck all that food and show talk. Just get a room and we gon' let it do what it do. The last time you and I were together, we did the oochie coochie. I'm a grown ass woman now, so I'ma have to show you how the 2013 Tashia get down."

*****

"You gotta put the pills in my ass."

"What!"

"You heard me, Redds. You gotta put the pills in my ass so they will dissolve quicker and shoot straight to my brain," Tashia said as she shed her clothes. "It's called boofing."

"They must've laced that loud with some PCP if you think I'ma put some pills in your ass. I ain't on that."

"Cool. Look, I'm high as hell and when I get this high, I need some pills and dick. In that order. If you ain't with the boof, that's cool. I can do that part myself. All I need you to do is fuck me real good after I put them in there. Can you handle that?"

"I think I can handle that."

Tashia unzipped her boots and pulled them off one by one and then her socks. "We'll see about that."

While he stood by the wall and watched, Tashia removed her panties and lay back on the bed. She opened her legs wide and played with herself. Before long she had worked a finger into her ass. After fondling her ass for several minutes, she got the pills and put each one in her ass. He watched as her ass swallowed the pills as if it were a hungry mouth.

Minutes later, Tashia closed her eyes and danced on the bed to a beat that only she could hear. Her pedicured toes curled up and she went back to fingering herself. When she pulled them out again, they glistened with wetness. He nodded and pulled out the gold box of Magnums, extracted one condom, and tore it open. Then with the wrapper in his mouth, he took his clothes off. Now completely nude, Khadafi slid the rubber over his hard on. He crawled up the bed until he slid in between her thighs. Grabbing both legs and cuffing them, he slid inside Tashia's wet pussy and went to work. As he slowly built up a rhythym, he thought about Ameen's daughter and Tashia's connection to the men who killed her. Anger gripped him. He threw her legs all the way back and stood up in the pussy to pound it senseless. He took all his frustrations out on her.

Later, they lay in the bed and talked about different shit. The weed and pills had Tashia loose, so Khadafi decided to start with the questions to learn what he needed to learn.

"Let me ask you something."

"Ask me anything," Tashia replied. "But hold on, are you gonna let me take the rest of the weed home with me?"

"No doubt, cuz. You can have that shit. I get that shit by the pounds."

"That's good to know. Okay, ask your question."

"When I came through the Avenue that day and saw you, I told you I needed to get in touch with D-Roc or Fella. You got me in touch with Fella. How did you do that? Did you talk to him and tell him?"

"Naw, actually I didn't. I told you before that I don't really fuck with them niggas. Why. I don't really know. I just don't. But my girlfriend Beauty that grew up with us been fucking Fella since we was teenagers. I called her and told her to call Fella. I was on the three-way when she relayed the message and gave him your phone number. I heard him ask her a rack of shit that she couldn't answer, and then finally he told her that he'd call you. That was enough for me. He did call you, didn't he?" Tashia turned to face Khadafi.

"Yeah, he hollered at me and we met and talked. Things didn't go as well as I had hoped, but that's how life goes sometimes. I need to meet up with him again. Do you know where he is, or where I can find him?"

"Why don't you just call him back from the number he called you?"

"Because to be honest with you, I need to see him in person. I'm tryna go to his house if I can."

Suddenly, Tashia sat straight up. Her breasts were extra perky and sexy and he couldn't help looking at them.

"Look, Dirty Redds—"

"Khadafi."

"Whatever. Listen, you asked me—naw—better yet, you paid me to get you in touch with Fella and I did that.

Irregardless of what was said or done, I did my part. I did what you asked me to do. And that's about as far as I'm willing to go. I don't like Fella and nem', but they are still my homeboys from my hood. And I ain't tryna see no harm come to them. So, please don't try to put me in the middle of nothing. Whatever y'all got going on is between y'all. Whatever we do is between us. Point blank period.

"So, I would appreciate it if you wouldn't ask me nothing about nobody from my hood. Let's keep things strictly dickly between you and me. Okay?"

"That's how you feel, huh? Even if I tell you that Fella threatened to kill me, and I'm just tryna protect myself? You would just say 'fuck me,' huh?"

"What I'm saying is please don't force me to choose between y'all. My loyalty is and always will be with my hood. I can get dick and weed from anybody. I'ma take my honor and loyalty with me to the grave. That's just the way it goes."

"Is that right?"

"Yeah, that's right!" Tashia replied with a lot of attitude. She swung her feet over the side of the bed and stood up. "Can you take me home now?"

Khadafi smiled, got out the bed, and walked over to Tashia and hauled off and smacked the shit out of her. She fell to the floor and lay looking up at him with a venomous look that left nothing to the imagination. He went to his pants pocket and pulled out a gun. "You said you are going to take your loyalty to the grave, right? Well, tonight you just might get that chance."

# Chapter Twenty-five

## Ameen

Ameen's nylon mask sat atop his head like a skully on a cold night, which it was. He had no idea if the stuff falling from the sky was snow, rain, or small iceballs. He drove through the night thinking about all the lies he had to tell Shawnay, just to avenge their daughter's death. In anticipation of the store opening in a few days, his main lie was something store oriented. Before long, he was pulling into the parking lot of the Econo Lodge and killing the engine. He picked up his cell and called Khadafi. "Assalaamu Alaikum, ock."

"Wa laikum assalaam. What's good, cuz? Where you at?"

"I'm in the parking lot. What room you in?"

"Drive around to the back. You'll see my Range parked outside. It's directly in front of my door. I'm in room 126. I'll be at the door waiting for you."

"That's a bet. Shorty ain't talkin', huh?"

"She says she wanna take her loyalty to her grave, but for some reason, I don't believe her. We'll see in a minute."

Ending the call, he followed Khadafi's instructions to the letter. It didn't take long to find his Range Rover and park beside it.

A few minutes later, Ameen was standing at the door to room 126. He knocked and pulled his mask down over his face. Opening the door, Khadafi stepped aside and allowed him to enter. The scene inside the room was something straight out of a movie. The woman named Tashia was sitting on the floor bruised and bleeding from the lip. Her partially nude body was visible, although she tried to cover herself with a sheet. She saw him masked up and instantly screamed.

"Shhhhh!" Ameen said, putting his finger to his lips.

"Please—please don't kill me," she begged.

"I won't, as long as you tell me what I need to hear. Are you gonna do that?"

Tashia nodded vigorously.

He walked over to her and kneeled, then pulled his gun and attached the silencer to the barrel slowly. The silencer gave the proper visual effect. Her eyes filled with tears, and she shook her head again.

"Please don't—kill me!"

"I'ma be honest with you, girlfriend, and tell you that I don't really give a fuck about you, one way or the other. I don't care if you live or die. I will kill you, go next door to IHOP, eat waffles and eggs and then go home and sleep good as hell. Now, what I'm trying to do is avoid having to kill you and a lot of other people by getting the few . . . well, mainly just one of the dudes that I need.

"Your homeboys killed my daughter, Tashia. And I can kill them all, or I can kill a few. It's up to you. I need a line on Tyger and whoever—"

"Tyger?"

"Yeah, Tyger. You know him, right?"

"I know him good. I knew this shit was gonna happen. That girl from the gas station was

your daughter?"

Nodding, he said, "Yeah. What do you know about her death?"

"I was with Tyger the night him and Tyjuan got into it at the movies."

"That was you?" Khadafi and Ameen both said simultaneously, which made Ameen look up at Khadafi, who'd stepped closer to Tashia.

Ameen turned his back to Tashia. "My daughter told me what happened that night."

Tashia's eyes lowered as her tears hit the hardwood floor. "What she couldn't tell you was that I mistakenly started the whole thing, and every day since, I've regretted it. I have always been in love with Tyjuan's lil' young ass. His swagger was larger than life and I wanted him. But for some reason, he wouldn't fuck with me. And that hurt me. Then when I started seeing him with that little girl, I was really fucked up." She paused, overwhelmed by the tragic results of her actions.

"That night at the movie, I saw them and hated. I told Tyger that Tyjuan be sweating me and stalking me for the pussy. Tyger got mad and decided to start something with Tyjuan. I didn't know he was gonna do that until it was too late. Tyjuan ended up spitting on Tyger. When we left the movies, all Tyger talked about was killing Tyjuan. I believed him, but then again, I didn't. I knew like he knew that him killing Tyjuan would start a war with the Circle and nobody really wanted that. I spent the night with him that night and left that morning. I forgot about the whole situation until

Tyjuan got killed a couple days later. Then I remembered and knew that Tyger killed Tyjuan. I was distraught about what happened. I felt responsible. But that didn't stop me from fucking with Tyger." She sniffled. "Days later, he admitted to me that he killed Tyjuan for spitting on him and that his cousin Choppa was with him. He mentioned that the girl from the movies was with Tyjuan, but she was in his car when the actual killing took place. He never said anything to me about wanting to kill that little girl. When it actually happened and the news broadcasted it and the girl's picture, I knew Tyger had killed her. I just didn't say anything to anybody. Then later, when they said the killer was seen leaving the gas station in a dark colored Maxima, my suspicions were confirmed. The morning of the murder, that's the car that they were in. Tyger and his cousin were together. Later that day, the Maxima was gone. I went to see Tyger at his aunt's house and stayed with him."

"Did he admit to killing my daughter?"

"No. He never said a word." Tashia swiped at the tears in her eyes. "Listen, I'm sorry about your daughter. I never meant for anything to happen to her or Tyjuan. I'm telling you the God's honest truth. I do my thing, but I'm not a bad person. I told you what happened. Please let me go. I didn't kill anybody."

"I appreciate all the light you just shed on the situation, but the fact remains that my daughter was killed by your boyfriend. Where is he right now?"

"I don't know. I swear to God I don't know. We just fuck every now and again, that's it. You gotta believe me." Her teary eyes were pleading.

"I do. But I need you to call him right now and try to get him here. Can you do that for me?"

Tashia's body sagged in defeat. She knew that it was Tyger's life or hers hanging in the balance. "I don't wanna do that, but to save my life I will."

"Where's your cell phone?"

"In my purse, over there on the dresser."

Ameen retrieved a Nokia phone out of her purse and handed it to her. "If your call is not to Tyger, or you say anything that I interpret as a warning, I'ma kill you. You understand me?"

Tashia nodded, wiped at her eyes, and dialed a number. The hand that held her sheet fell, exposing her body, which would have awakened something inside Ameen before, but not now. Kenya's death had stolen everything inside him. He watched as Tashia dialed and then redialed the number. He snatched up her phone. The number she was dialing was in fact stored under the name Tyger. He listened to a voice mail say that he couldn't be reached.

"He's not answering."

"Is that the only number you have for him?"

"It's the only one."

Dejected, he tried to think of what he wanted to do next. "You said something about going to see Tyger at his aunt's house. Do you know where Tyger lives? Does he live with the aunt?"

"Naw. Tyger has an apartment somewhere, but nobody knows where it is. At least that's what he always says. According to him, he doesn't take anybody where he rests his head. His aunt Linda, that's Choppa's mother. Her house is where I meet him at. Tyger stays there from time to time, but he doesn't live there. His cousin Choppa does, though."

"Where does the aunt live?" he asked.

"She lives on Burns Place."

"Where at on Burns?"

"Twenty-two thirteen. The red brick house with the black shutters and the black cast iron fence around it. It's the third house from the corner."

"What is Tyger driving now?"

"The last time I saw him, he was in a sky blue Acura. But it's hard to say because Tyger switches cars like clothes. His cousin drives an Infiniti Coupe, his girlfriend's joint."

Remembering the number that Tashia had for Tyger, Ameen programmed it into his phone. He stood and walked around the motel room, studying the drab beige comforter that had been discarded to the floor and trying to think of anything else to ask Tashia that might help him get Tyger. Ameen could think of nothing else, and he was getting hot under the mask, so he decided the inquisition was over. He tossed the silenced .45 to Khadafi.

"I'm not gonna kill you, although I believe you deserve to die. That decision is Khadafi's, and I'ma let him make it. Thanks for your help."

To Khadafi, he said, "I'ma be in the car."

*****

Somehow Ameen must've fallen asleep because he never saw Khadafi approach the car. He opened his eyes after hearing the tap on the window and then lowered it. "What did you decide?"

"That I needed to keep following what I always follow and that's my 'leave no witnesses' motto. I need you to help me with her body. We gotta put it in the Rover."

"Cool," he said as he exited the car. "But I bet not get no blood on my clothes. Shawnay will have a fit if she sees it."

"Don't even trip, cuz. You can just grab her feet then, because her head is damn near gone. That four-fifth with the silencer is a bad muthafucka."

# CHAPTER TWENTY-SIX

## DETECTIVE TOLLIVER

Stepping out of the truck, Moe had to button up his coat and pop his collar to fight off the chill. The sun sat high in the sky, but the cold over powered it. He glanced at his watch, noticing it was thirty-three minutes after 5:00 p.m. Moe walked into City Place AMC Movie Theater and flashed his badge on the first employee he spotted, who happened to be a short, white kid with bad acne, braces and three sizes-too large burgundy City Place AMC vest over a too small white shirt.

"Where can I find security around here, kid?"

The white kid was unimpressed by the shield. Without looking up from what he was doing, he jerked a thumb over his shoulder and said, "Go to the concession stand to your left and ask Katie to buzz them."

"Thanks, kid," he replied and followed his instructions.

Katie turned out to be a gangly, white female who resembled Elena Delle Donne, the basketball player for the Chicago Sky. She smiled as he approached, and it looked like the girl had forty teeth instead of thirty-two. "Hi. May I help you?"

He flashed the badge on Katie. "Metropolitan PD, I need to talk to anybody from security. Can you get someone for me?"

"I sure can," Katie replied and picked up the phone mounted on the wall behind her. After saying a few words into the phone, she hung up. She turned back to him. "Someone will be right with you, officer."

As he was reading the credits for a movie poster on the wall called *Beautiful Creatures*, a man walked over to him.

"You need to see someone in security, brother?"

He turned and completely faced the man. He was a high yellow dude with a played out high-top fade and lines cut into his eyebrows. He was about Moe's height, but outweighed him by at least thirty pounds.

"Yeah, Big Guy." He flashed his badge. "Moe Tolliver. MPD. Homicide. I'm investigating a couple murders, and I believe an incident that started here played a part in those deaths." He reached in his pocket and pulled out a notepad. Flipping the page, he found the entries about the movie incident. "On the night of the fifteenth, February 15, of this year, two men had some type of scuffle. One spit on the other . . ."

"I remember the incident. Mainly because of the spitting episode. I was here that night. I broke up the incident and literally kept the two dudes from tearing into each other."

"Well, I guess today is becoming a better day for me. Look . . . uh . . ."

"Gary. Gary Spencer."

"Okay . . . look, Gary, I know that y'all have cameras posted all over this lobby. I need to see the actual footage of the incident. The guy who did the spitting was murdered three days later on the eighteenth while his girlfriend watched. Then a week later, she was killed. We believe that maybe the incident here precipitated both murders.

"We believe the guy who got spit on is the killer of both victims. I need a visual of this guy to possibly get a name on him. Please tell me that y'all save what the cameras record for at least thirty days."

"We do, Officer Tolliver."

"Detective."

"Huh?"

"It's Detective Tolliver, Gary. But you can call me Moe."

"Uhhhh . . . okay. Well, we actually store footage for longer than thirty days. Our cameras are on a continuous feed, looped into a MPV conduit that automatically saves footage until we manually delete it. I usually do that after sixty to ninety days. Flash drives and memory cards make it very easy to do. Come on in the back with me, and I'll pull up the recording of that incident on the fifteenth."

Moe followed Gary into a room that would be better suited for surveillance of multiple cameras in a larger building like a casino. "There's a lot of equipment in here."

"I know, but the owners of the theater insist that it be here. After what took place in Colorado with that nutcase with the red hair, everybody got scared that something like that could happen in other theaters. I monitor all these cameras for eight hours straight. I only stop to use the facilities and eat. There's no exact science for it, but I've been trained to potentially spot a person who may want to become the next James Holmes. Let me get that video footage that you need."

He stood and watched Gary expertly navigate the computer's keyboard, and minutes later he found what Moe needed to see.

"Here we go. Sunday, February 15, 2013. If my memory serves me correctly, the incident happened somewhere between nine p.m. and eleven p.m. Let me see. Okay, here it is. Let me go back to the beginning . . ."

Leaning over to see the monitor better, Moe watched in real time as two men collided. Then the females intervened and attempted to hold both men.

"Here's where I enter the frame. I saw the initial collision and read the body language on screen. I immediately went to the lobby and intervened."

They both watched as the man with the shoulder length dreadlocks reared back and spit on the other man. Gary slowed down the feed and rewound it. Again they both watched in slow motion as spit flew in the air and landed on the other man's face. Moe watched the man wipe at his face. That man had to be his killer. Also, his eyes found the young girl whose face he had seen only in photos. Kenya Dickerson. She had grabbed for Tyjuan Glover's arm, but he shrugged her off.

"This is exactly what I needed, Gary. You are a lifesaver, buddy. Can you go back in and enhance the face of the man who got spit on?"

"Sure I can." Gary worked his magic and seconds later, forty-six inches of screen was lit up with the face of his potential killer.

"I need that face, Gary. Can you e-mail that image to my phone or computer? Or can you print it out for me?"

"I can do both if you want," replied Gary.

"That would be great, Big Guy. Make it happen."

Once the image on the screen was stored on Moe's phone and the paper image was in his hand, he was ready to leave. He thanked Gary again profusely. As Moe turned to leave, Gary called his name. "Yeah, buddy?"

"I just remembered something from that night. I remembered the last words the two dudes said to each other. As the one who got spit on wiped his face, he calmly said, 'I'ma kill you for that,' and the other dude said, 'Kill this dick, bitch nigga.' I held the one who got spit on and made the other dude leave. I threatened to call the cops if he didn't. I kept the dude who got spit on in the lobby for at least ten minutes to give the other dude time to leave the property and get some miles between them. It was all I could do that night, but I guess even that wasn't good enough, huh?"

"Unfortunately, it wasn't, Gary. Not if the man you held killed him anyway a few days later. But you tried. Take care, buddy."

Minutes later, back at the office, Moe scanned the photo of his suspect into the computer. As the system did its thing, he sat with his fingers crossed and silently prayed that the man in the photo was in the system. It took a few minutes before the system alerted him that no match could be found. His hopes instantly dashed. Again he decided to try the system, but this time he'd send the photo to the computer via e-mail. Once uploaded to his computer, he could send the photo through the system. He tried that, but again the screen beeped and displayed the 'No Match Found' icon. Moe even tried entering the name Terrell with the photo, but again, nothing. Dejected, he sat back in his seat and tried to remember anything he might've missed. Then something hit him.

While talking to Ronnie T, he remembered he'd said something about Tyger having a cousin named Choppa. Inwardly, he cursed himself out for not asking Ronnie T more about Tyger and Choppa. Leaning forward, he put the name Choppa into the system, spelled both with an A and the ER at the end. Several names and profiles came up on the screen. Moe typed the words Simple City and Alabama Avenue into the computer and waited. The system had one hit. Curtis Holloway with an address of 2213 Burns Place in Southeast D.C. popped up. He'd been arrested on Falls Church Terrace in Simple City, a few years ago with drugs and a gun. Moe's mood perked up as he decided to put the last name Holloway with Terrell to see what came up. Seconds later, the screen lit up with a profile. A large smile crossed his face. Not only was Terrell Holloway in the system, but so was his photo. Moe stared at an old mugshot of Terrell Holloway and the recent photo of Tyger and concluded that they were one and the same. And if he had any doubt about the photos, another thing that tied Terrell, Tyger, and Choppa together was the address. The system showed a home address for Terrell Holloway as 2213 Burns Place. Since he was suddenly on a roll, he decided to go for a threepeat.

Moe called the City Place movie theater and asked for Gary Spencer. A few minutes later, he was on the phone. "Hey, Gary, it's me, Moe Tolliver again."

"What's up, Moe?"

"I need you to go back to that night again and do the same thing that you did for me with the photo of the dude who got spit on. But this time, I need a good image of the female who was with the guy who got spit on. Can you do that for me?"

"You bet, Moe. Give me fifteen minutes, and you should be getting it on your phone. Do you need anything else?"

"Not right now, Big Guy. Nothing that I can think of. But if this guy turns out to be our killer, you might have to testify in open court about what took place in the movies that night. The spitting incident just might be enough to prove a motive for murder. Then add with that the fact that you heard him threaten the other guy three days before he was killed, and we might have a slam dunk conviction."

"I'm cool with testifying. I'll do anything to help the cops."

"Thanks again, Gary. I really appreciate you."

"Don't mention it. Give me fifteen minutes. Bye."

Not long after hanging up the phone with Gary, Moe's phone vibrated. He had picture mail. He uploaded the woman's face into the system, and then typed in the name that Nadiyah had given him. The system found a match instantly. He read the woman's profile on the screen. She had been arrested twice in the city. Once for assault and battery and once for fraud. Moe got up from his desk and walked down the hall to get a cup of coffee. One creamer, two sugars. He tasted the tepid liquid and grimaced. Coffee at the station always tasted bad. Like stale Irish lager. But he always ended up drinking it anyway.

Walking back to the desk, the wheels in his head were constantly spinning. Moe needed to talk to the cousin Choppa, the woman named Tashia, and the suspect, Tyger. He picked up the phone on his desk and dialed Dispatch. "Hello, this is Tolliver in Homicide. I need to put out an all points on three people wanted for questioning in two murders . . . Yeah. You ready? Here goes . . . Terrell Holloway . . . Terrell spelled with two r's and two l's . . . Yeah . . . Holloway . . . spelled with two o's and one a . . . correct.

"The next one is Curtis Holloway. Yeah, Holloway is spelled the same way, and they are of the same relation. They're cousins. You got that? Good. The last one is Tashia . . . spelled T-A-S-H-I-A Parker. Post those for me, buddy. Thank you. All info on them comes to me at this number."

Moe was reading over a file on his desk about an hour later when the call came through. The caller was a detective named Rio Jefferson. "What's up, Rio?"

"I just got the APB, Moe, and I think I got somebody here that you need to see."

"Where are you, Rio?"

"The city morgue. We just IDed a woman we found early this morning, shot and dumped on the side of the road near Southern Avenue."

A creepy feeling crept into the pit of his belly. It was the same one he always felt when a case was about to get crazy. "Who is she, Rio?"

"The woman that you're looking for. Tashia Parker."

# CHAPTER TWENTY-SEVEN

## SHAWNAY

The grand opening of the Islamic Sportswear Originals was a smash hit. After securing spots on the radio and the appearance of a local radio personality, people flocked to the store to be a part of the moment. With her hair wrapped in an Islamic traditional scarf for women called a 'hijab,' Shawnay sat behind the counter and rang up all purchases on the cash register.

Since Antonio had planned the opening during a weekend she didn't have to work, Shawnay volunteered to be the cashier for the weekend. It was the least she could do to show her support for her man. If she had to be honest, when he initially told her about his ambition to open the store and what type of clothing he'd sell, she wasn't optimistic about it.

She thought the last thing the world needed was another clothing store. Secretly, she wished that he'd go into something more secure like a franchise or a cleaning business. Something more concrete and durable, even in times of economic crisis. Something recession proof. But outwardly, she kept quiet and supported Antonio. But now to sit here and see so many people actually excited about purchasing his designs made her giddy. It made her feel proud. She couldn't stop smiling at all the people who came to the register and salaamed her as if she was Muslim.

Something inside of her Christian mind wanted to correct people and tell them that her husband forced her to wear the hijab and that she believed in Jesus, but she didn't. What the hell? It wouldn't hurt to be thought of as a different faith, as long as God knew what religion his child practiced. So, she kept smiling and returned the greeting every time someone gave it to her. A break in the action gave her enough time to check on her children, who were busy with one chore or another inside the store. Kashon was over by the shoe section sitting in a chair eating candy and watching all the people move around the store. Her heart swelled, and her love for the little boy grew deeper by the second. His curly locks were unruly and his gaze intense. He was dressed just like Antonio in an ISO sweatsuit with 'Property of Allah' emblazoned across the sweatshirt. A small, gray headband with Arabic writing accented his outfit and matched his tiny Jordans.

It took Shawnay a minute to find Asia, but she finally did. Her gregarious daughter was all over the place it seemed. She'd disappear in the back of the store for intervals, and then reappear with her arms filled with different colored folded shirts, T-shirts, and accessories. She couldn't take her eyes off Asia as she really noticed for the first time how much she'd seemed to mature since Kenya's death. Shawnay watched how she interacted with customers and her heart swelled for her as well. Then, sadness washed over her immediately. It was an emotion she'd grown to know well over the last couple of weeks. Sadness had been her constant companion ever since reality hit her the day she buried her daughter. It was Billie Holliday singing her song "Good Morning Heartache." This was a moment that she wanted Kenya to see, to experience. Her father opening a store had been a big deal to Kenya, and just the fact that she'd have to miss it, that alone crushed Shawnay inside. Without realizing it, a tear escaped her eye. When it hit the counter, she gathered herself and wiped her eyes. She'd promised herself that today she wouldn't cry, and she was determined to keep that promise, despite the one itinerant tear that fell. Out of nowhere appeared a line of people wanting to pay for clothes. *Saved by the bell. Thank you, God.*

Twenty minutes later, Antonio found Shawnay behind the counter as she straightened out a few things in the display cases and made sure they had enough bags. He hugged and then kissed her. She felt good. She felt proud. She felt love. "Hey, baby."

"What's good, wifey? How you holding up? Tired?"

"A little, but I'm good. We've been constantly moving since the opening this morning. I know I'ma sleep good tonight after a long bubble bath."

"And a long massage," Antonio added.

"Is that right? And what did I do to deserve all that?" she joked.

"I'll tell you what you did later, right before the massage begins. How's that?"

"That's fine. I'm looking forward to it."

"Good. Well, check this out, bay. I need to make a run right quick.You think you can mind the store for about an hour while I go pick up a shipment that never came? The supplier just called and asked if I'd pick it up. Furquan and

Tariq are here at your beck and call and my assistant Asia is all over the place playing hostess. You should be good until I return. You cool with that?"

Shawnay reached up and pulled him close. "Sure, go and do what you gotta do. But I can't let you leave here without telling you that I'm proud of you. You put in a lot of time, effort, and hard work. Look around you, baby. It paid off. Your store is a success and you did it all your way, on your terms. I never thought you'd get this type of a turnout. You did it, baby. You did it!" They kissed.

Afterward, Shawnay felt reflective and needed to vent, if only a little. "Not to kill the joyous moment, but I can't help thinking about what Kenya would be saying and doing right now. This was supposed to be her moment, too."

Antonio's face softened and his eyes glazed. Then he looked away. "I love you, Shawnay. Take care of things until I get back, okay?"

"Okay, baby. I will," she said, but Antonio couldn't hear her because he'd already walked through the crowd and out the back door.

She hoped one day they'd be able to mention Kenya's name and share their grief, but for now, she knew by the way Antonio had turned away, that the idea itself was improbable.

# CHAPTER TWENTY-EIGHT

## AMEEN

Ameen left the store and drove straight to the bottom of Benning Park where he met Khadafi. On D Street, he parked and looked around for Khadafi's Range Rover, but didn't see it. He wasn't even there yet. Annoyance was starting to creep in because he told Khadafi about his time constraint and the reason he picked today to put the work in. The grand opening of his store was the perfect cover for what he needed to do. His thoughts were racing a mile a minute when his cell phone vibrated. It was Khadafi. "Where you at, ock?"

"I'm where I said I would be. Look across the street."

Ameen's head was on a swivel as he looked all around for Khadafi. "What are you in?"

"I'm in a black Crown Victoria. The one with the Domino's pizza sign attached to the top of it. See it?"

He spotted the car. "Yeah, I see it."

"We gon' take this joint, so come on over."

As he exited the car, he couldn't help but smile and walk over to the Crown Vic. He ducked into the passenger seat and embraced Khadafi. He was dressed in an ill-fitting

Domino's pizza uniform with the hat to match. "The pizza man ruse, huh?"

"Why not, cuz? It's worked for me before, so you know what they say, if it ain't broke—"

"I can dig it, but slim, I ain't too fond of leaving my car out here. These niggas might steal my shit."

"If they do, cuz, we'll come back here and add their neighborhood to the list. But I don't think nobody will bother that joint. Now, if it was a Caddy, then I'd be concerned. Here, take these gloves. We gon' need 'em."

The gloves Khadafi handed Ameen were thin sports gloves that wide receivers wore. He slid them on.

"Before I called you, I rode through Burns Place and saw the house that Tashia told us about. I was hoping to make your day and tell you that Tyger's car was out there, but it wasn't. I did see a burgundy Infiniti Coupe parked outside. So, as of about twenty-five minutes ago, Choppa was there. Let's hope that he still is." Khadafi started the car and pulled off.

"And this is the plan that you told me about on the phone?"

"Without a doubt. But if you got a better one, let's hear it. Because we gotta get in and out of the house without looking suspicious. Did you bring me one of them silencer joints like I asked you for?"

Ameen reached in his pocket, retrieved the silencer, and then tossed it to Khadafi. "Good looking, cuz. Listen, just relax. This pizza man shit is gonna work. It worked for me before when I was hunting this nigga named Money. That's the dude that me and Boo hit and left for dead, but he survived. That nigga was hard as shit to kill for a while, but I finally got his ass. He's the one that put the money on our head and had that big nigga with the long braids on my ass. I still think he was the one that killed Boo and Umar."

"He was the one," Ameen said.

He could feel Khadafi's eyes on him without even looking his way. "How do you—"

"Do you remember when we was over the jail, and we got locked down for the murder in the stairwell? The dude that got put in the coat basket?"

"Of course, I remember that. Somebody fucked slim around real good," Khadafi commented.

"That was me. Me and my man Mike Boone crushed that nigga. He was the big nigga with the braids that you just mentioned," Ameen said. "He ended up getting locked up for Boo and his family."

"The dude, Cochise Shakur?" Khadafi asked.

Ameen nodded. "He bragged about all the people he killed. While we was on the tier down South-1, I baked a cake for his ass and followed him to SW-2 to get him. He even mentioned you and the fact that he was tryna get you."

"Damn, cuz, I wanted to kill that nigga myself. But it's all good. Damn. I didn't know that, that nigga was the—fuck it, he dead and that's all that matters. When we get in here, cuz, just follow my lead."

"What if the people inside the house don't open the door?"

Khadafi gave Ameen a crazy look. "Since when you've known black muthafuckas to not like pizza. Even if they didn't order a pizza, they'll trust the pizza man. Watch my work. Just wait for my signal and then come on in. Got that?"

"I got you, ock. Do your thing."

Khadafi stopped the car in front of 2213. Ameen saw the burgundy Infiniti still parked outside and smiled. Killing Choppa would do his heart some good. Reaching over his seat, Khadafi retrieved a nylon pizza case. He opened the case to reveal a pizza with sausage and pepperoni.

"You smell this shit, cuz? This shit smell like a nigga I killed back in the day named Big E. I shouldn't even touch this shit. I'ma really kill his ass now."

"Who? Choppa? Tyger?"

"Naw, the nigga whose clothes I got on. The real delivery man."

"And where the hell is he?" I asked, confused.

"He's in the trunk. Where else would he be?" Khadafi replied nonchalantly.

Ameen shook his head. *This wild ass nigga got a nigga in the trunk while we in the car.* "Whatever, ock. Let's do this, so that I can get back to the store."

He watched Khadafi as he opened the cast iron gate and climbed the stairs to the front door. While palming the pizza with his left hand, he knocked on the door with his right. A few minutes later, someone opened the door. The person, a woman, engaged him in conversation while he opened the pizza box. Then Khadafi made his move.

Ameen saw the play as it unfolded and was out of the car before he could signal.

# Chapter Twenty-Nine

## Khadafi

Khadafi heard the gate behind him and knew that Ameen was on his heels as he backed the woman into the foyer. The look on her face went from surprise to pure terror. Her hair, like black silk, was pulled into a ponytail that hung down her back. She reminded him of the singer Sade minus the big forehead. As they moved further into the foyer, he heard the front door shut and Ameen locking it. "Don't make a sound, or I'ma kill you right here. How many people are in here, and where are they?"

The woman was frightened, and as her hand reached her mouth, his gun came up to her forehead. "I'ma ask you again, one more time, and then I start shootin'. How many people are in here with you, and where are they in the house?"

"Uh . . . just the three of us. Me, Choppa, and his mother. She's in the basement washing clothes, and he's upstairs in his room."

"Okay, listen to me carefully. I won't hesitate to kill everybody in this house, but all I want is one of you. Call Choppa and tell him to come downstairs. Wait. Let's go to the living room first." He led the woman into the living room and made her kneel on the floor. "Call Choppa."

"Choppa! Choppa, come here!"

"Come up here!" a male voice shouted back. "I'm busy!"

"Call him again and say something to get him down here," he told her.

"Choppa, I hurt my ankle and I can't stand up. Come here!"

Ameen posted up at the side of the wall where he couldn't be seen by someone walking down the steps. A minute or so later, a dude with short dreads appeared. As soon as he saw Khadafi, he tried to run back up the stairs, but Ameen was quicker. He ran behind him and dragged him back into the living room.

"Get your bitch ass on the floor next to her before I open your shit up right here," Ameen said calmly. "Ock, you go get the mother and bring her back here."

Khadafi left the room and moved around the house in search of the basement. He found a door in the kitchen and saw a staircase that descended down and figured that was it. Softly he went down the stairs. He saw a heavyset woman dressed in jogging pants and a T-shirt separating clothes and putting them in a washer. "Hey."

The woman looked at him and said, "Who are you?"

He raised the gun and replied, "Death. Get your fat ass over here and up these steps before I kill you."

"Lord have mercy!"

"Lord have mercy is right. You better pray as you walk up them steps. Pray that I don't be the one to kill you. Let's go. Now!"

The heavyset woman moved with alacrity. She moved up the stairs as if she were twenty pounds smaller. With the gun to the back of her head, he led her into the living room. "Here's the mother, cuz."

Ameen took center stage like an actor in his favorite stage play. "Your son drove the car when your nephew killed my daughter. She was a pretty young woman who was only sixteen years old when she died. Your nephew Tyger decided that her life wasn't worth shit, so he took it. Have you ever lost a child?"

Tears welled up in the heavyset woman's eyes and then fell down her face. She shook her head no.

Ameen walked over to Choppa, who was on the floor on his knees with his hands behind his head. Before another word could be said, he raised the gun and shot the Sade look-alike in the head. Blood splattered and hit Choppa as her body fell to the ground. He went beserk and tried to go to her and comfort the dead woman, but his attempts were in vain. She was dead with half of her face missing.

Choppa looked up at Ameen. "You didn't have to do that. She wasn't with none of that shit. All she did was work—"

"Nigga, shut the fuck up! Do you think I give a fuck about all that? All my daughter did was go to school and be a teenager and y'all killed her."

"I didn't kill her!" Choppa screamed with spit in both corners of his mouth.

"You drove the car. Now you see how it feels to lose someone you love, huh? I take it that she was your girlfriend. Well, now that you've watched her die, now your mother can watch you die."

"Noooooo! Please! No! Don't kill my son! Please forgive him for what he did. Please! I beg you . . . oh God, please! Please don't kill my son!"

"If I could feel, this would be the part where I actually felt sympathy. But I can't feel anything. Right here where my heart used to be is pain. A pain that won't go away. My daughter didn't deserve to die, but she's gone. I can't bring her back and neither can you. So, it is what it is. But this is what I'ma do for you. Because I'm not a monster, I don't want you to have to watch me kill your son, so I'ma kill you first."

Ameen upped the silenced .45 and shot the heavyset woman in the chest. A crimson bloodstain appeared on her shirt as the force of the bullet knocked her back a few feet. Khadafi heard the dude Choppa scream, and Ameen shot him in the head. He walked over to the mother and dome shotted her to make sure she was dead. "Let's bounce, cuz," Khadafi said.

"Hold on for a minute, ock. I wanna send Tyger a message."

"A message? We gotta go, cuz."

"I'll be right back."

Khadafi stood fixed to the spot as Ameen left the room, then he returned with a large kitchen knife. He walked over to Choppa and cut off one of his fingers. Then like a man possessed, he took the finger and dipped it in Choppa's blood. He used the finger to write something on the wall. When he finished, the message read: *NOW, I'M HUNTING TYGERS.*

Ameen stopped to view his handiwork, and then dropped the finger into his pocket. "Now we can go." He picked up the pizza case and they left the house.

As soon as they were at the gate, approaching headlights signaled a car was coming. Khadafi stopped momentarily, seeing an Acura nearing. As it got closer, he could see the color. Sky blue. "Cuz!" he screamed. "It's Tyger!"

Ameen was already a step ahead because his gun was up and aimed at the Acura. Khadafi saw the driver's face briefly before the glass window shattered on the side of the Acura and it pulled off quickly. Ameen and Khadafi dashed to the Crown Vic and hopped inside. He started the car and pulled off headed in the direction of the Acura. At the corner, he made a right and tried to see taillights, but he couldn't. Erratically, Khadafi drove around the area in hopes of finding the Acura. He couldn't. Defeated, he gave up.

After dropping Ameen off at his Lexus, Khadafi drove the Crown Vic to a nearby park called Fort Dupont. In the rear of the park was a closed off area that used to be an amphitheater. He parked, hopped out, and changed into his street clothes. Khadafi balled up the Domino's uniform and walked it to the back of the car. He opened the trunk and looked at the cold, frightened man lying there bound and gagged. "Here's your clothes, cuz, but you won't be needing them where you're going." He shot the man in the face several times and then tossed the uniform inside.

In the back of the car, he retrieved the gasoline he'd put there earlier and methodically doused the car with it and then set it ablaze.

Walking all through the dark park until he reached Branch Avenue, he then walked upward, never looking back. But he heard the explosion and knew that the job was done.

# CHAPTER THIRTY

## TYGER

Paranoid and constantly checking the rearview mirror, Tyger sped through the streets all the while thinking, *What the fuck just happened?* By the time he pulled over, he was across the Maryland line in the rear of an apartment complex. He had evaded whomever it was that shot at him, but he still whipped out his gun as he got out the car. Tyger gave himself a rub down to check for blood or bullet entry wounds. He found none. But once he walked around to the passenger side of the Acura, he saw that it hadn't been so lucky. Not only was the window shot out, but golfball-sized holes were in the door. He counted seven total. A car approaching startled him.

The gun in his hand came up into the firing position, but the car kept going down the street. Still elevated, his heart rate wouldn't slow down. He paced the ground beside the car and replayed what had happened in his head in an attempt to make some sense out of it all. He had just turned the corner onto Burns Place with the intention of chilling at his aunt's house until he could reach Tashia and tell her to come over. She hadn't been answering her phone. As Tyger approached the house, he noticed two people coming down the steps out front. At first he didn't think anything of it because Choppa was always coming and going out of his house. He thought him and one of his men were leaving. But—as Tyger got closer, he saw faces and neither looked familiar. Their eyes found his, and then the bullets started flying. The window exploded, and he could hear the soft metal of the car being hit, but heard no gunshots. That's the part that was so baffling. And although he had a gun in his waist, he never thought to stop and exchange shots. Tyger ducked low, hit the gas, and got out of there.

That had all been about ten or eleven minutes ago, and he still couldn't figure out what was going on. His brain wasn't functioning right. *Who the fuck were them dudes, and why were they coming down the front steps of Aunt Linda's house? Why did they open fire on me? Had they been inside my aunt's house already?* He pulled out a new throwaway phone he purchased earlier and dialed his aunt's house, silently hoping they were okay. "Come on . . . somebody answer the house phone . . . answer the phone . . . Shit!" Ending the call, he redialed and willed someone to answer, just to let him know that everything was okay. But they didn't and his spirits tanked. Maybe nobody was home. Maybe that's why the two dudes started shooting at him. Maybe . . . Tyger dialed Linda's cell phone, knowing she never went anywhere without her iPhone.

His spirits soared as he tried to convince himself that everything was good with the family. But when his aunt's voice mail kicked in, his hopefullness took a nosedive. Once he called Choppa's cell phone and his voice mail came on, panic set in.

Tyger hopped back into the Acura and sped off heading toward Burns Place. He had to make sure his family was okay. As he approached his aunt's house, Tyger could see Choppa's girl's car parked out front. But damn, he hoped . . . he hoped that . . . "Shit! Fuck! Fuck!" He double parked in front of the house and dashed up the steps. He fumbled for the house keys in his pocket while turning the doorknob. The door opened and suddenly the keys became obsolete.

As he pulled his gun and crept up the steps that led to the living room, his heartbeat quickened. Tyger's worst fears were becoming a fast reality right before his very eyes. He saw a shoe and the first body. Then he saw them all. There were three. Choppa's girlfriend, Larcel, lay sprawled out on the carpet on her side. A small puddle of blood pooled beneath her head. Choppa lay beside her, his brains and blood splattered onto Larcel's clothes. The tears started then. All Tyger could do was cry and shake his head. Aunt Linda's body lay several feet away from the others. Blood stained her yellow T-shirt, and a neat little hole centered her forehead. Her eyes were open, glazed over in death. Tyger hadn't eaten since this morning, so when his stomach heaved, there was nothing to throw up. He smelled the potpourri that usually permeated Aunt Linda's living room, but he inhaled another smell. The scent of blood and death. And the heat made the odor worse.

Tyger stood in his spot stuck and surveyed the scene over and over again as if he were dreaming. But he wasn't. It was all real. His folks had been executed. And he had no clue as to why. *What had they done? What had Choppa done to make dudes come to the house and kill everybody inside? Had it been something that*

*Choppa and he had done together?* As if by epiphany, he turned and noticed something else, something written on the wall. Tyger inched closer, careful to avoid stepping in blood. The words on the wall were brief and concise. They were legible and clear. They were written in blood: ***NOW I'M HUNTING TYGERS.***

His questions had just been answered. The dudes who killed his family had been looking for him. Not finding him here, they killed all the people close to him. *Who were they? And what had he done lately?* Several things came to mind, but he couldn't figure out who would be so bold as to invade his peoples' house and kill them all. As his anger rose, something else invaded his head. The dudes who shot at him as he drove by had looked at him and immediately fired upon the car. That told him they knew who he was. And they knew he was in the Acura. If not, why open fire on a car that you didn't recognize and an occupant that you didn't know? It made no sense.

The truth of the matter hit him like a ton of boulders. The killers knew him. They knew exactly who he was. Knew what he was driving, and they had been looking for him. All kinds of questions came to mind. Somebody had told the dudes what he was driving, where to find him, and had either described him or shown the dudes his picture. And by process of elimination, that somebody had to be Tashia. Her freak ass had been the last person to see him in days. She knew where his aunt lived, and she had pictures of Tyger. He could think of no one else, so he pulled out his cell phone and dialed Tashia's number. Again, no answer. He called three more times and even left a voice mail. *Was she feeling guilty? Had she already known what the play was going to be and now she's ducking me?* Tashia wasn't answering her phone. That in itself convicted her in his eyes. And as soon as he found her, he was gonna kill her. Wiping tears from his eyes, Tyger said his final goodbyes to his aunt and cousin. They were gone, their souls off to another place, and there wasn't a thing in the world that he could do to change it. All he could do was kill the people who had killed them. The key to doing that was finding Tashia. Tyger dialed her phone again. Nothing. He dialed another number. Fella answered on the third ring. "I need to holla at you, slim."

"Tyger?"

"Yeah?"

"I almost didn't answer the phone. You know I don't pick up on numbers I don't recognize. Where you at?"

"Around the way. You?"

"Nearby. What's good?"

"Can't say over the phone."

"A'ight. Hideout spot. Thirty minutes.

*****

"You seen Tashia?" Tyger asked as he pulled up beside Fella on a block full of abandoned houses.

"Slim, I know you didn't call me here to ask me about no muthafuckin' Tashia. Park right in front of me." Fella waved him forward and took a seat on the hood of his car.

Tyger maneuvered his car into the parking space, got out and stood before Fella. "Tashia betrayed me. She gave some niggas my aunt's address . . ."

"What? She did what?"

"My peoples is dead. My aunt, Choppa, his girl . . . they're dead." Tyger told Fella everything that happened from start to end. It took him about fifteen minutes, and when he finished, the tears resumed. "I swear to God, slim. I'ma kill her ass! It had to be her. Tashia was with that shit."

Fella wasn't so sure Tyger's assumption was correct. "The last time I talked to Beauty, she told me she couldn't reach Tashia. She said Tashia had been drinking and drugging real hard and she worried about her. Maybe that's why.You saw the dudes on the steps clear enough to describe them?"

"Yeah. One was dressed in a uniform and he had a hat on. The other one had on a sweatsuit and ski vest."

"Hat on?"

"Naw . . . I don't think so. He had a baldhead, if I'm not mistaken."

"Baldhead dude, huh?" Fella asked, looking up at him.

"Yeah. Why? You know who . . ."

"Do you remember what Spock said the other day when we was in the spot?"

"In the spot? What Spock said?" Tyger searched his brain for an answer. "I smoke too much. What did he say?"

"He said the dude who killed TC and nem' was a baldheaded dude."

"Damn! You right. I forgot about that."

Fella got up off his car and paced the ground in front of Tyger. "I fucked up, slim. I fucked up bad."

"How?" Tyger asked, looking confused.

"I know who it was."

"What! You know who it was?"

"I know who *they* were." Fella stopped and looked him straight in the eyes. "I never told you this because I thought the nigga was bluffing. But now I see that he wasn't."

"Who wasn't? What the fuck are you saying, slim? Tell me what?"

"About a week ago, Beauty called my phone and told me that Tashia called her with a number for a dude I knew who needed to holla at me. He told Tashia he had some news that I could use. Beauty relayed the message to me and gave me the number. The dude's name is Dirty Redds."

"Dirty Redds?"

"Yeah, but you don't know him. He was over the jail with me and Roc when we was juveniles fighting some bodies. Anyway, I haven't seen or talked to slim in years. So when I got the message that he was tryna holla at me, I get curious and called him. We met at the Wendy's on Nannie Helen Burrough. He passed me a cell phone that had a picture on the screen. The picture was of you."

Tyger's face instantly screwed up. "Me?"

"Yeah. I don't know where he got it from, and I don't remember if he told me that or not. But what he did say was that you killed that girl at the gas station and her peoples was tryna see you about it. He told me the girl's peoples shot up the block and not the Circle. He said that her peoples was gonna come through and kill whoever they could find until they found you. They wanted me to turn you over to them and all the killing would stop."

Tyger couldn't believe what he was hearing. Why the hell would Fella not tell him all this shit a week ago? "Slim, why didn't you tell me about this shit when it happened?"

"Like I just said, I didn't take it serious. I thought the nigga was bluffing."

"Bluffing? You said that already. I can't believe this shit, Fella. A muthafucka told you that he wanted to kill me and you don't tell me?"

"Not him," Fella emphasized. "The girl you killed—*her peoples*. He said he was just relaying a message to me because the people heard that you be on the Avenue. And that he wanted to possibly spare innocent people. I told that nigga fuck him and fuck that girl's people. I told him we never give up our own for any reason and that the next time I see him, I'ma kill him. And that we were gonna find out who the people were and kill them all for shootin' up our block. Then he left and I left. I thought about letting everybody know what was up, but I decided that somebody could've been just tryna manipulate the situation and stop us from going at the Circle."

"By showing you a picture of me and telling you to give me up? That shit don't make sense, slim."

"So, what the fuck you tryna say to me, dawg? You feel some kinda way because I made a bad move? Because I fucked up? I made a decision that I thought at the time was the best one. It might've been one of them days when I was off that kush; I don't know. All I know is that whatever decision I made I'ma stand on it and say that I fucked up. I remember thinking about a lot of other shit that day. I was still fucked up about all my muthafuckin' men gettin' killed. I really thought the nigga was bluffin'. I should have, in hindsight, at least wised you up on what the nigga had said.

That's my bad. That doesn't bring your peoples back, but what the fuck? War is war.

"You knew something could potentially happen to your peoples when you decided to kill shorty from the Circle. Didn't I tell y'all niggas that this shit would get real in the field? Didn't I try to tell you to chill out and stop being so muthafuckin' trigga happy? This is that life you wanted to live. This that gangsta shit, lil' nigga. So wipe them fuckin' tears from your eyes and let's go and kill some muthafuckas. The dude Dirty Redds is from Capers. Let's go find him and make him tell us who the fuck sent that message, and then we kill them all. Fuck it. You ready to get turnt up?"

"Yeah, I'm ready," Tyger replied, drying his eyes as he followed Fella to his truck. He thought about everything Fella said, turning it over and over in his head, and every time he came to the same conclusion. Had Fella simply told him about the meeting he had with the dude a week ago, Tyger could've been more vigilant and possibly gotten Aunt Linda and nem' to lay back somewhere else for a while. Not telling him, for whatever reason, had crippled him. They didn't have to be dead. But Tyger's family wasn't Fella's, and at the end of the day he didn't really give a fuck one way or another. In Tyger's eyes, Fella was wrong. Dead wrong. So, he owed him. And one day soon, he'd come to collect what he owed. In blood.

# CHAPTER THIRTY-ONE

## DETECTIVE TOLLIVER

Glad you could finally join us, Moe," Captain Dunlap said as soon as he looked up and saw Moe standing across from him.

"Rough night, Cap. I overslept."

"We've been trying to raise you since last night. What's the sense in having a pager on your cell phone if you're not gonna pick up?"

"I'm sorry, Cap. What else do you want me to say?"

"What do I want you to say? Well, for starters since you are the one who put out the alert on Curtis Holloway and he's our victim here, I would like for you to tell me that you have a lead on this triple homicide. I need to keep the Chief off my ass. Tell me what's going on here."

When Moe woke up and learned that a triple murder had been committed at a house on Burns Place in Southeast, he knew what the outcome would be. Tyger and Choppa would be dead. But he was wrong. It was Choppa and two women. As he showered, dressed, and headed for the crime scene, he didn't quite understand everything, but he knew the murders on Burns Place were connected to the Kenya Dickerson case. "Did we ID the other victims?"

"We did. The mother is over there. Her name is Linda Holloway, her son, Curtis, and his girlfriend, Larcel Davis were found right here. They were all shot through the head. The mother through the head and heart. No signs of a struggle and no signs of forced entry. We've got fingerprints all over the house, but I doubt we'll find our perp's prints anywhere."

Tashia Parker. Choppa. His mother. His girlfriend. Eight people killed on Alabama Avenue. Five people killed in the F Street Circle. Seven people killed after Kenya Dickerson, but every murder connected to hers. Two of the three people that he wanted to question about her murder were now dead. Only one remained. Tyger Holloway. He had to find him. If Tyger knew what Moe knew, he would need his help. In fact, he'd need the help of the whole precinct. If Moe's gut feeling was correct, the men that he's up against, Khadafi Fuller and Antonio felder, were more than he could handle. But without concrete evidence, it would be hard to convince anybody that his hunch was accurate. He needed to actively pursue Antonio Felder for the murders on Alabama Avenue and possibly this case as well. But he needed Captain Dunlap on his side to do it.

"Are you listening to me, Moe?"

"Of course, I am. But Cap, I just thought about something, and I need to run it by you. Away from everybody else."

"Okay. But this better be good."

Moe led the way out of the house and walked Captain Dunlap past the media, gawkers, and onlookers. "Captain, I think I know who's doing all the killings. All the cases are connected. There's a few different scenarios and angles that I haven't figured out yet, but I'm sure that all the recent murders are connected and being done by three people."

He ran the whole spiel down to Captain Dunlap without leaving anything out. Starting with Tyjuan Glover at the movies, up until he was murdered. Kenya Dickerson's murder, up until the eight people killed on the Avenue. He told him about Tashia Parker, Choppa, and Tyger Holloway. "I found out that Antonio Felder, Kenya Dickerson's father was locked up for murder. He just got out a little over a year ago. He fits the description of the lone gunman that opened fire on the crowd on Alabama Avenue, killing seven. They were killed the exact same day that Kenya Dickerson was killed. He did it—"

"Can you prove that?"

"Not exactly, but it makes sense. I know he did it. The Avenue guys thought it was the Circle retaliating for Tyjuan Glover, so they went through and killed five people in the Circle. All the while, Antonio Felder is laughing at them and at us. And, Cap, he's not alone. He has a partner. One that he did time with and is just as ruthless and vicious as he is. This home invasion has his partner's name all over it. You've got to let me go after these guys. I can bring them down. I'm telling—"

Who is his partner?"

"Huh?"

"You said that Kenya Dickerson's father has a partner. Who is it?

"Luther Fuller."

"Luther Fuller? The same Luther Fuller that you've been obsessed with for the last five years? The same Luther Fuller that became your impetus to quit the force?"

He nodded. "It's the same one. But Cap, I—"

Captain Dunlap cut him off mid sentence. "No buts, Moe. My answer is no. And I'm really starting to second guess myself about putting you back in the field so soon.

"I will not sit back and let you go off on some wild goose chase after the father of that young girl. I will not okay you to throw away what's left of your career and mine with it. You will not pursue any leads that put that young girl's family in the crosshairs of your hairbrained conspiracy theories. You may not go anywhere near Luther Fuller."

"Captain, please . . . just listen to me—"

"I have been listening to you. I am not going to stand here and listen to any more of your paranoid ramblings and fanatical delusions. You're, effective immediately, off this case and any that involves Kenya Dickerson. And I want you to report to Dr. Gilbraith's office by tomorrow morning. Even though my gut is telling me to relieve you of your badge, I'm not going to do that. I want a psychological evaluation done on you before I let you back on any case in my office. I'm giving you a direct order to stay away from Antonio Felder and Luther Fuller. Do you comprehend that?"

"You know I do, Cap."

"Good. I'll see you tomorrow after you see Dr. Gilbraith."

There was no way for Moe to respond, so he simply walked away. For the record, officially, he understood why the Captain became irate and said what he said. Moe couldn't blame him for thinking that he may still be obsessed with

Luther Fuller. That was an inherent truth. While that may be true, everything else he said was on point and the investigation would prove it. But now, he couldn't continue down the road in which he traveled. Moe thought about what the captain said and about his direct order to stay away from Antonio Felder and Khadafi Fuller. Staying away from them didn't mean not talking to them. He had to find a way to bring them down.

While formulating a plan, he drove to the office. Nobody else knew that the Captain had put him off the case. That was Moe's ace in the hole. So, he could still gather evidence, just not in an official capacity. Then once he had something concrete, he could present it to the Captain, and he'd have to let him go after Khadafi. Moe needed something tangible, and his gut instinct told him that getting that tangible evidence started with Antonio Felder.

He picked up the phone on his desk and called the house number he had in his files for Shawnay Dickerson. He needed Antonio to verbally make a mistake. The only way to make that mistake happen was to turn up the heat under him. Moe needed him simmering, so that he'd boil over and get sloppy. As the phone rang, he crossed his fingers and hoped he was home. A female answered the phone. "Shawnay Dickerson?"

"This is she."

"Mrs. Dickerson, this is Detective Maurice Tolliver with the First District Police Department. Is your husband home? I need to speak to him."

"He is. Can I tell him what this is in reference to?"

"Just tell him I need to ask him a few questions about your daughter's murder."

"Okay . . . Please hold on."

A minute or so later, a deep voice came on the line. "Hello?"

"Mr. Felder, this is Detective Tolliver with First District Homicide. I need to ask you a few questions about your daughter's case. Do you have a minute?"

"Do I need to conference in my lawyer?"

"Not unless you have something to hide. Do you have something to hide?"

"Have you found the people responsible for killing my daughter?"

*You know who killed your daughter.* "Not yet. But we have some leads. That's why I want to talk to you. On the twenty-fourth of February, the day your daughter was killed, you IDed her body at the morgue, correct?"

"Correct."

"Where did you go when you left the morgue?"

"I don't remember. I was distraught."

"Did you know Tyjuan Glover?"

"I met him once. I forbade my daughter to see him, so she kept him away from me."

"Have you ever heard of a green-eyed dude named Terrell? The streets call him

Tyger."

"Never heard of him."

"Never heard a thing from your daughter about a possible beef between Tyger and

Tyjuan?"

"Naw."

"Does the name Curtis Holloway mean anything to you? The streets call him Choppa." "Should it mean something? Did he kill my daughter?"

*Good answer, you muthafucka.* "We don't know. The investigation is still in its infancy stages. But somebody killed Choppa, his mother, and a woman named Larcel Davis in his house last night. Know anything about that? Since Choppa may have been involved in your daughter's death."

"How could I know about something like that? Last night I was at a grand opening for a store that I own. I was there all day yesterday until late last night. We closed the store and came home. Me, my wife, and kids."

"What about a woman named Tashia Parker? She was at the movies that night too, she was with Tyger. Ever heard of her?"

"Never heard of her."

"Well, you won't because she's dead, too."

"Sorry to hear it. Is that all? I got shit to do."

"One more question and I'ma let you go. Do you know a man by the name of Luther Fuller? The streets call him Khadafi."

"Don't believe I do. Should I?"

"Yeah, especially since I saw you talking to him at your daughter's funeral. Reddish brown complexion, freckles—"

"There were hundreds of people at the funeral that I talked to. They were offering their condolences. I don't know hardly any of them."

*He's lying.* "You're right. You have a nice day, Mr. Felder, and I'll be talking to you again soon." Moe hung up the

phone and stared at it. Antonio Felder was lying about his connection to Khadafi. *Why?* If he lied about knowing Khadafi, it was reasonable to conclude that he was lying about everything. But it didn't matter, he had accomplished what he set out to accomplish. Antonio Felder knew that Moe was on his ass and that would make him cautious. But with all caution comes mistakes. He was sure of it.

Moe was just about to walk away from his desk when his cell phone vibrated. The caller was Rio Jefferson. "Rio, what's good, buddy? Anything new on the Tashia Parker murder?"

"You'll have to tell me. I got somebody I want you to talk to. Her name is Anteese Matthews, but her nickname is Beauty and it fits her, Moe. Tashia Parker was her best friend, and she's quite broken up over her death. She says that somebody picked Tashia up from her apartment the night she was killed. She believes that, that man had something to do with her death. In fact, she's sure of it."

"Did she get that man's name?"

"Of course. That's the reason I'm calling you and giving you the opportunity to talk to her. She said his name was Dirty Redd."

His heart stopped momentarily. "Khadafi . . . I'm on my way."

# CHAPTER THIRTY-TWO

## SHAWNAY

Shawnay waited until Antonio hung up the phone before she could hang up, or he'd know that she had been listening to his call. Although she felt bad snooping on him like that, she had to in order to ascertain certain truths. Because it wasn't like Antonio was going to tell her everything. She set the phone down and scurried back to the kitchen and pretended to be elbow deep in dish water for the last ten minutes.

It was early Sunday morning, and she had no plans of taking the kids to church, but even if she did, the phone call she just listened to would have dampened her rejoiceful spirit. Hadn't she told Antonio that his killing sprees would lead back to their front door? And she'd been right. The call from the detective was more a fishing expedition than a call to deliver news. His questions had been accusatory, more like an inquisition, and Antonio's replies had been mostly lies. *Why?* Maybe it was Antonio's self-righteous 'I'll never snitch to the cops' credo. Maybe he was afraid of where his honest answers would lead. Things that had been said in that conversation wouldn't leave her head.

*Why had Antonio immediately taken a defensive stance when the detective called?* The detective's statement echoed in her head. "*. . . killed Choppa, his mother, and a woman named Larcel Davis in his house last night. Know anything about that? Since Choppa may have been involved in your daughter's death.*"

Antonio's response made her shiver. "*How could I know something about that? Last night I was at a grand opening for a store that I own. I was there all day yesterday until late last night.*"

Antonio was smarter than the cops and that's what scared her. He had effectively established himself an alibi. He had not been at the store all day like he said. They both knew that he left the store before eight and stayed gone for a little over an hour and a half. That was more than enough time to get to D.C. and commit murder. Shawnay shook her head at the thought of Antonio killing somebody's mother. After she begged him to stop. *Hadn't I unequivocally explained the fallout from the storm that was brewing? Hadn't I vividly expressed what I thought would happen after all the smoking guns cleared?* And the really crazy part about it all was that deep inside, something wanted her to believe that her husband wasn't running around the city committing atrocious acts of murder to avenge their daughter.

"*What about a woman named Tashia Parker? She was at the movies that night, too. Ever heard of her?*"

"*Never heard of her.*"

"*Well, you won't because she's dead, too.*"

A few nights ago, Antonio had left in the middle of the night. He told her that his chest was tightening up, and he was going to CVS to get some over-the-counter medicine that he used to take while in prison. That night she believed him, but now, she wasn't so sure. He could've very well been the person responsible for killing that girl. The night Antonio left ISO on its grand opening day, he told her that he had to go pick up some stuff from a supplier who couldn't deliver. When he returned, he was emptyhanded. *Why?* Now, here's the part that really confused Shawnay. *"Do you know a man by the name of Luther Fuller? The streets call him Khadafi."*

Why would a detective, who knew nothing of the history between Antonio and Khadafi,

just out of the blue ask him about Khadafi? *How had he made a connection between them?*

Shawnay hadn't seen Khadafi in almost two years, and according to Antonio, the day he stabbed

Khadafi was his last time seeing him. *So, why link them to each other now? Why had Antonio*

*lied about knowing Khadafi, and was Khadafi really at Kenya's funeral? If so, how did he come without me seeing him? Why didn't Antonio tell me he was there?*

One side of Shawnay wanted to confront Antonio with all of her questions, but the other side begged her to leave things alone. *Why? Because you don't wanna know the truth*, her inner self said. Suddenly, three-year-old Kashon bound into the room and grabbed her leg.

"Mommy, Mommy, I play the game Dooty Caller."

Shawnay picked him up and hugged him. "You mean Call of Duty?"

"Yeah, yeah. I kilt them, Mommy. I kilt the people," Kashon exclaimed.

"You didn't kill people, baby. You played a game. That's all."

"Okay, Mommy, but I did kilt the people. Just like Daddy."

Just like Daddy. As much as she loved the bond between Kashon and Antonio, she cringed at what her son had just said for two reasons. One: she always felt she was duping her son by not telling him who his real father was. Although he'd met Khadafi once when he was a toddler, he didn't remember him. In fact, she dreaded the day when she'd have to explain that Antonio was not Kashon's father. She imagined the hurt look on his face and that tore her apart inside. Second: what her three year old didn't know was that the man he called Daddy killed people in games and in real life.

"Do you want some banana pudding, Kay Kay?"

"Yay! Nana puddin'! Yeah, Mommy!"

"Let's get you some then."

As she was scooping pudding into a small bowl for Kashon, Antonio walked into the kitchen. He hugged her from behind and let his hands linger around her waist. He kissed her neck. Shawnay turned so he could kiss her lips. "Hey, baby."

"Hey to you. What's good?"

"Nothing much. What did that detective say?" Shawnay asked.

"He asked me some questions about Kenya and Tyjuan. Then brought me up to speed on their investigation. They learned a lot in a short amount of time. They should be making an arrest soon," he said.

*Arrest who? You?* "That's good. We pay taxes so that the police can do their jobs."

"I guess so. What's on your agenda for today?"

"I'm thinking about taking the kids out to eat someplace. You wanna join us?"

"You know I'd love to, but I gotta get to the store and get things ready for tomorrow. It's bad enough that I let you talk me into closing on Sundays as if I'm a Christian or something."

"Boy, hush. There are plenty of people who close their businesses on Sunday and it has nothing to do with religion."

"Name one."

"People be in church anyway."

"That's religious. Try again."

She tried to think of something, but couldn't. Finally, she and Antonio just started laughing. He was right. "Okay. You got a point. How long are you gonna be at the shop?"

"Probably for most of the day. I'll call you later and let you know. Where's Asia?"

"In her room on her laptop, last I checked. That girl is addicted to social media. Did you see the pics she posted on Instagram at the grand opening?"

"Naw. But I know they were probably awesome. Let me go. I'ma see y'all later, Insha'allah."

Shawnay watched her lying ass husband leave and didn't know what to feel. Ambivalence was now her middle name. For some reason, she didn't believe Antonio was going where he claimed he was going. She wanted to believe him, but she didn't. "Asia! Asia, come here!"

"Yes, Ma?" Asia said as she walked into the kitchen.

"I need you to watch Kay Kay for me for about thirty minutes while I make a run. I'll be right back."

"Okay."

With no time to spare, she grabbed her coat and rushed out of the house. She wouldn't be but a few minutes behind Antonio, so he wouldn't be hard to catch up with. His Lexus was faster than her car, but there were only two ways to get to D.C. from Arlington, and she knew which route Antonio would take. It didn't take her long to hit the Interstate and spot him. Careful to stay at least three to four cars away from him, she followed him. Curiosity had simply gotten the best of her, and she had to see if Antonio was being truthful. Shawnay had to know. At some point Antonio would exit the interstate and head for the beltway if he was going to District Heights where his store was located. If not, he was headed to D.C.

Minutes later, she knew that her husband was headed to D.C. On New York Avenue in Downtown D.C., Antonio's blinker came on, signaling that he was about to make a left turn into a car dealership.

She read the sign above the entrance. Imperial Autos.

*Was Antonio buying a new car?* Shawnay pulled over and watched Antonio get out of the Lexus with his cell phone at his ear. What happened next, stopped her breath. The door of the trailer on the lot opened and out stepped a man she hadn't seen since that day at the hospital. He walked down a few steps and embraced Antonio.

Everything about him was the same, except his hair. Gone were his braids and cornrows. He was still handsome as hell and sexy. Shawnay couldn't believe her eyes. Two men who had sworn to kill one another were now friends. She thought about the peace she and Marnie brokered. *How had they put the past behind them and teamed up?* What the detective asked

Antonio came to mind: *"Do you know a man named Luther Fuller?"*

The detective knew about Antonio and Khadafi being friends. But how? At that moment sitting in the car watching her husband and her son's father talk, she knew. Shawnay knew that everything she feared to be true about Antonio was true. Not only was her husband still killing people, he had somehow managed to hook up with Khadafi, and together they left dead bodies everywhere they went. Tears came to her eyes as she thought about the dilemma she was in. All the lies, the ruses, the deception, she weighed her options. She had to decide whether the end result was worth the immediate risk. Shawnay wiped her eyes and made a decision.

# CHAPTER THIRTY-THREE

## KHADAFI

"You look like you gotta a lot on your mind right now."

Ameen shook his head back and forth. "Ock, I gotta get this nigga and then fall back. I'm out here wildin' out in the streets and tryna run a business. I'm tryna juggle that with being a father. That shit ain't easy. And on top of all that I'm still mourning my daughter. If that ain't enough shit on my plate, I get a call today from the detective investigating my daughter's murder, and this faggot gon' ask me a rack of questions like he suspect me of all the murders going on. How the fuck can he be that perceptive?"

"Cuz, some of them cops be like that. But what can he possibly have on you?"

"Yeah, I'm hip, but ock, that nigga making accusations like he know some shit. He knows that you and me know each other. He asked me about you?"

Khadafi zipped up his Northface coat to ward off the sudden chill. "He what?"

"You heard me. He came straight out and asked me did I know you. When I said that I didn't I know you, he told me that he had seen us together at Kenya's funeral. I'm glad he called and told me in so many words that we're being watched."

"I should've known the cops was watching the spot, but I don't understand why he asked you about me."

"He asked me about Tashia. He asked about Tyger and his cousin Choppa. He asked me about the murders on Burns—"

"Cuz, what's the detective's name? Do you remember?"

"Yeah. His name is Tolliver."

Khadafi couldn't believe it. His arch enemy was back on the force and on his trail again. His lawyer told him that after the trial and acquittal, Maurice Tolliver had quit the police force. The cop and witness getting killed blocks from the courthouse had fucked him up. "Maurice Tolliver. I can't believe it. He's back."

"You know him?" Ameen asked.

He nodded. "He was the detective on my last case. The double homicide. Seeing me again as a free man probably fucked up that nigga's day. He has a hard on for me because I beat every case he tried to cook me on. One day we had a face to face confrontation while I was in the holding tank at First District. He wanted me to tell on TJ and myself about some murders. I told him to eat my dick. He been on my line every since. But what I can't figure out is why he called you and revealed his hand like that."

"Beats me, ock. All I know is that he's somewhere trying to put the pieces together, and he not only wants you. Now, he wants me, too."

"You know what I always say. Fuck the police. Especially him. He can't touch me and he knows it. Other than that, what you tryna do now?"

"I just told you. I'm tryna get this nigga Tyger and then fall all the way back for a while."

"In that case, cuz, I got just what the doctor ordered," Khadafi told Ameen.

"And what's that?"

"A plan to cook this beef and get it over with. That is, after I settle a few scores."

"Talk to me, ock. What scores?"

"Last night somebody came through and killed two of my men. Deon and Wayne Wayne. They tried to be discreet, but one of my other men recognized one of the dudes. It was Fella. He must've come through looking for me, but found them instead. He knew them. Fella sent me a message and I got it. Now I wanna send him and whoever was with him—it was probably Tyger—a message of my own. I guess the one you left on the wall in his peoples' house wasn't enough."

"So, what's the plan?"

"We dress up like ladies and burn 'em with dirty three eighties. Rememeber that?"

Ameen just smiled.

*****

"I don't know about this one, ock."

"Don't trip, cuz. I read about this one in a couple of them urban novels. It'll work."

Ameen changed into his niqab and long flowing burqa dress. The only thing visible on his face was his eyes. The Islamic dress was designed to completely hide the shape of the woman wearing it. On Ameen's feet were black panty hose and ballerina slippers. His outfit was the same as Khadafi. "How do I look?" he asked.

"Just like me, cuz," Khadafi said. "Just like me. Let's bounce."

"People gon' think we terrorists."

"That's what we are, ain't we? Urban terrorist."

"I guess you right. Where to now?"

"First, I gotta pick up these choppers, and then we hit the Avenue."

*****

"The basketball court has become the hangout spot. I been riding through here every day off and on just to get a feel for the area. I knew that at some point we'd have to come back this way. I just wanted the heat to die down. It's been a while since the killings on the Avenue, and a few dudes think it's cool to come back outside. They're wrong. The court is fenced in with only one way in and out, so we just walk right in and put the work in. Dressed the way we are, they will probably think we just left the masjid down the street. You take the stroller in the back and push it like it's a baby, and I'ma act like I'm reading the Quran as we walk. We go in, bust and then get out. Burns Place ain't that far from here, so we gotta be quick. Hit as many niggas as you can and then get outta there. You feel me?"

"Let's do it."

They exited the car one street over from the basketball court, walked all the way down the block and then up and around to avoid suspicion. They had to look like they were coming from the direction of the masjid down the street.

Khadafi pulled out his book and acted as if he was deeply ensconced in reading it. Ameen was beside him pushing a stroller. As they got within feet of the basketball court, he looked over and spotted someone he knew. His heart rate quickened and he smiled to himself. "Aye, cuz, don't look now, but one of the dudes on the court is D-Roc. He sitting on the bleachers with the black Spyder ski coat on. He's my man. You hit everybody else."

"Got you."

A few eyes watched them as they walked by but then quickly turned away. To the people

in the court, they weren't a threat. How wrong they were. "Now, ock!" Ameen said.

He and Khadafi rushed onto the court and opened fire on the crowd. People tried to flee and duck but had no where to run. Khadafi kept his eyes on D-Roc and tracked his every move. He let some people run past as he went for D-Roc. He was trapped and reaching for a weapon, but he was too slow. Khadafi nailed his ass to the gate. He heard the screams and feet patter all around him as Ameen continued to chop shit up. The scene on the court was mass chaos. It resembled something in the papers that had happened in a place like Tel Aviv. Mission accomplished. It was time to go.

*****

"Aye, ock, pull over up here by East Capitol Street. In front of the carry out, I need to run next door to the convenience store." Ameen, who was now driving the getaway car gave Khadafi the head nod and pulled over. He grabbed the niqab out his lap and put it on, then left the car. As Khadafi walked into the convenience store, a bell chimed.

He looked around until he found the lone man in the store. He walked up to him and said in a feminine voice, "Frank Jasper?"

"That's me, ma'am. May I help you?"

"Yes, can you tell me—" Khadafi whipped out the handgun from under the dress and blew Fella's father's head open. "You can charge that to your son."

Somebody screamed as he left the store. Khadafi ran outside and hopped in the car. "Go! Go!" he screamed at Ameen, who mashed down on the gas and got the hell out of there. Once they were miles away from the two crime scenes, Ameen asked, "What the hell did you do back there?"

"Before Tashia died, she told me everything I needed to know about Fella. When he sold me all that death in the Wendy's that day we met, I decided right then to make it personal between him and me. That was his father I just killed in that convenience store. Tomorrow, we gon' visit his mother."

# Chapter Thirty-four

## Khadafi

"Answer the question, Khadafi."

"Marnie, I don't have time for this stupid ass shit. I told you this before I left the house, and you gon' call me on my cell and ask me the same dumb ass shit. Can't you just let it go? I thought we were past the insecure shit."

"Call it whatever you want to call it. I just wanna hear you say it. Be a man and keep it real with me. You can't hurt me no more than your non answers already have."

Exhaling deeply out of pure frustration, he ran his hand down his face. "Why are you doing this?"

"Why not ask? You are the one that keeps saying her name in your sleep."

"Unconsciously, Marnie, unconsciously. How you gon' hold me responsible for shit that I say when I'm sleep?"

"Nigga, fuck that. You ain't getting off that easy."

"A'ight, cuz. Cool. You want me to be real with you, huh? You just can't leave it alone, huh? Okay, I'ma answer your question. Do I still love Kemie? Of course, man. Cuz, it's too early in the morning for this shit. It ain't even nine o'clock."

"Fuck what time it is. Time could stand still for all I care. I wanna hear what you gotta say. Please continue."

"Yes, I still love Kemie. I'ma always love her. I spent over half my life loving her. Do I miss her? Yes, I miss her. I miss her a lot. Do I wish that I was still with her? A lot of times, yeah, I do. And no matter what happens in my life, I think I'ma always feel like that. She died because of me, because of what I did to Bean and Omar. She didn't deserve to die like that. TJ killed her to punish me. I can never forget that. That's probably why I been dreaming about her."

"Hold on, hold on, you fast talking me. What I wanna know is: if Kemie was alive right now, would you and I be together?"

"I . . . I don't know . . ."

"You don't know? . . . You don't know? Wrong answer, brotha!" Marnie said and hung up the phone.

Khadafi set the phone down on the middle console and ran his hand down over his face. When he looked up, he saw Ameen's Lexus pulling into the parking lot and then into the space in front of his store. He watched Ameen closely and thought about all the people that he witnessed him kill. He was as relentless and ruthless as he was. Then something inside him replayed the incident in the rec cage at Beaumont Pen. Khadafi saw the look on Ameen's face as he stabbed him through the fence. Instinctively, he rubbed the scars on his stomach and chest and where the shit bag had been. The beast inside him roared, then hissed, *Kill him, kill him right now. He's not expecting it.*

"I can't. I promised."

*You can*, the beast whispered. *You are an outlaw and outlaws break their word. Shawnay and Marnie will understand that. He tried to kill you and he failed twice.* The beast was right, but all in all he shook his head to clear it. His eyes still followed Ameen as he lifted the security grills on the store windows. When his cell phone vibrated, he picked up the phone knowing that the caller was Marnie.

"What's up, cuz?"

"Just wanted you to know that I'm pregnant—*before* I kill this baby. I already have one child by a man who doesn't give a fuck about me. I won't make it two. I was going to surprise you, being as though I know how much you want another son since you don't get to see Kashon at all. But you just killed my surprise. I thought you loved me, but now I see that you don't. My goofy ass thought I could suck and fuck you into loving me the way I wanted you to love me."

"Marnie, damn, cuz. We just went through this shit. I—"

"I thought that enough time had gone by and maybe you had forgotten about your past, about Kemie, and all the pain she caused you. I tricked myself into thinking it was truly just you and me now and that we'd live happily ever after. But I was a fool. Then again, I'm more than a fool because they say it takes a fool to lose twice. I've lost more than twice, so what does that make me? I needed to know whether what we had was real and you just confirmed that it's not."

Khadafi took a quick breath before speaking. "I didn't say—"

Deep in her feelings, she talked over him. "I was there for you when nobody else was, but that don't mean shit to you. I have been the only good and constant force in your troubled world and this is how you do me? My appointment at Hillcrest is for one o'clock. So, if you want another son, I suggest you go to Harmony and dig your girl up, fuck her, and see how that works out for you."

"Marnie, don't make me kill your ass—"

"You can't kill me, nigga! I'm already dead. I'm just not in a coffin. You killed me already. You killed my spirit when you chose a dead woman over me. And knowing that in itself kills me slowly as each minute passes. I can't keep living like this, with you."

"Cuz, if you kill my baby . . ."

"It's as good as dead. Fuck you!" Marnie hung up the phone.

Slowly, he inhaled and exhaled several times before dialing Marnie back. Her answering machine picked up each time. Frustrated, he tossed the phone into the rear of the van. Marnie's revelation about being pregnant weighed heavy on his mind. *She knows how bad I want another son, and she gonna play with me like that. That's crazy.* Khadafi wanted to start the van up and rush home to talk and then eventually smack some sense into her hard ass skull, but he decided against it. He needed to finish what he and Ameen started, and he'd deal with Marnie later.

In his heart he didn't believe she'd really get an abortion, if she was even pregnant at all and not only trying to hit him where she knew it would hurt most. "She knows I will slump her shit. Marnie ain't crazy," he said to himself as he stepped out of the van. The wind chill rushed in like a caged UFC fighter. He had to zip his coat all the way up and pull down the Prada skully on his head. The expression on his face told the story of his sour mood as he crossed the parking lot and entered Ameen's store.

Although he had been to the store a few times in the last week or so, he'd never been inside. The store was spacious, yet it felt cramped, as if there was too much stuff crammed into a storage space. Everything was organized and brightly colored. On the wall behind the counter was a framed photo poster of the Kabah in Mecca. Other than that, the walls were bare. The store reeked of scented prayer oils. "Assalaamu Alaikum, cuz."

"Wa laikum assalaam. What's up, ock?"Ameen looked up from something he was reading on the front counter. "How you?"

"I'm good, cuz, despite the fact that Marnie is trying my patience. Talkin' 'bout she's getting an abortion today, and she knows how I feel about that abortion shit."

"You never told me shorty was pregnant, slim. I would've left you outta this shit."

"Cuz, I would've rolled regardless. You know I live for this gangsta shit. I never knew that Marnie was pregnant until about thirty minutes ago when she sprung that shit on me. I don't even know if she's really pregnant, or if she's just tryna hurt me because I hurt her."

"What did you do this time, ock?"

"Something I never do. I told her the truth. She asked me did I still love Kemie and whether I'd be with her if Kemie was alive."

Ameen shook his head. "Ock, please don't tell me that you told that woman how you really feel. That, being—that you still love Kemie, and if she was alive, y'all would be together. Please tell me you didn't tell that woman no shit like that."

His non answer said it all. He walked over to one of the mannequins and inspected the outfit on it. Behind him, Ameen began lecturing, but Kadafi wasn't listening. Suddenly his mind was on his son, the one he couldn't be with because of Ameen. That thought resurrected the whispers of the beast within. Again, he shook his head to quiet the beast.

"You got some slick pieces here, cuz. I didn't know you had it in you to design clothes."

"Years of solitary confinement bring out things in a man that he never knew was in him. I'm glad you like 'em, though. Go ahead and pick you out some stuff and take it. It's on me."

"Naw, cuz, I can pay my way. Let me support the hustle. Besides, I still owe you."

"You don't owe me shit, ock. I told you that already. We even all the way around the board. End of discussion."

"Respect, cuz, respect."

"Before we get down to business, let me tell you what happened to me yesterday after I left you. I stopped down the wharf to get some seafood for the fam' and dump them niqabs and burqas that we had on. While I was walking back to the car with the bag of seafood in one hand and my phone in the other. I was watching the news on my phone. They were broadcasting live from the basketball court talking about all the violence in the area, despite a heavy police presence in the last few weeks. The next thing I know, somebody snatches my phone and takes off running."

"Get the fuck outta here!" he said and laughed.

Ameen put his right hand over his heart and said, "Wallahi, ock. All I could do was stand there and watch this nigga run down Water Street with my phone. I was so shocked that I never even thought to chase him down. When it finally dawned on me what had happened, all I could do was stand there and laugh." Khadafi and Ameen cracked up laughing. People told him before that laughter was good for the soul. At that moment, it sure felt like it.

In mere seconds that moment passed, and they focused on the business at hand. "Before Tashia died, she told me a lot about Fella and Tyger. The stuff she said about Tyger, we already knew. Not only did she tell me where Fella's father worked, she also told me where his mother works, what she drives, and what she looks like. She told me her name and everything. My plan is that we use her to get to Fella. Once we get Fella, we get Tyger. You know what happens after that."

"I kill Tyger. You kill everybody else."

"Exactly. Let me break the whole plan down to you."

For the next fifteen minutes, he went through the plan with Ameen. The look on his face after the fact concerned Khadafi. "What, cuz?"

"The idea in itself is cool, but the execution is what troubles me. The plan is filled with holes and unknown variables."

"What plan ain't? I need to know if you're with me on this, doing it like this or not. I'm talking to the street Ameen in you and not the professor side. Talkin' 'bout variables and all that geekin' ass shit."

Ameen laughed. "You right, ock. My bad. Every move we made had a flipside to it. But what if the mother is fucked up about the father and isn't at work? What if she doesn't surface for weeks? I need to get this nigga now, and then fall back and repair my marriage."

"I'ma call the school and see if she's there. We can settle that right now," he said and reached for his phone before realizing that he'd left it in the back of the van. Let me use your cell? Damn, my bad, cuz. Your cell phone got snatched. You got a business phone in here, right?"

"Of course. It's on the wall over there," Ameen replied and pointed out the phone.

He called 411 first and then got the number to Alton Elementary School. A minute or so later, he replaced the receiver onto the base. Turning back to Ameen, he said, "Evidently, moms didn't mess with Pops because she's at work. Next concern?"

"What if we get the mother but can't get her to call Fella?"

"Never say can't, cuz. You and I know that all things are possible as long as we think positive thoughts. She'll call him. I guarantee it. If not, I'ma kill her and then we hunt Fella and Tyger. Straight like that. It might take us a while, and I know what you said about tryna put the rush on and find these niggas so you can fall back, but you gotta put it in your mind that this might be one of them long movies. No matter the length though, it's still gonna end the same way, R rated. It's red rum all day. You feel me?"

"How could I not?"

"That's what I'm talkin' bout. Let's go buy ourselves some new clothes for the premiere."

# CHAPTER THIRTY-FIVE

## AMEEN

The transformation took less than forty-five minutes. It was a little after ten a.m. by the time they pulled into the elementary school parking lot. Khadafi was now dressed in a royal blue Department of Public Works uniform with the hat to match. Ameen adjusted the Rastafarian crown with the fake dreads sewn into it atop his head. A pair of personality glasses changed his appearance drastically.

"Remember, cuz, get in, say what you gotta say, and then get out. When you come out, the keys will be in the ignition. When she comes out and goes to her car, wait for my signal and then come to me."

"And the signal is you touching the bill of your cap, right?"

"Right. When you see me do that, make your move."

Nodding, Ameen got out the van and snatched the push broom out of the back. In character, he started sweeping the parking lot as he made his way over to the school. The entrance door was unlocked. He pulled it open and went inside. Then he swept the halls as if he belonged there. At the security desk behind him, he saw a heavyset black man sitting and reading a magazine. He glanced in Ameen's direction, but quickly turned back to his magazine. He swept the long hall until he saw the sign over the door that read, 'Main Office'. Ameen walked into the office and got the attention of a lady behind the desk on the other side of the counter. The lady was slim and mature, but she was attractive. "Security asked me to tell you to call one of your teachers down here and tell her that she needs to move her car. DPW is outside, and they're trying to work on a water main in the parking lot. Her car is in the way."

"What teacher would that be, baby?"

"Uhhhh, a Mrs. Jasper. Drives the forest green Cadillac CTS."

"Okay. That would be Donna Jasper. Our English teacher. Let me call her classroom."

Sitting behind the wheel of the van fifteen minutes later, Ameen watched a short, petite woman, stylishly dressed, walk out of the school's door and head for the Cadillac CTS. Khadafi stood next to it as he wrote something on a clipboard. Ameen watched Khadafi engage her in conversation. Starting up the van, he waited for the signal. A few minutes later, he saw it. The side panel door was open. He pulled alongside Khadafi and Fella's mother and called out to her to get her attention. As soon as she turned her head, Khadafi made his move. In one swift motion, he scooped the woman and tossed her into the van. Then he leapt in. Ameen burned rubber getting out of there.

Khadafi held his gun to the woman's head while Ameen taped her wrists and ankles with duct tape. Tears fell down the woman's eyes. The look on her face was one of pure terror, but she didn't utter a word.

"Don't put tape on her mouth, cuz," Khadafi said.

Ameen left her mouth uncovered. After inspecting his handiwork, he climbed back into the driver's seat and pulled the van away from the curb near Deanwood Station.

"Go to my lot and pull into the garage all the way in the back."

Careful to obey all the laws of the road, he drove through the city. He thought about Kenya, but he could still hear Khadafi talking to Fella's mother.

"If your hands were free, I would tell you to wipe your eyes, but they're not, so I won't say that. But what I will say is this: I don't want to hurt you. But I will if I don't get what I want, and who I want. To me this is real simple. It may be a little difficult for you, though. If it is, you die and it's nothing to me. I don't care one way or the other. I need your son to bring somebody to me. A friend of his named Tyger. Do you know Tyger?"

"Yes."

"Do you know how to get in touch with him?"

"No."

"Well, that's okay. Fella knows where he is, and I need you to convince him to bring Tyger to me. If he does, you live to breathe again. If not, he can pay to bury you. It's his choice. I'ma hold you for as long as it takes. Your life for Tyger's. If you start acting crazy, I'ma kill you. If you try to escape, I'ma kill you. If I get mad about anything, I'ma kill you. Do you understand me?"

"Y-y-e-s-s."

"Do you have a cell phone?"

She nodded yes.

"You do? Do you have it with you?"

"It's in my coat pocket."

"That's good. We can call Fella from your phone, and he'll know that this is not a game. As soon as we get to where we're going, you can make that call to Fella. And if you wanna make it through this, you better hope and pray he answers the phone and does exactly what I want him to do."

An hour had passed and still no sign of Fella or Tyger. Ameen sat on the car across from the van where Khadafi and Donna Jasper sat and ate Chinese food. He grabbed the last General Tso boneless wing and ran it around the rim of the red and white paper basket that the food came in to get all the sauce. Then he popped it into his mouth.

"Call him again. He must be sleep," Khadafi told Donna Jasper.

Her ankles were still bound, but the tape around her wrists had been cut and now her hands were free. One of her shoes was missing, probably left in the back of the van as she was hastily dragged to the side of the van and made to sit right next to Khadafi. Donna Jasper dialed a number again and put the phone on speaker. The other end of the phone rang a few times and then someone picked up.

"Hello? Ma, what's up?"

"Fellano, I've been kidnapped!"

Khadafi snatched the phone. "Fella?"

"Dirty Redds?"

"It's Khadafi now, cuz, but for now, Dirty Redds will do. How you doing, cuz? Sorry to hear about your father."

"Aye, slim, you playing a dangerous game now. You taking this shit too far."

"Naw, cuz, I haven't taken it far enough. You ain't seen shit yet. Yesterday, I blew your father's shit clean off in that store. If you don't give up Tyger, I'ma do the same thing to your mother. And then I'ma hunt your whole bloodline and kill it. It's gonna be like the Jaspers never even existed. So, naw, this ain't going too far. Killing everybody that's some kin to you is going too far. But it's the dangerous game that you wanted to play. So, let's play."

"Slim, if you kill my mother . . ."

"What? If I kill your mother, what? What you gon do, cuz? Kill mine? Well, you too late for that. Somebody beat you to that already. My mother been dead since I was seven years old. If you want your mother to live, you need to give me Tyger. Sorta like a trade off. Your mother for Tyger. Then after that, we can do it however you wanna do it. You and I can meet up, pull hammers, and blaze it out like the cowboys did back in the day."

"If you touch my mother—"

"Nigga, fuck your mother!" Khadafi exploded. He stood up and shouted into the phone. "This shit is bigger than your mother, so stop tryna make it about her. You keep talking that tough shit, I'll smoke her ass right now. Say something else besides what I wanna hear and I'ma do it. Go head . . . talk that killer shit. Run your mouth and be the reason the cops come and have to scrape her brains up off the sidewalk. Talk that shit that you talked in Wendy's that day—and watch—no—listen how fast I blow your mother's brains out.

Tell me that 'meeting at the opposite ends of a smoking barrel' shit again . . . I'm listening . . ."

"I'm begging you, slim. Please don't kil—"

"Now you begging. You went from hard to soft in seconds, and all I had to was threaten to kill your mother. Bitch ass nigga, we could've avoided this shit had you just gave up Tyger."

"I didn't think you would involve the innocent."

"Innocent? Cuz, ain't nobody innocent. Nobody. Everybody's guilty of something. Whether they die for their sins or not, nobody is ever completely innocent. The last time we talked I practically begged you to do the right thing and turn Tyger over for what he did. But he wasn't innocent, and neither was all them other muthafuckas that we killed on that basketball court yesterday. Again, you wanted to play rough, so we played rough. Your father and a lot of your men lost their lives in this dangerous game, as you call it. Shall we continue to play rough, or do you wanna hand over Tyger?"

"You got it, slim. You win . . . just don't hurt my mother. I'ma do it."

"I got what? You gon' do what? Break it down for the *message boy*. I'ma little slow. You gon' do what?"

"You said you want Tyger, right? I'ma deliver him to you."

"Glad to hear that, cuz. Now you talking like you got some sense. Give me Tyger and we'll swap out, your mother for him."

"My alive mother, right?"

"Of course. Don't you trust me?"

"When and where?" Fella asked.

"I'll call you back with the details. You just focus on getting Tyger. Leave your phone on and answer it when I call. Your mother's life depends on that one phone call."

# CHAPTER THIRTY-SIX

## TYGER

The world around Tyger had a way of becoming too loud at times, so he had to seek peace and serenity wherever he could find it. And that ended up being at the last place that anyone would ever look for him. At the backdoor of his aunt's house on Burns place, he paused before opening the door. The lights were still on in the living room and kitchen. The house smelled like old cigarettes, chemicals, and blood. A powdery substances had been sprinkled on the rug. Stickers had been placed on all the surfaces, and abandoned coffee cups littered the carpet along with bloodstains. He saw the message the killer left for him on the wall. Sitting down on the steps, he surveyed the whole scene ending with the crime scene tape that he had to duck under to sit on the stairs. Tyger's eyes grew heavy and threatened to shut at any moment. Grief inside his tortured soul wouldn't let him sleep or rest or eat. His haggard appearance would have been shocking at any other time, but he didn't care. Too much had happened, too many lives had been taken for him to care about anything. The knots in his stomach had finally reached his heart and made him empty inside. The dull throb behind his eyes wouldn't subside. He pulled the gun from his waist and turned it over in his hands. Ejecting the clip, Tyger stared at the bullets and imagined something the size of a thimble ending his life, his pain, his suffering. But for some reason, he couldn't bring himself to end it all. He was still the coward that he'd known once as a young boy. He still lived inside him. Tears came to his eyes, and again, he felt the need to apologize to all those whose deaths he'd caused. He repeated the apology over and over again, while hoping that his aunt and cousin could hear him. Tyger hoped that D-Roc and the rest of his homeboys could hear him also. He hoped that Tashia could hear him. After finding out that she was dead, he forgave her for what he thought she might've done. Either way she was dead because of him. Altogether, over twenty people were now dead because of what he had done.

*Was God punishing me for what I did to that teenage girl?* Tyger thought about the scene at the basketball court around the way. The way things had looked twenty minutes after the shooting spree that claimed so many lives, lives of people that he'd known all his life. People he loved. He remembered somebody telling him later that day that Fella's father had been killed at the store where he worked, minutes after the basketball court had been shot up, and that the killer was one of the same two women dressed in black flowing Islamic dresses. He listened to different people describe the two women, and something inside him told him that the two women weren't women at all. They were two men dressed in women's clothes to hide their identities and bad intentions.

"The only thing visible were their eyes," one witness had said.

The cell phone in his pocket vibrated, startling him, breaking his reverie. He pulled the phone out of his pocket and recognized Fella's number. He answered the call. "What's up, slim? I'm sorry to hear about Pops."

"Me too, youngin'. Me too. How you doing?"

"I'm hurtin', slim. I'm hurting bad."

"You ain't the only one. Everybody's hurting and fucked up about what done happened. Who would've thought it, slim? Who would've thought that this would be the year so many of our friends and loved ones died? I mean, it was all good just a week ago. I keep asking myself how do we go on and where does this shit end? Feel me?"

"I feel you, big homie."

"We gotta find this nigga Dirty Redds and find out who that girl's family is. Then we gotta kill them all."

"My thoughts exactly," Tyger whispered.

"Well, I think I gotta line on this nigga. I might know where he's hiding out at."

Tyger's spirits rose instantly. "Is that right?"

"Yeah. That's why I called. I'm waiting for a bitch I know to call me back and tell me if he's still at that spot in Park Chester. If he's there, we'll only have minutes to get there to make sure he doesn't leave. So you come on and hook up with me and we'll check on that line, then kill some shit."

He stood up and wiped the tears from his eyes. "That's what I'm talkin' about. Where are you?"

"Meet me on Shannon Place. In the back of the Big Chair."

"I'm on my way."

******

Tyger spotted Fella as he pulled onto the block. He was standing outside beside his Navigator. His head was down at first, but it rose as he parked. The fact that his family was dead and that it was partially Fella's fault crossed his mind. This made him renew the vow to kill him after everything was said and done and all his enemies were dead. He walked up the street toward Fella.

As soon as he was within earshot, he heard him say, "Me and my father were never really close, but he was still my father. We didn't agree about how I should live my life. Can you believe that shit? Me and that man never really saw eye to eye, and I hadn't spoken to him in months. Had I known, slim, that some shit like this was gon' happen, I would've treated him better and told him I loved him more. He just wanted me to do right, that's all. Now to know that my lifestyle got that man killed, that shit hurts like a muthafucka. Niggas gotta treasure their loved ones more while they're here because no one knows when this shit is gonna end. And when it ends, that's it. My man D-Roc is gone, slim. Shit is all fucked up."

Tyger looked at Fella crying. His shoulders sagged and his body language showed defeat. He could visibly see that the big homie was crushed behind the most recent deaths of their friends and his father. He felt his pain one hundred percent, but he stood there in the street, speechless.

"Blue is in the hospital. They saying that he might not make it . . ." Fella continued. "D-Roc's mother and sister blame me for his death. Why? I don't even know." Fella looked up at Tyger, his eyes wet with tears. "You ready to put this work in?"

"You don't even have to ask."

"Good, because I heard back from the broad, and she says that Dirty Redds is there. He's at an apartment in Park Chester. You gon' ride with me. Leave your car parked here and it'll be safe. Let's bounce."

They rode about seven blocks to the bottom of Barry Farms projects. Fella stopped the Navigator and double parked by a patch of woods near the fence that surrounded the rec center. They both exited the SUV. Tyger knew that Park Chester projects were up the street from them, but he couldn't understand why Fella picked the small desolate street called Firth Sterling to park on. The walk to Park Chester was easily three city blocks, and the run back to the truck would be like running a marathon in Boston, but again, he kept his mouth closed.

As if he'd read Tyger's mind, Fella walked around the truck to his side and explained, "I don't want to drive through Park Chester and take the risk of somebody knowing one of us. We gon' walk straight up Sumner Road and hit Wade. We can go through the cut on Wade and be in the back of Park Chester. On the way back, we can cut through the woods that lead to St. Elizabeth. They'll lead us right back here. I—hold on a minute, I left something in the truck."

Fella disappeared around the side of the truck.

Down the street, Tyger spotted a single vehicle parked by the curb. It was a dark colored van that stood out on the desolate street, but he paid it no mind and mentally prepared himself for the business at hand. Suddenly, Tyger felt cold steel tap the back of his head and knew that it was a gun.

"Get down on your knees, youngin', and don't make me say it again."

He heard what he heard and knew that it came from the mouth of his homie, but confusion and shock made him stand still. A crushing blow rained down on his head, opening a gash that instantly sent blood down onto his neck. "Slim, what the fuck are you doing?" Tyger muttered, trying to overcome the wooziness.

"Get on your knees, Tyger. I'm not playing with you. Do it, now!" Fella hissed. "Put your hands straight up and fall to your knees."

Through the brain fog, his inner self warned that if he complied with Fella's demands, he'd be a dead man. He couldn't go out like that. Whatever Fella was doing, or going to do to him made no sense, but his voice and his actions told Tyger that he was serious. His life was his own to guard, and he couldn't let it be taken without a fight. He launched a wild elbow to where he perceived Fella's midsection to be. The offensive action caught Fella completely off guard. It connected with his body and he heard the air escape his lungs. Fella was a few inches shorter than Tyger, but he outweighed him by thirty pounds of pure muscle. First Tyger felt Fella's fist connect with his side as he turned to face him, and then he bear hugged him. By then, Fella's hand was reaching for the gun in Tyger's waist. Fella threw him to the ground and grabbed his right wrist. With his other hand, he pummeled Tyger's face and head until he was semi-conscious. Still, Tyger's hand edged toward his waist, but the grip Fella had on his wrist wouldn't allow him any progression toward the gun. Then Fella had it. Tyger felt the Ruger leaving his body. He closed his eyes, knowing that any more fight would be in vain.

Fella kicked him repeatedly. "Didn't-I-tell-you-to-just-get-on-your-knees? Now-look-at-you! Hard headed ass nigga! All this shit is because of you! Stupid ass nigga! You killed that little girl and started this fuckin' war with these niggas, and now every fuckin' body is dead! The whole hood is fucked up and lost. All because of your hardheaded ass. Showing off for that whore ass bitch, Tashia! That bitch was obsessed with Lil' Tyjuan. Did you know that? Pussy whipped ass nigga! Tashia told Beauty everything and she told me. All that shit could've been avoided. You started that shit tryna show off for that bitch. My father is dead because of you. My best friend in the world is dead because of you. All my homies and homegirls died because of you. Now them niggas got my mother because of you. I wanna kill you for every reason that I just said, but I can't! You know why?" Fella stooped all the way down and looked him in the eyes. "Because they want you alive. That girl that you killed had a father and he wants you dead, but he wants to kill you himself. I agreed to let him do that, so I can get my mother back. You for my mother. And since you got my father killed, she's the only parent that I have left. Don't look at me with that betrayed look in your eyes. You knew that one day death would come for you. It's gonna come to claim us all."

An abundance of pain filled Tyger's body, but no pain felt worse than the sting of deception and betrayal. The fact that Fella snaked him, beating him to the punch, hurt worse than any punch, kick, or blow with a gun that Fella could ever inflict. There was a lot that Tyger wanted to say, needed to say to Fella before he left this world, but for some reason, no words came out his mouth.

All he could do was lay there and watch his betrayer pull out a cell phone and dial a number, with his own gun trained on his face.

"Hello? . . . What? I got this under control. He's right here. Now bring me my mother!"

# CHAPTER THIRTY-SEVEN

## AMEEN

"Bring you your mother!" Khadafi spat into the phone. "You gon' get your mother back, cuz. I promise you that. But first thing's first. I need to make sure that that's Tyger you got down there. That could be anybody for all we know."

"It's him. I wouldn't gamble with my mother's life like that," Fella replied.

"I hope not, cuz, because if that dude you got down there on the ground doesn't have light green eyes, I'ma let you listen while I kill your mother. Then I'ma throw her body out in the stre—"

"I just told you it's him!"

"Cuz, shut the fuck up and listen. My man is on the way down there to check slim's eyes. I know you strapped, so take your gun and toss it in the grass to your left. Then get down on your knees beside your man."

"No can do. Didn't you just see me damn near beat slim to death to get him on the ground? If I toss my gun, he gon' try something, and then we gon' have a problem."

Khadafi put the cell phone on mute and turned to face Ameen. "What you think, cuz? I think he's being straight up.

The fight could've been staged, but what would he gain from that? Where could he hide reinforcements? If he involved the cops, they would be all over us by now. It's up to you to go down there while he strapped, but I think he really wants his mother back."

Ameen thought about everything Khadafi said and agreed. Facing Tyger was long overdue, and that blinded his ability to rationalize. "Fuck that nigga and that gun he got, ock! He says that that's Tyger down there, and I'm going down there to see if it is, so I can kill him." Ameen shrugged. "If it's a trick, you know what to do." Without another word, he exited the van and walked down the street toward the two men. He pulled the compact Mac-90 from under his coat as he walked. When he got close enough to Fella, he aimed the Mac at him, seeing one handgun in his hand and another in his pocket, the butt of the gun visible. "Drop your gun, slim."

The gun in his hand clanked as it hit the ground. "You're the dude that shot up the avenue, huh?"

Ameen nodded. "That was me. Plus, I killed Tyger's family and all y'all homies on the basketball court. When your man decided to kill my daughter, everybody he knew became food in the food chain. Take that other gun out of your pocket and drop it, too." He waited for Fella to do what he said before finishing. "You could've stopped all the killing a long time ago, but you didn't. You refused. Now you gotta live with that. Walk down the street until you reach the van. Khadafi and your mother are waiting for you."

He watched as Fella walked, wondering if he even had a clue that he was about to die.

"I hope they kill you and your mother!" the condemned man on the ground shouted to Fella's back. "Coward ass nigga!"

"Shut the fuck up!" Ameen bellowed, walking over and kicking the dude on the ground. Then he stood over him and looked into his light green eyes. Finally, he had found his Tyger.

"Fuck you!" Tyger spat venomously. "Do what you gotta do. Your daughter was a witness against me. She was in the wrong place at the wrong time. And she chose the wrong nigga to mess with."

"Is that right?"

"It wasn't personal. Killing her was necessary. You're a street dude, what would you have done in my position?"

He reached into his pocket and pulled out a small plastic bag. Dumping the contents of the bag onto Tyger's face. His cousin Choppa's severed finger roll onto his chest. Tyger recoiled as he realized what had just hit him. "That's the same thing I thought as I killed your cousin's girlfriend and your aunt. Choppa was guilty but they wasn't. But like you said, they were at the wrong place at the wrong time."

"Fuck you, nigga!"

"Naw, ock," he stated calmly and aimed the Mac at Tyger's face. "Fuck you!" Ameen said, unleashing a burst of .45 bullets into Tyger's face. His head exploded and became a bloody pulp.

It was over. Ameen looked into the sky as tears fell from his eyes. "I got him, baby. You can rest in peace now."

# CHAPTER THIRTY-EIGHT

## KHADAFI

"Face to face again, huh, cuz?" Khadafi lifted the gun at his side and aimed it at Fella. "You said the next time we met it would be at opposite ends of a smoking barrel, right?" He shot Fella in the thigh.

"A-a-r-r-g-g-h!" he yelled out. As the smoke from the gun rose upward, Khadafi said, "I guess that makes you something like a prophet."

Fella clutched at his leg, but kept his eyes on Khadafi. "That was the past, this is the present. You killed my father to get my attention. I didn't get the message. You snatched my mother and now I get it. I'm here. You got me and I gave you Tyger. Let my mother go."

"I can't do that, cuz. She saw too much. Heard too much."

"C'mon, slim," Fella pleaded. "You gave me your word. What's a man without his word?"

Khadafi responded by laughing. "Whoever said that I was a man? I'm not a man anymore, cuz. I'm an animal. Hear me roar . . ." He tilted his head and howled at the moon. "You should've taken my deal when I offered it. Had you just taken your gangsta hat off for a little while, your mother wouldn't even be here now. I was tryna chill, but just like the song says:

*niggas test you when they think your gun got cold.* You and your man made me turn it back up and I'm mad about that." He fired the gun again. This time he hit Fella in the stomach, and feathers exploded out of his North Face coat. Fella clutched at his stomach as if he could somehow stop the flow of blood now seeping out of him. His terrified eyes found Khadafi's.

"Kill me, but let my mother go."

Ameen walked up then and stood beside Khadafi. "Was it him, cuz?"

"Yeah, ock. I finished him."

"Well, it's time for me to do the same." Khadafi's next bullet struck Fella in the face and knocked his head back. When his body collapsed, he walked over and put three more bullets into his face. Then he shook his head. "Tsk, tsk, tsk, another tough guy killed by a message boy."

"Ay, ock?" Ameen shouted from the side of the van.

Khadafi walked over. "Yeah, cuz?"

"What did you do with the mother?"

"What do you mean, 'what did I do with the mother?' I didn't do shit with the mother."

"Well, she ain't here," Ameen said.

He peered into the van from the side. It was empty. Two cut strips of tape lay in the spot where Donna Jasper had once been. "What the fuck? How in the hell—" How long had Fella's mother been gone? Five minutes? Ten? And where the hell had she slipped off to without him noticing? Khadafi dropped down and looked under the van. Nothing. He dashed around the van in search of a possible escape route. It didn't take long for him to spot one.

On the same side of the street where the van was parked, were two dilapidated buildings. Right where the two buildings met was a small cut. It ran all the way through to the highway.

"Fuck!" Khadafi said. "Cuz, let's bounce. Ain't no telling how long she been gone."

As the van pulled away from the curb with Ameen behind the wheel, Khadafi felt robbed. Robbed of his chance to kill again.

"Fella's mother can't really identify us, but she did hear Fella call you Dirty Redds. That might be enough to put the cops on your line. Especially that detective . . . what's his name again?"

"Tolliver. Maurice Tolliver."

"Yeah, him."

"Fuck the police, cuz. They better find me before I find her ass. Bright and early tomorrow morning, I'ma start hunting her. She's living on borrowed time, and she don't even know it."

"Ay, ock, I appreciate you sticking your neck out for me like that. I called and you came. I will never forget that. I couldn't have pulled this off without you."

"Don't even trip, cuz. That's what I'm here for. You would've done the same for me, and we both know that."

The next ten minutes passed in silence. Ameen finally turned into the parking lot where his Lexus was parked. He put the van in park, turned to Khadafi and said, "Call me tomorrow, ock, but call the store. I gotta get a new cell."

"A'ight, cuz. I'll do that."

Ameen slid out of the van. A voice whispered in Khadafi's ear. He called out to Ameen. "Ay, cuz?"

He stopped in his tracks. "What's up, ock?"

"Gimme them guns you got so I can get rid of them. The less evidence the cops can find, the better."

Ameen thought for a minute, then said, "Yeah, you right, ock." He pulled the compact sub machine gun from under his coat first, and then handed Khadafi two handguns. Khadafi tossed the guns under the passenger seat and waited until Ameen was all the way out of the van before climbing into the driver's seat. He watched Ameen walk to his car and get inside, despite what he'd just said and how he replied to it. Khadafi couldn't shake the impulse to give in to his demons, the voices inside his head. Blowing the horn to get Ameen's attention, he jumped out the van and approached Ameen's Lexus on the driver's side. Pulling the gun as he walked, Khadafi cuffed it by his side out of sight.

Ameen let the window down. "What's good, ock? Forgot something?"

"Yeah . . ." Khadafi went to lift his arm and bring the gun up, but for some strange reason, it didn't move. His arm felt immobile. With his other hand, he pulled out a cell phone and tossed it to Ameen. "Here, take this. Just in case I really need to reach you. At least until you cop something else."

"Good thinking, ock. One love."

The Lexus pulled off, and all Khadafi could do was stand there and watch it leave. "Dammit!" he muttered as he walked back to the van. What had just happened had him vexed. It was something that he would never understand. It was as if a force greater than Khadafi had stopped him from killing Ameen. To him that was an omen. He could never try to kill Ameen again. He had to finally let the past go. It was time to focus on the present and the future. And Marnie. He got in the van and headed for home, but then he stopped the van in the middle of the street. Something told him not to go home because if he did and Marnie had gotten an abortion like she threatened, he was sure there was no force great enough to stop him from killing her. Khadafi made a U-turn and headed for the lot.

# Chapter Thirty-nine

## Ameen

Music calms the savage beast, and Ameen needed to calm down. He put on a song in the Lexus that he needed to hear. The Mariah Carey and Boyz II Men classic always made him feel better. Mainly because Ameen truly believed that one sweet day, he'd see his daughter again. And that belief always conflicted with his Islamic faith, but he held on to it anyway. Otherwise, he'd go crazy. Killing the green-eyed dude, Tyger, lifted a load from his shoulder, but it did nothing to patch up the hole deeply embedded in his heart. He could still see his daughter's face, hear her voice in his head. Tears formed in his eyes again, and he wiped them away. The heat in the car was making him sweat, so he turned it all the way off and cracked the window a little. He picked up Khadafi's cell phone and dialed home. What Ameen needed was to hear Shawnay's voice. When the phone went to voice mail, he hung up and dialed again. The voice mail clicked on a second time. Checking his watch, he saw that it was only 9:57 p.m. Shawnay would be at home getting Asia ready for school the next day, and tucking Kay Kay in, but up walking around nonetheless. So why wasn't she answering the phone? He decided to try her cell phone and see if she had stepped out or something. The voice mail on her cell picked up, and suddenly he got a funny feeling in his gut. Ameen pushed the Lexus to do the limit so he could get home as fast as he could. All kinds of wild thoughts entered his head along the way, and he prayed to Allah to protect his family. Even though all of his known enemies were dead, he could still imagine someone at his home doing unspeakable things to his family. Then something told him to calm down and that he was overreacting. Taking a couple deep breaths, he dialed home again. Still no answer. With his heart now racing uncontrollably, he bent the corners in his neighborhood, fast and furious.

Minutes later, he pulled into the driveway. Shawnay's car was not there. Killing the engine, he searched the block for Shawnay's car, but didn't see it anywhere. Again, he glanced at his watch: 10:13 p.m. "Where the hell . . ." Ameen picked up the cell phone and dialed Shawnay's cell. No answer. He looked at the house and noticed all the lights out. He reached for his gun as he stepped out the car, but then he remembered that he'd given all the guns to Khadafi.

"Shit!" he muttered as he approached the house from the side. He let himself in the back door and turned on all the lights as he walked through it. The house had that empty ass feeling, but he checked the whole house anyway. For the life of him, he couldn't figure out where his family could be. He tried a different angle and called his daughter's cell phone. Asia's cell phone went straight to voice mail. That was strange. But things got even stranger in the bedroom. All he could do was stop in his tracks and stare at the drawers. Each was extended and empty. As if they left in haste.

A look of pure confusion crossed his face as he walked into Shawnay's walk-in closet. It too was empty. All of her things were gone, her shoes, handbags, and accessories.

Everything was gone. Turning, he quickly rushed into Asia's bedroom. Her dresser and closet were empty as well. As the realization of what had happened dawned on him, he slowly walked into Kay Kay's small bedroom, knowing exactly what he'd find. His things were gone, too. All Ameen could do was lean against the wall and wonder where he had gone wrong. And how had things gotten so incredibly bad so fast? All the strength left his body, and he allowed himself to drop to the floor. He sat on his butt and pulled both of his knees in close, hugging them as he cried.

And then suddenly he was back in the cell in Beaumont Pen, the day he found out that Shawnay had betrayed him and slept with Khadafi. Ameen sat in the same position then, and cried as he did now. The pain he felt was exactly the same. Abandonment was the same as betrayal. He wanted to pick himself up off the floor, but he couldn't. His limbs wouldn't cooperate. They had a mind of their own, and they knew that Ameen's family was gone. Shawnay had made good on her threat to leave, and just the acceptance of that alone broke his spirits, killed his soul. He knew deep inside that trying to find her tonight would be fruitless. Her decision to leave, and following through with it was well executed. No telling how long she'd been gone. The last time he'd seen Shawnay and the kids was that morning at breakfast before he'd left to go meet Khadafi at his shop. He had been so caught up in finding and killing Tyger, that he never noticed anything wrong with Shawnay. He never saw her exodus coming. As the tears now rushed down his eyes unabated, he thought about what Shawnay had said to him in the basement, days ago: *I can't go back to those days when I lived in fear, Antonio. Not for you, not for anyone. I won't regress back to being afraid. I can't. I won't. And that's what I'd be doing if I allowed myself to stay in this situation.*

Ameen could hear her voice as clearly as the day she had uttered every word. *I have to protect what family I have left, since you have so little regard for us . . . If you continue to let your puffed up pride, narcissism, and ego cause you to continue killing people in my daughter's name, I'm leaving you. I'ma leave Arlington, and I'm taking the kids with me. I have already lost one child and my grandmother. I'll be goddamned if I'm gonna stand by and wait to lose you. And this time when I move, I'm a make sure that it's far, far away.*

His every thought turned to everything Shawnay had done to him over the years, then settled on what she'd done now. He wiped at the tears in his eyes, and his heart turned cold. The resentment and hurt was replaced by anger. Then an uncontrollable rage. That rage lifted him off the floor and onto his feet. He looked around at Kashon's bedroom, devoid of anything personal to remind Ameen of him. Shawnay had no right to abandon him at a time when he needed her most.

# CHAPTER FORTY

## DETECTIVE TOLLIVER

"Now that you've had the chance to sit and pick my brain, doc, what's the verdict?"

"You mean diagnosis?" Dr. Sandra Gilbraith asked, but continued to write in a notepad and folder on her desk.

"Yeah, that's what I meant. The diagnosis. What is it? Am I insane, or was one session not enough for you to make that determination?"

"Oh, you're definitely sane, detective. A bit obtuse, but sane. I am gonna prescribe you a mild sedative to relax you when your OCD kicks in."

"Obsessive compulsive disorder!" *Ain't that a bitch? Now I'm a nutcase with OCD.* Moe shook his head as he thought about the psychologist's diagnosis yesterday. Finished with answering the call to nature, he shook his package, put it back in his boxer briefs, and washed his hands.

His cell phone belted out the ringtone he'd programmed for all phones at work. "Shit!" he cursed, trying to dry his hands on his pants. He answered the call after grabbing the cell phone from his pants pocket.

"Captain Dunlap, Moe. Gotta minute?"

"I did what you told me to, Cap—"

"I already know that, Moe. I have Gilbraith's report on my desk. That's not why I called."

"That's what I was afraid of. You're suspending me?"

"Suspending you? For chrissakes, no. Today, earlier this morning, a woman was kidnapped from the school where she works. Called to the parking lot by a person impersonating a janitor and a man disguised as someone from the Department of Public Works. Told her she needed to move her car. She was snatched and thrown into a dark colored cargo van. We have been all over the case since it was discovered that she was missing. Well, about forty minutes ago, a motorist called in to report a woman running down the freeway on 295 frantically waving down cars. We send out a few cars and guess what? The woman turns out to be our kidnapped teacher. She managed to escape her captors. The woman's name is Donna Jasper—"

*Why is the name Jasper ringing a bell in my head?* Moe thought.

"—has been here at the station talking to her since she walked in the door. She said that her captors—neither that she could positively ID—forced her to call her son—"

Moe's heart sped up. "Fellano Jasper!"

"Now you see why I called you? Before coming in, the woman took officers to the place where she escaped the van. On Firth Sterling. We found two bodies out there, Moe."

"Khadafi!"

"I think you were right about what you told me, Moe."

"Fella ran the Avenue. Wait, you said two bodies—the other guy was Darius Queen?"

"No, it was the guy that you put out the all points on. Terrell Holloway."

"The guy that killed Kenya Dickerson. Khadafi is friends with Kenya Dickerson's father. The two men who kidnapped that woman were Luther Fuller and Antonio Felder. I'm sure of it."

"You're sure of it, but can you prove it?"

"Give me the case back, and I'll do all I can to prove it."

"You got it. And you need to start by talking to Donna Jasper. She's hysterical about her son, but she's lucid and willing to talk. Another reason I called was to tell you that you were right, and that I should've listened to you when you told me your theory on Burns Place. Rio Jefferson told me to let you know that the woman told him that her son called one of the captors, Dirty Redds. And we both know who the hell that is. C'mon in, we need to talk and not over the phone."

*****

"Donna Jasper thought real hard and remembered the man dressed in the DPW uniform was a cinnamon complexion with freckles speckled across his cheeks and nose," Captain Dunlap told Moe as they walked through the precinct. "We showed her a picture of Luther Fuller, and she said that it could be him. She's only like eighty percent sure. According to her, the man called Dirty Redds by her son was wearing a hat with a bill the entire time. The other man wore a crown of some kind and had long dreads sticking out from under the—"

"It's a hat that they sell in stores. Real popular with criminals because of the fake dreads sewn onto the back of it. I'm familiar with them."

"The ID won't stand up in court, but we both know that it was Fuller. And here's the kicker: we can't connect Fuller to the murders on Firth Sterling. Donna Jasper wasn't there when the killings happened. Unless forensics can connect the dots, we're shooting a blank on nailing Fuller on anything."

"So why did you call me down here, Cap? I'm confused," Moe asked.

Captain Dunlap stopped in his tracks and looked around the precinct. He spotted a sign that led to a fire exit. He jerked his head in that direction. "In there."

The two men walked into the fire exit stairwell. Once the door was shut, Captain Dunlap said, "You have the most intel and insight on Fuller. I've had it up to here"—the captain raised his hand high over his head—"with that scumbag. I'm tired of his shit, Moe! And I'm frustrated that the system doesn't work in regards to him. So, I want you to take him down. Do whatever you have to do, but goddammit, I want you to take him down. All the way down, if you have to. Am I making myself clear?"

Moe nodded.

"Officially, we can't touch him until we can prove he did something. But unofficially, we know he did something, so I'm giving you permission to nail his ass. Are we on the same page?"

"Definitely," Moe replied, feeling like Pat Garrett being told to shoot Billy the Kid in the back if he had to. He turned to leave the small confines of the stairwell, but stopped in his tracks. "Thanks, Cap."

"Don't thank me until it's over. That muthafucka has to be stopped."

*****

"Rio, did you find any guns at the scene of the murders on Firth Sterling?" Moe asked.

"Nein," Rio replied and smiled. "That's German for no. I've been working on my German for a trip to Germany this summer. No guns recovered from the scene. Just the bodies and shell casings. Two different kinds of casings that suggest there were two killers. Which makes even more sense when you consider that the two men were killed almost a block away from each other."

"That far?" Moe asked incredulously.

Rio nodded. "One was killed about twenty feet away from where the vehicle we believe they both arrived in was parked. Double parked. It was a silver Navigator registered to Donna Jasper. We also found a severed finger—"

"Curtis Holloway was missing a finger, right?"

"Right. It was the finger used to write the message left on the wall in the house on Burns. Hopefully, we can pull a print off it, or the plastic bag that we found. Then compare them to the prints we found in the Navigator."

"And what you've already told me is all that Donna Jasper could remember about the second captor?"

"That's it."

"I'm willing to bet you that it was Antonio Felder."

"The most likely suspect if your theory is true, and Terrell Holloway killed his daughter."

"He did it. And he had serious help. Did you put the APB out on Fuller yet?"

"I did it about twenty minutes ago."

"Is Donna Jasper still in the building?"

"No. Why?"

"I need to talk to her myself. Did she say anything about where she thinks she was before they went to Firth Sterling? What she heard while waiting in the van? Conversations that she heard? Anything like that?"

"Let me think . . . she said she was in a garage of some kind when they forced her to call her son. They fed her Chinese food. That's about it."

"They took her to Khadafi's car lot on New York Avenue. Get a search warrant, Rio. There's a small garage on the premises. Donna Jasper might recognize it." Moe grabbed his coat and hat. "I'm also thinking the dark colored cargo van might still be there, too."

"And you? Where're you going?"

"Guess. You get the warrant. I'm going to get Khadafi."

*****

It was almost eleven o'clock at night and the chains that locked the fences around Imperial Autos were unlatched and hanging. The entrance fence was open. Why? It was too late to be still open for business. There had to be somebody inside, somewhere. And that someone had to be Khadafi. Moe's pulse quickened. From his position across the street, he could see the garage at the rear of the lot. Climbing out the truck, he walked across the street, careful to stay in the shadows. He needed a closer look at everything.

The acre of land that facilitated rows of cars and trucks was well lit. The double wide trailer had to be where the office was. He didn't see any vehicle parked directly in front of the trailer, but that didn't mean that one wasn't nearby. One that Khadafi was possibly driving. Moe didn't see the

Range Rover anywhere. Neither did he see a dark colored cargo van. Again, his eyes focused on the garage. Was the Range Rover and the van in there? He crept along the fence until he was near the rear of the lot. Then Moe climbed the fence to look into one of the windows of the garage. The lights in the garage were out, but enough light from the lot allowed him to see inside. He smiled as he made out what appeared to be a van inside the garage. A cargo van. Leaping down from the fence, he pulled out his cell phone and dialed Dispatch. "This is Detective Maurice Tolliver. I need you to send back up to Imperial Autos."

*****

"This guy is extremely dangerous. He's more than likely armed and he won't go down easily," Moe announced to the crowd of uniformed police officers gathered around him, down the block from the car lot. "He's a stone-cold killer wanted for kidnapping and assault. Let's bring him in effectively by the book, but if he so much as moves without permission, do not hesitate to put him down." He let his words resonate for a minute, before continuing. "If it's him on that lot, we gotta get him. It's just that simple. Let's go."

They stormed the car lot like ants in search of food. A lone figure appeared in the doorway of the trailer. Moe's heart rate increased. "You in the trailer, keep your hands completely visible and step out onto the front now!" he bellowed. The lone figure complied. The light shined in his face and Moe's heart sank. It wasn't him. The man in the trailer front wasn't Khadafi. "Stand down! I repeat. Stand down! It's not him. Good job, men. Sir, walk to me," Moe told the man on the front. When he was within earshot, he asked, "Is Luther Fuller on the premises?"

"No. I'm here by myself."

"Somebody get this man's name for me. I need to take a look in that garage."

# CHAPTER FORTY-ONE

## KHADAFI

At the line where D.C. stopped and Virginia started was a bridge. The Woodrow Wilson Bridge. Khadafi parked the Range Rover and hopped out on the trail that led directly under the bridge. In his hand was a bag with five guns inside. Murder weapons that needed to be disposed. He followed the trail to the water, totally unafraid of the darkness that surrounded him. At the water's edge, he stood on a small embankment and tossed each gun into the Potomac River. All in different directions. Discarding the Mac-90 hurt him the most. She was a beauty and a bad muthafucka. From his position on the embankment, he could see the bright lights of the city. Nostalgia kicked in and suddenly, he longed for the days of old. The days that he'd spent with Kemie. The questions that Marnie had asked him that morning came to mind, and he remembered the answers he gave. They were the truth. His truth. Khadafi's eyes watered, and he had to wipe away the tears. Then as quickly as the melancholy hit him, it left. Leaving wrath in its place. Kemie wasn't supposed to be dead. He put his hand in his waist and massaged the .45 ACP under his shirt. Khadafi needed a quick release to ease the tension. He pulled out the Trac-Fone he purchased from CVS and dialed a number.

After the third ring, a female voice said, "Hello?"

"What's good with you, sexy?"

"Who is this?" Erykah asked.

"Khadafi."

"Oh . . . what's up?"

"Damn, you said that like you don't wanna talk to me. Was you busy? In the middle of something or somebody?"

"Naw, you good. I'm cooling. What made you decide to call me now?"

"What you mean?"

"What you mean, 'what I mean?'"

"I don't know what you talking about. What did I do wrong?"

"I never heard from you after we did what we did. You were supposed to call."

"Oh, my bad. I was on some other shit that was top priority. I wasn't ducking you. I was just busy. In any event, I'm thinking about you now and I called. What's up with you?"

"Ain't shit up with me. I just told you that I'm cooling. What you want to be up?"

"I'm tryna come through and recreate a few magical moments. What's up?"

After an eternity of silence, Erykah replied, "Yea, a'ight. Come on through. You know the address. I'll see you when you get here."

"You want me to stop and get you something?"

"Naw, I'm good. Just make sure you bring some protection."

"You got that. But hey, let me ask you something."

"What's up?"

"Are your toes polished?"

"Are my toes polished?" Erykah repeated. "Why you ask me that?"

"Because the last time we were together, they weren't."

"You never told me that they needed to be. What? You gotta foot fetish, huh?"

"Something like that."

"Well, they aren't polished, but they could be by the time you get here. What color do you want them to be?"

"Red, baby. Blood red. That's my favorite color."

"I'm on it. I'll see you in a few."

As he ended the call with Erykah, he thought about Marnie. He thought about calling her, but then he changed his mind.

*****

The next morning he woke up to breakfast and head. After a long night of animalistic sex, he thought that Erykah's insatiable appetite for all things Khadafi was sated, but he was wrong. He looked down at his body and watched Erykah as she watched him, all the while twisting, stroking, and sucking his dick. Khadafi's eyes opened and closed and his body responded accordingly. His toes curled and his fingers gripped the satin sheets. He felt like he was on a wild roller coaster ride with Roxy Reynolds and Pinky, both sucking his dick and he was about to fall off. Khadafi held on for dear life until he couldn't any longer. He had to let go. Khadafi let go. And when he did, Erykah swallowed every drop of semen that left his body.

*****

"Let me see your cell phone."

Erykah looked at him as if he'd gone crazy.

"Cuz, your pussy is good and your head is even better, but don't ever get it twisted. It's gon' take way more than that to make me act like a sucka. I'm not tryna check your phone. I need to use it to make a couple calls."

"Where your phone at?" Erykah spat.

"Last night I called you from a throwaway joint. I just tried to use it and that shit ain't even picking up a signal."

Erykah disappeared into the back room and reappeared a few minutes later. She tossed her phone at him. He caught it in the air.

"Don't be calling none of your bitches on my phone. I'm not tryna be getting my shit blown up by jealous hoes."

Ignoring Erykah, he dialed voice mail and entered the access code. The mailbox was full. Eighty percent of the missed calls were from Marnie. He skipped them all. One message was from Ameen. He called from his house phone, knowing that Khadafi would check his messages. He told him to call him when he got the message. Then there were at least five calls from Pee-Wee, all marked urgent. Khadafi called him immediately, but got no answer. All of Pee-Wee's calls were from last night. He left him a message to call the Trac-Fone as soon as possible. Then he called Ameen, who answered on the second ring. "Assalaamu alaikum, cuz. What's good?"

"Shawnay left me, ock," Ameen said.

"Shawnay left you how? When?"

"When I got home last night, she was gone. Her and the kids. All their stuff. They're all gone."

"But how? Where?"

"Everything that happened was too much for her. And me doing what I was doing—it scared her. I told you she put two and two together and came up with four. The day she told me she knew that I was—"

"Watch the jack, cuz."

"My bad. The day she came clean about what she knew, she gave me an ultimatum. Either stop what I was doing or she'd leave me. Those were her exact words. I didn't believe her."

No matter how hard he tried, Khadafi couldn't find the words to comfort Ameen. Last night he had almost killed the man, and then today he felt his pain. Life is a fickled bitch that loves getting fucked around. "Cuz, I'm sorry. I don't know what else to say."

"That's the thing, ock. There ain't nothing that you can say. There's nothing that no one can say. But I know what I gotta do. I gotta find my family. I can't live without them." And with that said, Ameen hung up the phone.

With Khadafi's mind still befogged with Ameen's situation, he called Pee-Wee back. This time, he answered.

"Man, slim, where the fuck have you been? I been calling you since last night."

"I don't have my phone. But what's up? What's so urgent?"

"The cops are looking for you, slim. They raided the lot last night after you left."

All Khadafi could do was smile. The cops work fast and apparently, Donna Jasper had told them enough to come after him. “Did they say what they were looking for me for?”

“Naw. But they came back this morning and impounded that black van in the garage. They had warrants and everything. What did you do?”

“I'ma call you back, cuz,” he said and quickly ended the call with Pee-Wee.

Khadafi dropped Erykah's phone on the couch. He stood up and went after the rest of his clothes and coat. “I gotta bounce, E. Something came up. I'ma call you when I get free later.” He pulled out a wad of money and peeled off a few large bills and dropped them on the coffee table by the couch. Erykah didn't say a word as he left, and he was glad that she didn't.

Outside in the Range, he thought about the fact that he was now a wanted man. Khadafi had been so preoccupied with getting rid of the guns that he never even thought to get rid of the van. That was his mistake. The van wouldn't be much help to the cops’ case, though, if they could build one. The floor of the van had been stripped bare of carpet, so no fibers belonging to Donna Jasper would be found. There would be no blood to detect. All they would get from that van was fingerprints. His, Ameen's, and the other ten to twenty people who had probably been inside the van before he bought it at the auction. So far, the key to whatever case the cops had was Donna Jasper. So, she had to die.

As he drove through the city, he wondered how had they ID’ed him so quickly when he was wearing a disguise? All kind of thoughts were going through his head until a horn blowing snapped him out of the musing. He happened to look in the rearview mirror, and his survival instincts kicked in. A black Camaro drove behind him, and it was the same Camaro that pulled behind him once he pulled off Erykah's street. Pulling out the .45 ACP, he set it on his lap and kept his eyes on the Camaro as his ire surged. He decided right then and there to cook whatever beef the occupants of the Camaro had. Up ahead was a stop light. If it was time to cook the beef, at the light, he'd fire up the grill.

# Chapter Forty-two

## Detective Tolliver

"I told you to get Fuller, Moe, but I didn't tell you to take half the fuckin' department with you to do it! Remember the conversation we had? Remember where we had it?"

"Captain, I had a hunch—"

"A hunch? It stopped being a hunch when you involved everybody else in it. You wasted time, resources, and manpower on a fuckin' hunch. You fuckin' made me look bad. That's what you did."

"I'm sorry, Cap. I saw the van . . . the fence was unlocked. I thought Khadafi was there."

"Get the fuck out!"

"Cap, I—"

"I said get the fuck out! Now Moe. Get out!"

Last night had gone badly, and he didn't blame Dunlap for being upset. Moe fucked up and placed the blame where it belonged, with himself. He knew better than to proceed like he did with no visual of the suspect. All morning he sat and wondered where Khadafi could be. He needed to get him off the streets before somebody else died. Donna Jasper's life was in danger as long as Khadafi was free. Moe glanced up at the homicide board on the wall in front of him. Tyjuan Glover and Kenya Dickerson's names had been scratched out because their cases were marked closed with the death of Terrell Holloway.

But now his name, along with Fellano Jasper, was up on the board. Their names were right below Linda Holloway, Larcel Davis, Curtis Holloway, and Frank Jasper. He reread the list of names and shook his head. There was no doubt in his mind that all the names left on the board were in fact killed by two men. Antonio Felder and Khadafi. But until he could prove that, he had nothing. Moe opened a file on his desk and searched again for a possible address where he might find Khadafi. Then he remembered something, and didn't know why he'd never thought of it before. Picking up the phone on his desk, he dialed a friend. "Hey, Marjorie. I need you again. Imperial Autos is registered to a Ms. Mary Henderson. Yeah . . . Imperial with an 'I.' Right. I need an address for her . . . Yeah. I'm at my desk . . . Yeah. Call me back."

While he waited for Marjorie to call back, he dialed Rio Jefferson.

"Hey, Moe, I swear you must be psychic. I was just about to call you."

"They say great minds think alike. What's up on your end?"

"I hear that you're sorta a curse right now. I can end up in Smiley's doghouse by just talking to you."

Moe feigned mock indignation. "Who, me? The dog house is big enough for all my dawgs. Seriously though, I called to ask you about that case that Khadafi caught out Maryland a few years ago."

"The domestic beef?"

"Yeah, that one. Tell me about it."

Rio ran the whole story down.

"Was that Monica Curry?"

"Naw. Back then he was with Rakemie Bryant."

"You're right. I remember now. I spoke to her before. Do you think you can get me a copy of that report or at the very least, the address of the house where that happened?"

"Sure. But what are you up to?"

"Nothing. Just following a hunch."

"A hunch? From what I hear, your hunches will get a guy canned around these parts. I want no parts of it, but I'll get back with you on that info."

"You do that, buddy." Moe had just hung up with Rio when Marjorie called him back.

"Hey, Marj. What do you got? . . . Is that right? Let me grab a pen . . ."

# CHAPTER FORTY-THREE

## KHADAFI

What Khadafi thought was cooked beef turned out to be paranoia. He couldn't help but laugh at the situation from earlier when he thought the black Camaro was following him. At the light, he'd hopped out just as planned. But when he ran up on the car, what he saw made him smile. The driver was a woman that looked like a man, and the passenger was an old man. Taking his hand off the gun under his shirt, he walked away laughing.

Before he could even get his key out the door, he heard his daughter shout, "Daddy!" and then turned the corner at full speed. She ran up to him and leapt into his arms. He hugged her tight and kissed her face. "Now what if I wouldn't have caught you, pretty girl? What would you have done then? Huh?"

Khadajah didn't respond. All she did was giggle and hug his neck tight. Her laughter warmed Khadafi's soul. He never thought he could love another person as much as he did Kemie, his mother, his uncle. But he did. His love for Khadajah was unparalleled. Khadafi looked past his daughter and suddenly saw her mother. Marnie leaned on the wall with her arms folded across her chest. Her hair was different. A different color. When he'd seen her last, her hair had been red. Now it was two different shades of brown. It matched the polish on her fingers and toes and the brown and white scrubs top that she had on. From the waist down, Marnie wore only white lace boy shorts. His eyes instantly dropped to the middle of her shorts. Her pussy was so phat that it bulged out as if it were permanently swollen. Aroused, his dick stirred in his pants and then a pain shot through him, reminding him about the Olympic-styled sex he'd had for most of the night with Erykah.

"You pulling all nighters, now, huh?" Marnie spoke, killing his vibe.

"Don't start with the bullshit, cuz. I'm not in the mood."

"Stopped answering your phone and shit. Stayed out all night . . . That must've been some pretty good pussy you was in. Couldn't even get up out of it long enough to check on your girl and your daughter. This must be a new bitch."

Khadafi put Khadajah down and watched her run back to her mother.

Marnie reached down and picked her up.

"Think whatever you wanna think. Somebody snatched Ameen's phone, so I gave him mine."

"Ameen? Since when did y'all become busom buddies again?"'

"That's neither here nor there. Listen, the police believe that we did something, and I gotta bounce for a while until shit calms down. I'ma grab a few things and leave. I'ma cop a new phone so you'll be able to reach me."

"You don't need no excuses to leave, nigga. Just leave. You ain't gotta make up no stories."

"Did you get the abortion?" he asked.

Marnie's response was to walk away.

He turned and jogged up the stairs to their bedroom. Khadafi moved through the room grabbing stuff he thought he'd need. He shed his coat and pulled his sweater over his head. Deep in his heart, he felt bad about the way he was treating Marnie. She hadn't done anything but love him and take care of their daughter. Why should he be mad because she didn't wanna birth another child by a no good nigga like him? Hadn't she been by his side when he needed her every time? The answer was yes. Khadafi sat down on the bed and dropped his head in his hands. Again, he was headed nowhere fast, and it was starting to affect the people he loved. He heard footsteps and then felt soft hands under his tank top, massaging his shoulders. Marnie stepped off the bed and stood directly in front of him. Their eyes connected and melted him. "Marnie, I'm sorry—"

She put her finger to his lips. "Shhh! Don't talk. Let me. This is what I signed up for, remember? I love you so much, Khadafi, that sometimes I feel like I can't breathe without you. I have never felt like this for no other man in my life. And sometimes, I don't get enough attention from you. So, that makes me do and say stupid shit just to get under your skin. I would never kill a child of yours, of ours. No matter what you do or how mad you make me. This baby inside of me deserves to be given a chance at life just like we had. Whatever you did—"

"Somebody killed Ameen's daughter. The sixteen year old. She witnessed a murder, and the dude who committed the murder thought she would tell on him. So he killed her after the funeral she attended—"

"I heard about that. The teenage girl that got killed at the gas station a few weeks ago."

"Yeah, that was Ameen and Shawnay's daughter Kenya."

"Oh my God! That poor girl. Her poor mother and father . . ."'

"Ameen been on a nut about that and I been with him. He came to me and asked for my help because despite what we went through, I'm the only person he trusts. We did some shit and it backfired. Now the cops are looking for me."

"Baby, whatever it is, we gon' deal with it. The same way we did last time. No matter what, I'm with you. Ride or die. Whether it's a year, or life in the pen. You know how I'm built. Plus, we got lawyer money, so fuck the police. Go ahead and bounce and do what you gotta do. Me and Dada gon' be here regardless, and we gon' come running when you call. I love you, boy, with all my heart. Don't ever doubt it or forget it."

His heart swelled with love for the woman standing in front of him. Khadafi pulled her in close and inhaled her scent. "I love you, too, cuz. Where's Dada?"

"She's across the hall in her room. After she saw you she decided she wanted to sleep. I let her take a nap."

"Good. Because I need to make mad passionate love to her mother."

"Handle your business then, brotha. Handle your business."

*****

Khadafi left Marnie curled up under the covers with her eyes closed. His dick was like Kryptonite to her Superwoman ass. He put the keys to the Range Rover on the dresser and swapped them out for the keys to the Escalade off Marnie's key ring. Then he grabbed his bag and gun and looked in on his daughter. Khadajah slept just as peacefully as her mother. He kissed her face and left.

Outside in the carport, he tossed the bag into the back of the Escalade and then walked over to the Range to retrieve his .45 ACP. Tucking it in his waistband beside the Taurus 9-millimeter, he climbed into the Caddy truck and started it up. Music instantly blared through the speakers. The display screen said that the song was Miley Cyrus' "Adore You." Khadafi listened to it and decided that he liked it.

It didn't take him long to reach Upper Marlboro, Maryland. In the middle of the block on Montrose Avenue was a beige brick three-story house. It was one that he didn't visit often, but he knew it well. He bought it for his aunt right after his uncle was killed.

Khadafi parked the Escalade and walked up the walkway to the front door. It took him a second to locate the right keys, but a minute or so later, he was inside the house. He called his aunt's name to see if she was home. When he received no reply, he walked over to the window to see if her car was parked on the side of the house. It wasn't. That meant she wasn't home. Silently, he thanked Allah and kept it moving. Aunt Mary was Khadafi's heart, but she always asked too many questions. Whenever he visited her, he felt like he was being interrogated by the CIA. Upstairs in the attic, it didn't take long to find what he was looking for. His safe was in the corner behind several boxes of who knows what that his aunt never unpacked.

Opening the safe, Khadafi pulled at a couple bundles of money and dropped them in the bag that he carried on his shoulder. He thought about the money in the safe at the car lot. It was over forty thousand dollars in it. He'd leave that for Pee-Wee to purchase more cars at the auction. Back downstairs, he dropped the bag on the carpet and went to the kitchen to get a snack. His stomach reminded him that he hadn't eaten since that morning at Erykah's. As he turned the corner, he spotted something moving past the window outside. Although, he figured he was tripping, he still walked over to take a second look. Khadafi didn't see anything, but since the window was cracked a little, he could hear leaves or sticks being crunched under someone's weight. *Could it be a dog or something?* he wondered as he pulled one of his guns and put his back on the wall.

Quietly, he made his way out of the kitchen and toward the back of the house. Unlatching the lock on the back sliding glass door, he pulled the ACP and stepped into the backyard. His guns came up simultaneously, as a lone figure stepped into view from the side of the house. Khadafi recognized the person instantly. He had one gun in his hand, pointed directly at Khadafi. He expected to see other cops come from every corner, but to his surprise, none materialized. A smile crossed Khadafi's face. "Trespassing is a crime, ain't it, detective?"

"Put the guns down, Khadafi!" Detective Tolliver replied.

"What about stalking? That's definitely a federal offense. How long you been here waiting for me? Or did you follow me here?"

"In a few minutes, Khadafi, this place is gonna be crawling with cops. If they see you with them guns pointed at me . . . you know how trigger happy PG County police are. Lower your weapons and let's talk this out."

"Talk it out? It's a little too late for that. You're outta jurisdiction. You're behind my people's house, all alone and threatening me. What's there to talk about?"

"Don't be stupid, Khadafi. Put the gun down!"

"The last time I checked, cop, I never gave you permission to call me Khadafi. It's Mr. Fuller to you."

"Whatever you say. Just put the guns down before you make us both do something that we don't wanna do. Nobody has to die here today."

"Why not? It's a little cold, but other than that, the sun is shining. It's a beautiful day to die. But the thing is, I don't plan on being the one who dies today. You put your gun down and I promise I'll let you live. You walk away. I walk away. Nobody will ever know. How about that, cuz?"

The detective shook his head. "I'm not gonna be able to do that, big guy. At the end of the day, I'll know and I'd never be able to live with myself. You've killed too many people, and it has to stop. Here. Now. You have to be stopped."

"And you plan on doing that how?" he asked.

"By taking you in. By any means necessary on the kidnapping charge . . ."

"There's no way in the world I'ma let you arrest me. You must be putting gun powder in your coffee in the mornings, if you think I'ma lay down like that. I'm never going back to prison. Besides, I play the odds and at the moment, the odds ain't in your favor. You got one gun. I got two. Do the math. Then walk away."

"I told you I can't do that. I need you to drop them guns and get down on your knees. Then lace your fingers together behind your head. I—"

Khadafi laughed out loud. "You must be crazy, cuz."

"I've been told that a time or two. C'mon, Khadafi, let it go. You don't want shooting a cop on your record. Do you? Do the right thing and drop the guns. Think about your little girl."

"Fuck you, cuz! How 'bout that?" he spat at the detective. "You don't know me. Or nothing about me." The detective's comment made him ponder the position he was in. It was a catch 22 situation however he looked at it. Khadafi had two options and he couldn't get around them. Either he and the detective gunned each other down, or Khadafi went to jail. One or the other. It didn't look good either way. Right then, everything he had ever done flashed before his eyes. He read somewhere before that in humans, fear increased the metabolism. Which is why things seemed to happen next in slow motion. In super slow motion, Khadafi saw his mother again and then he saw her being killed. He saw himself killing her murderers. Saw himself burying his uncle Marquette. Saw himself killing Bean, Omar, Devon, Lil Cee's mother and sister, the dude in New York, Shayla, Liyah, Ronald Moten, Mark Johnson, Big E. Miller, Chris Bowman and his family and so on. Khadafi thought the images in his head would never stop. He relived every moment in just a few seconds. The next thing he knew, he heard music. DJ Khaled's "No Surrender" featuring Scarface, Meek Mills, and Jadakis. The lyrics to that song made the decision for him. He saw Queen Latifah go out blazing her guns in the movie *Set it Off*. He smiled, looked the detective dead in the eyes and said, "Let's see what's written in the stars for us, cop!"

"Khadafi! Don't do it. Don't make me—"

Khadafi mumbled, "Bis'millah" and went out like a real gangsta, blazing his guns.

# EPILOGUE

## MARNIE

"Marnie!"

"Hey, Ma. What's up?"

"What're you doing?

"I'm feeding Dada her dinner. Why?"

"I need to ask you two questions, but it may be nothing."

"Go 'head."

"Do you remember when Khadafi first came home and his aunt had a cookout?"

"Of course, I remember that."

"Does his aunt still live in that big beige house on Montrose Avenue?"

"His aunt Mary. Yeah, she still lives there. Why?"

"And is Khadafi driving your Escalade?"

Marnie broke the last piece of chicken patty into small pieces and dropped them on her daughter's tray on her high chair. "Ma, you're starting to scare me. Why are you asking me all of this?"

"I saw a house on the news that looks like . . . There's a black Escalade parked outside and there's been a shooting..."

Suddenly, she remembered. Marnie ran out of the kitchen and peeked out the side door. Sure enough, Khadafi's Range Rover sat in the driveway. Khadafi had told her that he was taking the Escalade. She remembered the phone in her hand as panic set in. "Ma, you said you saw something on the news?"

"Baby, it's on the news. Go to channel 7."

Marnie sat on a barstool and clicked on the TV that was mounted on the wall by the cabinets. She put the TV on channel 7. A female news reporter stood outside on a residential street filled with cops, emergency personnel, and other plain clothes people. As a camera shifted, Marnie could see a black Escalade and she really couldn't say that it was hers, but a deep, dark, foreboding feeling sat in the pit of her stomach. Then the camera panned the beige brick house that the news lady stood in front of, and it came into focus.

Although she had only been to Mary Henderson's house two or three times, she could still pick it out of a line up, and the one she had stared at was indeed hers. Marnie's heart rate quickened as she focused on the words that came out of the news woman's mouth.

". . . authorities are trying to to determine exactly what happened here at the rear of the residence behind us. Nothing has been confirmed yet, but a source close to the scene here tells us that a decorated D.C. police officer, and another man, identity unknown, were involved in a gun battle that left both men suffering from gunshot wounds..."

Slowly Marnie rose up off the stool and put her hand over her mouth. Her eyes watered instantly.

"NO!NO!NO!NO! Nnoooo!" she screamed. A startled Khadajah saw her crying and followed suit. Her screams louder than Marnie's.

"Marnie . . . I'm on my way over there," her mother said and hung up. A feeling that she never felt before descended upon her as she dropped the phone. Tears rolled down her cheeks unabated, but she still told herself that it couldn't be Khadafi that the lady was talking about. He was Superman. He couldn't be dead. As her daughter screamed beside her, she stood there in shock. Total shock. Then Marnie snapped out of it. She reached down and picked up her phone and dialed Khadafi's phone, but then she remembered he'd said his friend Ameen had it. Ending the connection, Marnie felt helpless, so she walked over and picked up her daughter and tried to comfort her as best she could. But who would comfort Marnie? As she rocked Khadajah, Marnie prayed that Khadafi was okay. That could be anybody dead in the rear of his aunt's house. It didn't have to be him.

Dressed in jeans, a sweatshirt, boots, and a Gortex ski coat, she rushed out the door of her house, leaving Khadajah with her mother. All the while still telling herself that Khadafi was alive and good. Marnie pushed the Range Rover around the Capital Beltway at break neck speed in route to Upper Marlboro. The sun had gone all the way down by the time she reached Montrose Avenue. The middle of the entire block was cordoned off, and yellow crime scene tape was all around the beige house, Khadafi's aunt house. Throngs of police, both from Maryland and D.C. congregated all around the house. Different news outlets were there as well, with all the equipment and vehicles. Marnie found a place to double park and got out the truck. She walked down the block, past all the curious onlookers, and other people and walked straight up to the grassy area that led behind the house. As she ducked under the yellow tape, a voice yelled, "Ma'am, you can't go back there!" But she kept walking, almost as if in a trance. In seconds, strong hands grabbed her arm.

Marnie turned to see the face that the hands belonged to. Her eyes were filled with tears. "My boyfriend . . . this is his house. I need to know if he's one of the people dead here."

"I understand, ma'am. I really do, but I still can't let you go back there. This is a crime scene, ma'am, but I think I know who can help you. Hey, Detective Jefferson? Can you come over here for a minute?"

She stood and listened as the young looking cop from Prince George's County explained her situation to the detective, who was dressed in urban winter gear. When the other cop had gone, the detective turned to her and said, "My name is detective Rio Jefferson, from the D.C. Police Department. What is your boyfriend's name?"

"Luther Fuller. His name is Luther Fuller. He's driving that black Caddy over there," she said, noting that she spoke of Khadafi in the present tense, hoping to will him to still be there and not in the past. When the detective looked in the direction in which she pointed and turned back around, she noticed his eyes. They were puffy and reddened as if he had been crying himself. Marnie wiped at the tears in her own eyes.

"I'm not supposed to do this because a next of kin hasn't been notified, but I understand your situation." He paused before continuing, "Khadafi is dead. He was pronounced dead at . . ."

That's all Marnie heard before things faded to black.

*****

The next time she opened her eyes she was sitting up on a gurney inside an ambulance. A female paramedic was attending to her. The ambulance door was open, allowing the bitter cold to creep in and envelope her. But she didn't feel a thing. Inside, Marnie felt hollow.

"Ma'am, are you okay?" the paramedic asked. Marnie nodded and lied, "Yeah, I'm good, thanks."

"Do you want to go to hospital for observation?"

"No," she said and stood. Then she climbed out of the ambulance. Without a backward glance, she walked away and headed for the Range Rover. Once she was safely inside the truck, the dam broke. Marnie banged both fists onto the steering wheel as she cried, "Why? Why? Why? Did you have to take him now? I'm pregnant!"

"So what are you gonna to do now?" a voice to her right said.

Her head whipped to the right so fast, she almost gave herself whiplash. At first she didn't see anything, but then right before her eyes, her pain materialized and sat in the passenger seat, staring back at her.

"Not you again? You're not real."

"I'm back, baby, and better than ever. As real as can be. But this is not about me. We talkin' about you. Khadafi is dead, and you're hurting more than ever. It looks like I'm here to stay now. What are we gonna do?"

Marnie couldn't believe this was happening again. She hadn't seen or heard from the pain that lived inside her for years. She shook her head violently to clear it, but it wasn't meant to be.

"You can try to shut me out, Marnie, but it won't work. Your heart is hurting now more than it's ever hurt before. That's why I'm here. And that's why I'm here to stay."

"No! I'm not listening to you. I'm-not-listening!"

"You don't have to listen to me, but you will hear me. The man you love is gone from this life, never to return. The only thing you will hear from now on is my voice."

Marnie covered both of her ears with both hands and shook her head.

"You're acting like a child, Marnie. No matter how immature you act, I'm still here. And I'm not going nowhere." Her pain stared forcefully and laughed.

"We'll see about that," she replied finally and started the truck.

Ignoring her pain for the rest of the ride, she drove home, trying not to cry anymore. But she couldn't get her pain's maniacal laugh out of her head. Her cell phone vibrated and vibrated, but she ignored it.

Twenty minutes later, she was pulling into the carport. Looking around, Marnie saw her mother's car was gone. That meant that she had taken Dada whereever she went. Marnie would be alone.

She leapt out of the truck and rushed into the house. In the bedroom, she saw her work uniform across a chair. Marnie stopped in her tracks and stared at the brown and white scrubs, her white crocs, and the white boy shorts she had taken off in haste earlier when Khadafi and she made love. The hours they spent sexing one another just hours ago replayed in her head. Tears started anew. She turned away from her clothes and found a photo. One of Khadafi and her at the Howard Theater for a comedy show. Katt Williams and Mike Epps had cracked them up until she almost pissed herself. Marnie smiled at the thought, then focused on Khadafi holding her around the waist, both of them dressed impeccably. Her heart fluttered in her chest as she heard the detective say, "Khadafi is dead."

Marnie remembered the scene from earlier when she walked into the bedroom and found Khadafi sitting on the bed with his head in his hands. She remembered what she'd told him.

". . . I love you so much that I can't breathe without you."

And she meant every word she'd said because at the moment Marnie felt like she was suffocating. She felt like at any moment she'd choke. To get away from that and to hide from her feelings, she knew what she had to do. She fortified her resolve and walked into her walk-in closet. It was like déjàvu. Marnie scrambled through her drawers until she found what she was looking for. Looking up, she saw the pain right there, staring at her with accusing eyes.

"Don't do it, Marnie. We can get through this together. Think about it."

"I already have." Marnie put the gun to her head and pulled the trigger.

THE END